NONE THE WORSE FOR A HANGING

NONE THE WORSE FOR A HANGING

Jonathan Ross

St. Martin's Press ✿ New York

Library of Congress Cataloging-in-Publication Data

Ross, Jonathan
    None the worse for a hanging / by Jonathan Ross.
        p.   cm.
    ISBN 0-312-13572-6 (hardcover)
    1. Rogers, George (Fictitious character)—Fiction.   2. Police—
England—Fiction.   I. Title.
PR6068.0835N66   1995
823'.914—dc20   95-34499
                                                                CIP

First published under the title *The Body of a Woman* in Great Britain by Constable & Company, Ltd

First U.S. Edition: December 1995

10   9   8   7   6   5   4   3   2   1

1

Detective Superintendent George Rogers, the ancient town of Abbotsburn's most senior CID officer, was a man who refused to believe that he was all that decayed and over the hump at the age of forty-three. His ex-wife, apparently finding in a bull-necked hairy-faced rugby-playing primitive that which she had failed to find in a more civilized Rogers, had left him for the many years of their separation in a generally unsatisfied sexual void. It had driven him to probably the same conclusion as the biblical Hebrew cove who had pontificated that all flesh was grass, doomed to wither or to be cut down; that it mightn't be too bad an idea for him to interest himself seriously in a woman. A woman, he qualified in his mind, not objecting too determinedly to being married to a pipe-smoking, whisky-drinking, addictively fond of playing a poor game of golf detective living virtually from the investigation of one violent and bloody death to another. The latter bore its obsessional fruiting in a repetitive nightmarish dream of travelling an endless shadowed corridor lined with doors, each opening on to a bloodied body.

Rogers, something over six feet in his charcoal-grey suit and his size $10^1/2$ Oxford brogues, black-haired, brown-eyed and with a swarthy skin that didn't pale below his shirt collar, had been fitted by his inherited genes with a thrusting wedge-shaped nose and a mite difficult-to-please temperament in any investigation of violent crime. Too, he could be more than a mite difficult when he met – as he did often – with acts of cruelty to animals of whom he thought more highly than their persecutors.

He was, however, generally quasi-amiable with a more than occasional showing of his white teeth when not brooding on

5

the sequestered fifty per cent of his salary being squandered in supporting his ex-wife and her ape-man lover's buying of the embrocations, the genital protection boxes and the gallons of black Irish stout he apparently needed to do his face-stamping stuff on the rugby field.

Living on his own in four tiny box-like rooms called an apartment because he could afford no better, he occasionally erupted into gusts of frustrated irritation at the injustice of it, throwing to destruction into his mock fireplace items of the wedding gift crockery that his wife had omitted to take on leaving him.

In some stagnant periods when he wasn't hunting out the vile, the wicked and the godforsaken, his mind was inclined to boredom and, in it, to contemplating the procreative functions presented to his body by an apparently unthinking and not wholly friendly Mother Nature. There was a simple answer to it, though not to be met by the first understanding and compliant woman attracted to him. His need could be provoked most effectively by tallish, almost lanky women with black hair and small breasts and owning to a touch of feminine arrogance backed by a well-programmed intelligence. That they might be a decade or so younger or older than himself, swathed in a tastefulness of jewellery and playing a low handicap club golf would not, he was certain, induce nausea in him.

It was nine fifteen in the morning and he was preoccupied with this thinking at his office desk, unloaded for once of anything requiring immediate action, when his telephone bell rang. His caller was Detective Inspector Coltart, telling him in his rumbling bass voice that he was at a house in High Ipstone View, Thurnholme Bay – his departmental car was standing outside it – where he had an apparent suicidal death by hanging in an empty garage about which he was seriously unhappy.

Replacing the receiver with all thoughts of black-haired women with small breasts fled, Rogers accepted that he had a murder on his hands. Coltart, just short of being monosyllabic but quite definitely taciturn, had, he knew, the ability to direct his attention to a chosen objective with all the subtlety and delicacy of a charging rhinoceros and come up with the irrefutable truth of it.

2

Thurnholme Bay was a short run of twenty minutes in Rogers's dark blue automatic car – chosen for its inconspicuousness among the multiform tens of thousands of its kind – during which he found that the sun had lost little of its heat from the summer so recently departed. Dropping down the steep gradient into the town, his ever questioning nose identified the rankness of exposed seaweed and fetid mud and the escaping smells of late breakfasts, anticipating in imagination the repugnant odours of the death he was going to meet. He knew that it would contain – as always – the strong elements of unease and what might be called dread, his wryly orientated mind relating it to his own physical dissolution, with his main concern being the probable absence of a golf course wherever he was sent.

Climbing further steep gradients of streets the other side of the town, he found that the destination address, High Ipstone View, given him by Coltart, was the topmost road and therefore probably the most expensive in which to buy property. The six villas lining its length all overlooked the sea below and were in a pseudo-Spanish style of white walls inset with arches, red clay roof pantiles blotched with lichen and black wrought ironwork on almost everything else.

The CID so-called Q-car, even more anonymous and nondescript than Rogers's though much older, stood outside the arched wrought iron gate of the villa called San Jose. A detective constable stood by its open door, manifestly tending to its radio transmissions. In front of it was parked an aluminium-coloured Metro, dulled with dust. Having pulled in behind the Q-car, Rogers could see through the gate in the high white wall a garage with its up-and-over door open. Climbing out and nodding at the DC who had opened the gate for him, he passed through to a yellow gravelled drive and yucca-planted garden. Detective Inspector Coltart, a born-again non-smoker and thus a bloody nuisance to those who weren't, was waiting for him outside the garage. Built on lumpish lines, he was sandy-haired with small green eyes in a fleshy freckled face that showed all the emotions of a painted wall. He made the garage in which he stood look smaller than it was. He wore an elderly dun-brown suit which hung loosely on his big frame like an elephant's hide and was reputed to have been run up for him by an Arabian tent maker who was having a bad day. He had an unsettling mannerism of jerking his head sideways as though expecting somebody to creep up on him from behind and lay him low. A man of trammelled thinking, he was of the opinion that very nearly everybody was guilty of something if only he could find out what. Though without question heterosexual, he was wholly indifferent to the attractions of women, managing only a sort of filial affection for those of, and above, the age at which his mother had died. As a consequence, he was generally referred to appositely in the department as the as-yet-undetected Abbotsburn Rapist.

Beside him, Rogers felt almost frail. Not looking for more than a short second into the windowless and lightless garage from which he could already detect the offensiveness of a body's putrefaction, he said, 'Don't tell me the why of your opinion, let me do my own thinking. How was he found?'

Coltart, the apotheosis of undisturbable phlegm, looked at his wrist-watch. 'Report received at 9.30 a.m., sir, from Mr Stephen Cruickshank. He's the son of the deceased and he's waiting in the house. He lives in Abbotsburn and was currently concerned about his father. He's Philip Cruickshank, aged sixty-two and a retired farmer. The son's been here twice because his father's not been contactable for about a week. This was apparently unusual and he worried as his father had apparently been threatened in the past. He came up early this morning, knocked on the door, broke a window at the back, found nothing and looked in the garage – he said he had a hunch – finding his father hanging. He was obviously very dead so he left him there, ringing emergency on the house phone. Since when he's been tanking up on Father's whisky. When I arrived he was emotional, wasn't really much with it. He said that he'd be inside until wanted. I sent for DC Lewis who's now out checking other villas for who lives where. DC Cole who came with me is manning communications outside.'

While Coltart had been speaking at such an unusual length for him, Rogers had filled his pipe – his recklessly-bought expensive meerschaum – and lit it as a fumigant against the coming smell, noting with an inner amusement that his uncompromisingly tobacco-hating detective inspector had moved with a ponderous discretion to the windward side of the pipe smoke. 'No notification to anyone but myself?' he asked.

'No need'. Coltart jerked his head at the interior of the garage. 'He's already been there long enough for you to decide.'

Before entering it, Rogers reminded himself of his long-held tenet that, in any investigation of a violent death, very little would be quite what it might seem to be either to himself or to anyone else. 'Right,' he said. 'Let's see whether I can be as seriously unhappy about it as you say you are.' There was no window in the garage and Coltart switched on a light against the change from daylight to semi-darkness as he followed. 'No car?' Rogers queried.

'I asked. He doesn't have one.'

Rogers stood well back from the body he saw suspended from a roof joist by a nylon rope. Though dressed in expensive-looking midnight-blue pyjamas, it was not a pretty sight and did nothing to make violent death anything but horrifying. Rogers thought again that the Somebody in charge of Things Material should have ordered the decomposition of living matter left behind to present itself elegantly and pleasantly scented in place of its existing ugliness.

Detaching himself from his unsettling appraisal of the body and regretting that he had breakfasted, he took in the interior of the garage. With a dusty cement floor and a heavily cobwebbed open roof space, it was empty but for some folded house removal cartons, a fat green and white bag of golf clubs likely to spark envy in his golfer's soul and a motorized trolley. Patently,

9

there was nothing there from which a suicidally determined man could step to hang himself.

'I see what you mean,' he said to the close-in-attendance and lightly breathing Coltart. 'I'm assuming that there'd never been anything in here for him to stand on?' He guessed that its absence had been the basis for Coltart's suspicion.

'Never, according to his son,' Coltart growled. 'But there's more.'

'I'm sure there is.' Rogers inhaled deeply of his anaesthetizing tobacco smoke and moved close – too bloody close, he told himself – to the hanging man. Overall, he seemed to be of an unusually slight build for a one-time farmer, though, he supposed, like the rest of *Homo sapiens*, they must come in different sizes. Studying the face intently – he had not seen it in its life – he felt that it had not been too happy in its encounter with death. The tightly ridged brown hair showed the dullness of an applied dye, the half-closed eyes a glazed and swollen pale grey. The nose, small for a man, was stubby like a transplanted bent thumb. A neat moustache and a small pointed beard, also dyed, gave the features the look of an Elizabethan courtier. The hands, hanging at the sides of the body, though discoloured and engorged, suggested that they were not unused to handling tools and such things. Rogers noted spots of blood on the floor beneath them without coming to any conclusion about their origin, though also noting that there was no bloodstaining visible on the pyjamas.

Rogers believed that he could sense the emptiness of the body from which personality had fled. He also imagined unwillingly something of the terrible anguish there must have been in the process of its dying. Though, in a sense, the dead man was now a client of the services offered by the CID to the criminally dead, Rogers guessed from his appearance that he would probably not have liked him in life.

He moved to the rear of the body, examining the faded yellow rope from where its end had been knotted to an adjacent joist to its throttling noose. Well-worn from use, it had sprouted broken fibres. At the rope's point of contact with the joist the direction of the angled fibres showed him that an already dead or unconscious man had been hoisted from the rear to

10

its present position by an outside agency. He looked with questioning eyebrows at the verbally constrained Coltart who nodded his agreement.

From where he stood, he examined the rope's fastening at the back of the neck. It looked to be a common reef knot and only its position caused the detective to frown. He then scrutinized the pyjamas, nothing the traces of cement dust visible on the backs of the jacket and trousers and on the arms. 'That too?' he asked Coltart who nodded again.

Taking out his handkerchief and grimacing his revulsion, he looped it around the ankle of one of the legs hanging nine or ten inches from the floor, lifting it to an acute angle and examining the foot's sole. Apart from minimal amounts of smeared cement dust and dirt on the broken skin of the heel it was clean, though grossly discoloured. Releasing the leg and allowing his handkerchief to drop with it, he said to the impassive Coltart who had patently missed out on the feet, 'For certain, he didn't walk from his bed to the garage, but was carried perhaps over the gravel outside and then dragged on his heels to here. Agreed?'

'Agreed,' Coltart replied. 'I'm told his bed's been slept in.'

Rogers grinned companionably at his solidness. 'You were right, of course. It's almost certainly a murder that's been faked to look like a suicide. He's been lying on his back on the floor here and never could he have lifted himself into that noose without something to stand on. And the knot tied at the back of his neck isn't right, is it? Nor the rope fibres that are forced in the wrong direction either.' Wrinkling his nose at the pervasive smell of death he relit his gone-out pipe. 'Whoever did it . . . not a very clever bastard, eh? It's just as well you were right about it, because I'd left instructions at the office for Dr Twite to be called out, in addition to Inspector Millier, Sergeant Magnus and the Coroner's Officer.'

He turned, grunting, 'I've to get out from under, it's choking me,' leaving the hanging body for the less suffocating atmosphere outside in the morning sun. From where he stood at the drive gate, breathing untainted air into his lungs and doing some necessary thinking, he could look down on the amphitheatre-like tiers of heat-shimmering red tiled roofs and green pocket-handkerchief-sized gardens dropping down to the town's harbour and marina and meeting the gently heaving blue-green sea, its shallows scored with the frothy wakes of sailing boats and glaringly white motor launches. Though much like a woman wearing heavy make-up with distance showing her to be more attractive than she actually was, the body behind him seemed a wholly unwelcome and appetite-destroying hindrance to his getting anything from what should have been a reasonably satisfying view.

To Coltart, who had followed him out, he said with a little allowable familiarity on his side, 'It leaves a bit of a problem, doesn't it, Edward? If it wasn't the rope that killed him, what did? I couldn't see a hole in him or any obvious signs of violence.'

The big inspector wagged his head. 'Nor me, sir. Except, I think, the blood on the floor.'

'Not, I feel, criminally shed blood,' Rogers said, 'but possibly the result of decomposition. Still, there might be something under those pyjamas when they're stripped by somebody less likely to upchuck than I am at the moment.'

He had been chewing thoughtfully at the stem of his pipe, beginning to show signs of irritation with himself. 'That aside,' he continued, 'I'd guess he'd been hanging in there for more than a week, and looking to me as if he'd actually been strangled . . . or, at least, dying an asphyxial death. It doesn't fit, does it? So I must be wrong.' He shrugged. 'Ah, well, it'll be Wilfred Twite's concern when he arrives, so you stay here until he does and while I have words with Mr Cruickshank. He's upset, of course?'

'If pushing back more than a glass or two of his father's single malt and crying into it, then yes he is,' Coltart replied, not unsympathetically. 'And there was an unspecified something in his mind. Something about somebody having it in for his father.'

'You didn't press him about it?'

'No. He was getting maudlin and I knew you'd want to.'

'What does he do? What is he?'

'A dentist. I've seen him about Abbotsburn often enough.'

'A decent chap?'

'He seems to be. I wasn't with him long enough to know.'

'Shouldn't he be in his surgery pulling out some poor bugger's teeth about this time of the morning?' he called back to Coltart, not expecting an answer and already heading for the villa and the always unwelcomed face-to-face encounter with tearful grief.

3

Rogers, tugging at the black iron bell-pull and producing inside the villa a carillon of bell-like sounds, waited several last-minute inhalations of tobacco smoke before rapping his pipe empty on the opening of the door. The man who was certainly the bereaved Stephen Cruickshank appeared to be about thirty years, leanly masculine without being bullish and almost eyebrow-to-eyebrow with the taller Rogers. Beneath dark brown hair, his pouched eyes were an oily chocolate with the pink suffusion of recent weeping in them, his mouth small and thin-lipped, exposing in repose his upper teeth in what could be taken as a mirthless half-smile. Unlike his father's nose, his seemed to take up a lot of room in a white stricken face.

He wore an expensively tailored white suit with nothing unconventional about it, and a blue silk open-neck shirt with a growth of chest hair climbing around an ankh cross hanging below his throat. Two gold bangles occupied the wrist that wasn't sporting what appeared to be a black-dialled space age watch. Rogers thought he might look different in a white surgical jacket to a pain-anguished eye but, now off duty, he was unlike any dentist he had so far met.

As Rogers produced his warrant card, a strong odour of whisky reached his nose and, behind it, a perfume. Possibly, he thought charitably, one designed for male wear. 'Detective Superintendent Rogers,' he said with a suitable gravitas. 'I'm sorry to have to intrude, but I need to speak to you.'

'Yes, of course.' His voice was high-pitched and breathy as if he was managing it on half a lung.

With Cruickshank turning and preceding him into the villa, a suspicion of a stagger in his walk, Rogers saw that his hair was pulled and tied behind his head in a finger's-length pigtail. It confirmed his already held opinion that he was an oddity.

The sitting-room into which he led the detective was large, low-ceilinged and clinically white-walled, the three windows, through which the sun shone, barred outside with Spanish-style black iron grilles. The furniture was of an unpleasant raw-ochre stripped pine, the curtains and upholstery fabrics in abstract patterns of primary colours. To Rogers, it represented a bachelor pad ordinary and whatever measure of good taste he held in his soul suffered.

The pictures scattered over the expanses of white wall were stereotyped landscapes and nineteenth-century hunting scenes. A large wall cabinet with an opened service flap held an almost empty bottle labelled *The Sgurr a Mhaim Single Malt* and three cut-glass tumblers, two with a quarter-inch or so of whisky still in them. A small square revolving bookcase, a television set in a partly opened cabinet and a closed secretaire were possibly the only interesting items in the room. There were no house plants, no fireplace and the parquet flooring – not very well polished – had neither carpets nor rugs. Rogers, admittedly no authority on it, thought the room lacked a woman's touch.

Cruickshank folded himself almost arthritically into one of the gaudy easy chairs and flapped his hand at Rogers to do the same, then waited, his chin sunk in the collar opening of his shirt.

Rogers, sitting, thought, Apathetic? Stunned? Dissociating himself from the reality of grief? But one of them for certain. Waiting for a few silent seconds that seemed to stretch far too long, he said, 'This is a sad happening for you, Mr Cruickshank, and I'm sorry that it's necessary for me to intrude on your grief . . .'

'My sister,' he muttered, the smell of exhaled whisky fumes reaching out to the detective. 'I've just telephoned her . . . she's taking it so badly.' He was blinking his eyes. 'Father didn't take his own life, you know.'

'I'd like to know why you think that,' Rogers said. 'But first, tell me how you came to discover his body.'

Cruickshank was silent for long moments, palpably fighting for normality. When he spoke, his voice was held under control only with the carefully spaced out articulation of a man who had had three or four drinks too many. 'Father hadn't been fit lately, having had a bit of trouble with his hip and b-being on the waiting list for a replacement joint.'

When he paused, Rogers nodded for him to continue. He had, thank God, moved away from shedding emotional tears, doing little more than sitting sloshed under his own personal black cloud. Rogers considered that his occasional hesitation and slurring of his consonants might be brought on by his drunkenness and his bereavement.

'F-Father,' Cruickshank continued, 'wouldn't allow me to do anything for him to minimize the discomfort – well, pain, I imagine – he suffered. He often joked that so long as it wasn't terminal he intended not to worry about it. But of course I did keep an eye on his progress – or lack of it, actually. Though I admit it irritated him, I telephoned him r-regularly; as, naturally, did Veronica, my sister.'

His head tipped backwards as he lapsed into silence and Rogers could see the thick vein like a pale blue worm that throbbed jerkily at the side of his exposed throat. 'So you called here?' he asked, wanting him to get to the point of what he was saying.

'Yes, but I'd telephoned him twice recently and there'd been no reply on either occasion, which wasn't all that unusual. And I did pop up here on Thursday, finding him out.' He was peering at Rogers as if from behind misted glass. 'Normally that wouldn't have worried me because he lived his own life and it was generally an active one where he would often be away from h-home for a few days. Not too often, but often enough, you understand. But with his hip acting up . . .' He trailed into a lip-biting silence, looking down at his fingers restlessly twisting themselves on his lap.

'And you waited until today before you came up again?' He was careful to make it a question, not an accusation.

Cruickshank apparently thought that he had been remiss in

15

this and he screwed his expression into a grimace. 'I d-didn't wish to upset Father. He could be . . . well, could be awfully difficult should Veronica or I appear to be fussing about him, or trying to interfere with what he did. And it's difficult having my associates standing in for me at the surgery.'

'But you did return today?' Rogers edged him along. 'Five days later.'

'Yes, we'd been away and I'd worried myself sick about him, thinking he may have died in his sleep, or fallen over and been unable to move to get help. So I came up this morning fairly well . . . well, determined to settle my mind – and V-Veronica's as well, of course – one way or another. First, I did what I should have done before. After I'd rung the bell and hammered on both the front and back doors without getting any answer, I looked through the letter-box, seeing the newspapers he hadn't picked up.'

Cruickshank bit at his bottom lip. 'That didn't mean too much because when Father went off on his occasional days away the same would apply. But it did give me a kind of.licence to start seriously worrying about him.' He was manifestly working hard against an occasional stumbling over words and the putting of what he had done into a proper sequence.

'I went around the back again and broke the glass in the kitchen window with a stone and unlatched it and climbed in. He wasn't in his bedroom, though I saw that his bed had been slept in and the clothing he'd taken off hung up in the dressing-room next door to it.' He swallowed, squeezing his eyelids together. 'And his w-walking-stick; that was there too. I mean, in his bedroom. So far as I know he still uses it even in moving around the house. That meant to me he could either be somewhere close at hand or that he had been taken away against his will.'

Rogers said, 'That would be his only stick?' He badly wanted to smoke his pipe, but non-smokers – and Cruickshank looked every inch one such – seemed to have equated smokers with pariah dogs and to have made what was but a minor acceptable vice into an anti-social misdemeanour. He feared that the same rabidly inclined prohibitionists might soon move on to the banning of his more-or-less freelance sexual activities.

16

'Definitely. Even then, I don't believe that he'd have used it unless it fitted in with how he wished to be seen by his friends; and where the alternative would be a crutch or similar.' Cruickshank fell silent, his eyes closed, one of his hands active behind his head and presumably doing something to his pigtail; brooding, it seemed, on the issue of the walking-stick.

'The garage,' Rogers prompted him. 'Was that next?' With the windows closed the air in the room felt dead and stale. There were no ghostly traces of smoked tobacco or of a woman's perfume; only, he thought, the fading smell of a dead man's corruption lingering in his nostrils with the stronger fumes of the whisky Cruickshank had drank.

'Yes. Father clearly wasn't in the house and that left only the garage.' His hands clenched into fists and he shook his head violently. 'Christ, I can't go in there again. P-Please don't ask me . . . I don't wish to think about it.'

He suddenly pushed himself from his chair, moving unsteadily to the window behind him, turning his back on Rogers who waited patiently, avoiding staring at a man whose body, seen now in dark silhouette against the outside sunlight, was being shaken by the rigors of his grief.

When he turned back to the detective his face had been set in what appeared to be emotion concealed, only his pink-rimmed eyelids indicating the turmoil that had passed behind them. 'Sorry about that,' he said in a steadier voice as he reseated himself. 'It won't happen again.'

'It's understandable,' Rogers said commiseratively. 'I take it that in view of your breaking into the house you don't have a key to it?'

'No. Neither of us.'

'Has it occurred to you that in order to gain access, whoever it might have been would either be in possession of a key or have been known well enough to be let in by your father in his pyjamas, he having presumably been in bed?'

Cruickshank looked vaguely surprised. 'I hadn't thought of that,' he said.

'Now tell me why you don't believe that your father did this thing to himself.' Rogers leaned forward in his chair. In his continued appraisal of Cruickshank he had decided, hoping that he wasn't wrongly denigrating the man, that his small mouth could probably be indicative of a meanness of spirit.

Cruickshank blinked as if the words had been shouted at him. 'No, he couldn't. He isn't a man who'd remotely consider such a terrible thing. In any case, I saw at once that there was nothing . . . noth . . .' He drew in a deep shuddering breath and started again. 'Th-There was nothing on which he could stand to do it.'

Rogers nodded his agreement, wanting to ask him why he had not attempted to cut his father down, but thinking it might sound too much like an accusation of having not done the right thing. In this instance, as Rogers knew, he had actually done the right thing in not touching his obviously dead father. 'You saw that he was dead, that he'd been dead some time, of course,' he said.

'Yes.' He shook his head as if to banish a recall of what he had seen. 'For God's sake,' he whispered to himself.

'I'm sorry,' Rogers said, disliking anyway this grubbing around in a man's grief. 'Seeing what I have seen, I do have to investigate your father's death and that means asking questions; some of them painful, some of them possibly embarrassing to you and your sister. Was there anything else you think might be suspicious? You mentioned to Inspector Coltart about somebody having it in for him.'

'Yes. Perhaps I shouldn't have mentioned it, for it doesn't now seem to me to be too important. It was about six months ago when I saw him in town and we had a drink together in the King William pub. He said – it was out of the blue and he was kind of laughing about it – that he was becoming one of n-nature's endangered species because a lady-friend's husband – who he didn't name – had taken exception to a quite innocent friendship and had promised to smash his face in or something similar. Knowing Father I could see that he wasn't altogether too happy about it, though he wasn't a man who got frightened easily.'

'No names, I suppose?'

'No. That was Father too. He wouldn't ever take me completely into his confidence.'

18

'Forgive me,' Rogers said as diplomatically as he was able, 'but did your father have other lady-friends?'

Cruickshank was silent for long seconds. 'I don't know,' he said at last, Rogers believing that he damned well did. 'At least, not recently.'

'Is there anything else?'

'Yes, I believe there is. When I returned here to telephone for help I saw that the b-bureau . . .' – he indicated the closed secretaire – '. . . was open and the papers in it were in disorder, definitely looking as though they'd been gone through. Father would never have left it in that state; he was too terrifically meticulous.' His eyes searched Rogers's features as if for some assurance. 'You do agree that he didn't – he couldn't – do it himself?'

'At the moment, yes.' Rogers was, for the moment, cautious in his commitment to murder. 'So, would you tell me about him? About his background, his associates; anything which might help us to find out why and how he met his tragic end.'

A subdued Cruickshank measured him up with a suddenly guarded look, creasing his forehead. 'Yes, I'll try, though I know very little about whatever friends or associates he has here in Thurnholme. For the past six months or so, since he threw out the woman who was living with him, I've seen even less of him than before. And that, I'm afraid to say, hadn't been very frequent.' His brown eyes darkened and he winced as if a raw nerve had been touched. 'He and Mother separated a few years back and he had lived on his own ever since, both at the farm and here. Then, over a year ago, he took up with this woman who came to live with him . . .' – his face flushed red – '. . . and she turned out to be a tart. It didn't work out, of course, and I can't say that we were upset that it didn't.'

'We?' Despite Cruickshank's emotional state and the desensitizing whisky he had taken on board – Rogers had judged it to be more than enough – his speaking seemed a little more under the control of his tongue.

'My sister and I,' he said shortly. 'It's because it didn't work out that he was now living on his own again.'

'I think that tart or not she'll need to be informed of his death. Where does she live?'

19

'I don't know. I don't wish to know.' His expression was ugly. 'We didn't like her and she apparently didn't like us. We tried not to visit while she was here and unfortunately my father realized that, and things became difficult.'

'Why didn't you like her? Because she was living with your father?'

Cruickshank shot him whatever soft brown eyes could manage in a look of resentment. 'That wasn't the whole of it. We got to hear that she was going out drinking with young men – studs, for sure – behind his back, though neither of us could get around to telling him.' He shook his head, it seemed in frustration. 'All hell would have broken loose and he'd never have forgiven us for knowing, let alone telling.' He looked down at the parquet flooring. 'I have to say that he could be most short-tempered and very very difficult at times. Still, he must have found out for himself, for I heard later that he'd thrown her out – which she would have deserved – or that she had left him.'

'Might she have been the woman whose husband had threatened to smash your father's face in?'

Cruickshank's eyes widened in surprise. 'That hadn't occurred to me, I must say. She might have been, though to be fair I'd never heard any suggestion that she might be a married woman.'

'Was there anything else about her I should know?'

'I heard that she d-drank too much, but I'm sorry to say that Father was much the same in that respect.'

'You knew her reasonably well, I expect? Sort of off and on?'

'No; I did not.' He had spaced the words out. 'I told you, I hardly knew her. How could I? Or Veronica? Neither of us were ever invited here by her and I doubt that we would have gone even had we been.'

'That's sad, isn't it?' Just socially tongue-in-cheek words, Rogers admitted to himself. Cruickshank seemed to him more bloody-minded about his father's live-in girlfriend than otherwise.

Cruickshank lowered his eyebrows in a scowl. 'No, it isn't at all. I'm telling you why we didn't like her. She was a mercenary uncaring b-bitch and . . .' He punched a closed fist on his thigh, then clamped his mouth shut.

'And?' Rogers encouraged him.

'And nothing.' His face was again suffused with red. 'It's just that he shouldn't have messed about with a woman like her at his age. He was sixty against her being something over thirty and it wasn't decent.'

'A not unknown combination of ages though,' Rogers said cynically. 'And it does usually lead to big spending if the money's there, and some younger lovers on the quiet. What is her name?'

'Eunice Parr, though while she was with Father she had the nerve to call herself Parr-Cruickshank with a hyphen. Parr was what she was called before she met him.'

'And her present address?'

Cruickshank shook his head irritably. 'How the hell would I know? We weren't exactly on visiting terms. She'd been working in some club in Abbotsburn, and I think she's an Australian, so I expect she went back there.'

'I still need to find her. Can't you give me any information at all about where she is? I can't pluck her whereabouts out of thin air.'

Cruickshank shook his head, weary irritation in the way he did it.

'Does she have a car?' Rogers persisted. 'Is she licensed to drive one?'

'I wouldn't know about her having a licence, would I, but she does have a car. I saw it parked here once, which meant that I went away without calling on my father. I think it was a Mazda; a small red one, though I'm not sure.'

He put a hand over his eyes as if in pain. 'I'm sorry, but I don't wish to talk about her. It makes me feel ill. So is there much more? I do need to go to my sister and see how she's taking all this.'

'I've nearly finished,' Rogers assured him, recognizing his apparent fatigue and continuing mental perturbation. 'Your sister is who?'

'Mrs Veronica Cummins. She's associated with the G-Goatacre Horse and Pony Sanctuary, but lives with me. I'd rather

21

you didn't speak to her before I do. She can be so easily upset.'

Rogers nodded his agreement, though storing the deferring of the interview in his mind for future consideration. 'I understand your father's a retired farmer?'

'Yes, he is. He farmed land at Lower Penruddock until four years back. He had to move then and has been here ever since.'

'I've finished for the moment,' Rogers said, recognizing Cruickshank's returning agitation, though feeling the need to mention that people didn't normally get murdered for nothing and that there was a something existing he had to find. 'It means,' he said, 'that there'll be more matters concerning your father to be gone into and I shall have to see you again. I assume that you live in Abbotsburn and that you're in the phone directory?'

'Yes. Any time after today and I'd be grateful.'

'I shall need to have the villa secured for the examination of its contents. You may be present if you wish, or have someone here to attend in your place. Also . . .'

'Do what you have to do,' Cruickshank interrupted him. 'I've locked up Father's private papers in the drawer of the bureau. If I find anything I think you should see I'll let you know. Otherwise, I'll be quite satisfied with what you choose to do just so long as you leave the villa secure.' He stood from his chair, swaying slightly. 'I must go now.'

Rogers stood too. Putting friendliness in his voice, he said, 'I assume that the Metro outside is yours, so if you'll give me your ignition key I'll have one of my chaps drive you home.'

Cruickshank frowned, then looked puzzled. 'Th-Thank you, but I'd prefer to do that myself.'

'I'm sure you would.' Rogers still kept it fairly light. 'Unfortunately, I can't help but be awkwardly official about this. Understandably, you're dreadfully shaken up about your father and, again understandably, you've been drinking to anaesthetize your grief.' He held out his cupped hand. 'I'm sorry, old chap, but it's for your own good.'

Cruickshank stood mute for long enough for Rogers to retrieve and hold his pipe in his hand and to start anticipating

22

the filling of it. Then, fumbling in his trouser pocket and producing a key, he said, 'No, *I'm* sorry and you are quite right. I wasn't thinking.'

Taking the key, Rogers thought that despite the seemingly decent apology Cruickshank's eyes had shown a touch of malevolence as he said it. And that had been contrary to the detective's overall opinion of him as a bit of a dried stick who had secrets of his own in addition to an oddball liking for wearing an ankh necklet and a small 'with-it' pigtail. On the other hand, he could understand his taste for his father's single malt whisky; a civilizing vice if there was ever one.

4

With Cruickshank gone, Rogers stuffed as much tobacco into his pipe as it would hold, applied a flaring match to it with a hand that shook slightly and then inhaled deeply of the pacifying smoke. With the nicotine infiltrating his blood he felt more at peace with his fellow man, though not with what he was anticipating to be a bitch of an investigation.

There was a bareness about the villa he was about to examine which he didn't like. Its walls and uncarpeted floors echoed the sounds of his walking as if the late occupier were following behind him. Opening uninformative cupboards *en route* and entering the kitchen, he examined the window through which Cruickshank had said he had gained access. It was open with a large hole punched in its glass near the inside catch. Shards of glass and smears of garden soil littered the sink draining board below the window. Among them was an unwashed cup and saucer, the cup containing what appeared to be the dried dregs of coffee. Looking out through the window, he saw overlapping footprints and a large stone in an unplanted border beneath it. On opening the refrigerator and freezer, he saw that they contained good quality convenience foods; survival stuff, as he well knew, for men living on their own.

By passing a small dining-room and a combined shower

and lavatory, he spent time in the bathroom fitted with a floor-level jacuzzi sporting chunky gold-plated fittings. The contents of a double wall cabinet included an electric shaver and beard trimmer, quantities of expensive French scents, body lotions, creams and soaps for *l'homme*. Separately stored were varieties of sprays, jars and tubes of scents and cosmetics which Rogers considered might have been for the use of the departed Eunice Parr or overnight visitors. Two of the scents, both looking horribly expensive and opened in the vicinity of Rogers's susceptible nostrils, held the promise of exciting any unneutered male's eroticism. The dead man, he concluded, had had a taste for women and apparently the means to satisfy it.

Moving along a short passage, still with his footfalls echoing behind him and accompanied by a backward trailing ribbon of tobacco smoke, he came to two bedrooms. One was fully furnished with a huge double bed, an empty built-in wardrobe and a bare-topped dressing-table. It held no evidence of recent occupation. Between it and that which proved to be the dead man's bedroom was a small windowless dressing-room with a small wardrobe racked with male clothing and a narrow full-length mirror on one wall. A row of clothes hooks held a greenish-coloured linen jacket and trousers and a shirt, and a straw laundry basket contained male underwear. A search of the jacket and trousers revealed only the small bits and pieces a man might carry. There was, perhaps significantly, no wallet or cheque book.

The other smaller bedroom, in which the older Cruickshank had apparently been killed, had in it a threequarter-size bed with a patterned fabric canopy in poor taste over its head, and a bedside table holding a green-shaded lamp, a television and video remote control pad, a paperback novel, an elderly Tissot wrist-watch and a pair of wire-rimmed half-moon spectacles. In the compartment beneath there was a round tin of tobacco, a well-charred briar pipe, a half-empty box of matches and an ashtray of dottle and matchsticks. Rogers could think of him as not such a bad chap after all. A large and extremely slim television unit had been secured at eye level to the otherwise bare wall opposite the bed. A ruby light in its base showed that it had been switched to stand-by. There

24

was no dressing-table and no stool or chair, and the parquet flooring was rugless.

The bed in which Cruickshank had seemingly slept his last sleep was a jumble of disturbed wine-coloured linen and purple satin coverlet. A pillow, creased and with a faint staining on it, lay on the floor at the side of the bed. Close to it was a twisted rubber band about six inches in diameter. Without touching anything, he leaned and smelled at the sheets and pillow. He could detect no odour of a woman's scent, but then, he told himself, if there had been it would have had days to waste its fragrance on unresponding air. Opening the drawer of the bed-side table, Rogers was unsurprised to find in it four blatantly pornographic magazines and a few packeted condoms.

The bedroom was one that required the early attention of Sergeant Magnus, the meticulous Scenes of Crime officer for whom the finding of an eyelash on a thick pile carpet seemed to pose no special difficulties, and Rogers was careful to leave it exactly as he had found it.

He was already tangling his thinking with variations on the bloody theme of the older Cruickshank's death, for, throughout his search of the villa and apart from the window broken by Stephen Cruickshank, he had found no other evidence of a forcible entry. Only one thing seemed to be reasonably clear. With the dead man having been found in his pyjamas, then the odds were that he had been in bed immediately prior to his death. From that, it might be reasonable to suppose that he had known his killer well enough to have let him into the villa; accepting for the time being that his killer had been male because of the strength needed to carry the body to the garage and there to suspend it. Or, he had to qualify, he could have been sleeping with a woman who had subsequently let in a male accomplice. Or, he again qualified, only this time irritably, why not a cuckolded husband having access to a house key in the possession of his promiscuous wife? Or, indeed, he thought lastly, putting a brake on a mind that was going round in circles, why not the odd ball Stephen Cruickshank? There might be a motive for patricide should he dig deep enough, though that wasn't logical with his disbelief in his father having committed suicide.

Returning to the sitting-room in which Cruickshank suffered not so stoically his questioning, Rogers dropped the flap of the secretaire to expose the muddle of documents in it. So far as he could see, and assuming that that which had been of significance or private interest to Cruickshank and the killer had already been taken, they were the common accumulation of a householder's lot, though he did see included in them several handwritten letters which might yield some later profit.

Closing the flap on its contents, destined for another's scrutiny, he tried the drawer beneath it, finding it – as Cruickshank had said – to be securely locked. He was moving over to the square revolving bookcase when he heard cars pulling up in the road outside, feeling now that his investigation could be getting itself into a higher gear.

The twenty or so books held in the case were uniformly and beautifully bound in pale blue pseudo leather, each identified on its spine by an elaborate art nouveau poppyhead design and sequential numerals in gold blocking. Opening two of them and leafing through, even Rogers, hardened over the years by his necessary examination of obscene publications, thought them grossly depraved in their text and photographic illustrations. Fitting them back into the case to decent anonymity, he said, 'Bloody hell!' under his breath. Life obviously didn't necessarily become uninteresting just because one had reached the sixties. Whether the books were *pour encourager les autres* or a jog to the dead man's memory was another matter.

He was at the wall cabinet admiring with held-back envy its almost pub-sized stock of spirits and liqueurs when he heard the front door being opened and a woman's footfalls rapping on the wooden tiles of the passage.

She who entered was by any standard disconcertingly attractive with pale blonde hair worn short, dark blue eyes and a smoothly sensual mouth that for any man's peace of mind should have been covered by a yashmak. Too, her breasts were on the large side which, Rogers thought, was overdoing it a bit. She was Detective Inspector Helen Millier, formerly a detective sergeant in his department where, in Rogers's angst-struck opinion, she had been a disruptive element, even if an unwitting and apparently chaste one, among her male colleagues.

26

Rogers thought highly of her as a detective, but in her junior rank as a sergeant he rarely had personal contact with her. Much as a priest would with a nun, though heedful more of Police Discipline Regulations than whatever it was that held back a goatish priest, he repressed any below the waist thoughts he may have had of her as a woman with breasts and a kissable mouth.

When she had been promoted to the rank of inspector and transferred to the uniform branch he was pleased for her but relieved to see her go from a department of mainly males acting out too often the ritual clashing of the antlers of stags in rut. Then, a week ago, after nearly a year out of the department, she had been posted back as a detective inspector with a remit to Rogers to give her some experience of higher level crime investigation as a preparation for a Police College senior course. Her assistance was fortuitous and doubly welcome, for he was without his second-in-command, Detective Chief Inspector David Lingard, unhappily absent from his office suffering in a car smash-up a lineal fracture of his now encased in plaster left arm. Fortunately, he had told Rogers, not the one he used for the presenting of credit cards or for the periodic feeding of Golden Cardinal snuff into his nostrils.

While she had now to distance herself from her former colleagues, Rogers hoped that the higher ranks with whom she would now work would be less subject to any disruption caused by her undoubted sexual attractiveness. For himself, he was hoping that he would stay proofed against whatever feminine witchery emanated from the body that refused to be made at all ordinary by the conventional though elegant clothing she chose to wear.

Of one thing he was wholly ignorant and, had he not been, it was certain that he would have reacted to it like a badly startled horse. It was that Millier suffered a sort of off-and-on infatuation for Rogers and, as a consequence, the posting to serve under him, to be in frequent contact with him, was, perversely, not wholly welcomed.

So far as the happily unaware Rogers was concerned, sexual infatuation was something he distrusted, a condition to be somehow avoided. He much preferred the lesser emotion of warm affection for the few softer moments in his life.

He smiled as she came towards him. 'Miss Millier,' he greeted her, not having yet decided on calling her Helen, a friendly one-sided familiarity to which he might or might not later come.

Her smile back at him was reserved. 'I came as soon as I was told,' she said. She wore a moss-green linen suit that set off her blonde hair, carrying a small leather clutch bag to accommodate, among other things, her notebook and handcuffs.

'Has Dr Twite arrived yet?' he asked.

'No,' she said, 'but Sergeant Magnus came in behind me and he's in the garage unpacking his equipment.'

'I've to be quick,' Rogers said briskly, closing the drinks compartment of the wall cabinet and giving her a rundown on the finding of Philip Cruickshank's body, and an abbreviated account of his interview with Stephen Cruickshank. 'First of all, I'd like you to introduce yourself to the dead man who I hope is still hanging in the garage. Take him in, get to know what he's telling you and then later let me know what you've concluded from his being found where he is.' He tried not to look too hagridden, speaking to her much as he would to a second-in-command replacement. 'I've already gone around in circles about it and a fresh approach, a look at it from your viewpoint, would be helpful. When you've done that, I want you to find into which hole Eunice Parr seems to have dropped since she and Cruickshank parted. She has a car so check with the D and V Licensing Agency for her present address in addition to our own records and NIB. When you've found where she is – perhaps you'll have worked out some sort of a description of her by then – confer with me and we'll see what she knows about the life style of her late lover. That is,' he added, 'if Stephen Cruickshank has his facts right.'

Once she had gone, Rogers felt an inexplicable relief at being free from the steady regard she had been directing at him while he was speaking. On his way to the hall to check on the delivered mail and newspapers, he grunted to himself that her staring at him had been bloody unsettling and nothing to which he wanted ever to become accustomed.

Rogers, leaving the villa for the garage, saw that Cruickshank's dusty Metro had gone and only just caught a glimpse of the rear end of Millier's new racing-green Rover Mini leaving the road with its canvas sunroof open. Somehow, he thought, its appearance of an immaculate mechanical femininity reflected Millier's own felicitous style and taste.

Coltart was standing monolithically at the entrance to the garage, its interior now shut off from public view by canvas screens. The uniformed Coroner's officer stood waiting inside with his body and coffin shell while Sergeant Magnus exploded electronic light as he took photographs of the hanging body and the apparent artifices of its death.

Coltart, following Rogers into the garage and visibly disliking it, rumbled from the depths of his chest that DC Lewis hadn't finished with his checking detail in the road, but had dug out a Mrs Angharad Rhys Pritchard, a neighbour of the dead man who lived in the villa called Casa Griot. 'She's been here already,' Coltart said, 'because she's got some sort of an interest in Cruickshank. She asked me if he was all right and I said he'd had an accident and was no longer with us. That sort of thing, though she must suspect it's something more serious. She said she thought she could help as she'd known him a long time. Been friendly, she said, but a bit more than that I'd say.' His face had twitched to a lesser stolidness in saying that. It may have been due to the stifling atmosphere inside, but Rogers didn't think so. 'Thinking you'd want to speak to her yourself, I asked her to return home and wait for you to call.'

'I'll be there,' Rogers said, knowing that any woman not being grey-haired and plainly matronly would fail automatically to get his unqualified approval. 'How old is she and what's she like?'

'Forty-ish. Well spoken, but tarted up. Lots of bangles and rings and things. Lots of scent, too. Dresses in trousers meant for somebody younger. And money. I reckon she's got a fair bundle.' Coltart had spoken without apparent malice and, in Roger's opinion, as if he genuinely accepted that the no doubt normal Mrs Rhys Pritchard was a sex-mad harpy.

'I'll still see her,' Rogers said amiably, deliberately so in his dig at his inspector's misogyny. 'You make her sound a very attractive woman. Any news of Dr Twite?'

'He's on the way.' Coltart seemed oblivious of any pricking at one of his tangled complexes. 'He should be here any minute unless he's got himself lost.'

'Good. While I'm with him, take the PC with the coffin shell with you and have a look around the garden and see what there's to see. Lewis can also help you when he gets back.'

The ginger-haired Magnus had finished his chores – Rogers had often said of him that he was as efficient as all hell at finding evidential microscopic particles in a suspect room, but could then trip over an unnoticed dustbin on his way out – and reported to Rogers that he thought the nylon rope suspending the unfortunate Cruickshank from the joist had discoloured oil on it and that due to the decomposition of the hands he was unable to take satisfactory elimination prints from the fingers. Directing him to take his camera, powders and sprays to the villa to lift from it what marks, dust and stains a murderous intruder may have left behind, Rogers couldn't help but add with a smile, 'And mind you don't walk into the screens on the way out,' which mystified the sergeant into thinking that his senior officer had been early at the bottle.

Having told the Coroner's Officer to wait in his van, Rogers was now alone, his necessary thinking processes interrupted by the carelessly fast entry into the drive of a cream-coloured shark-nosed Citroën Safari, a model after which he had long lusted, but which he had decided was beyond his present means to support. But, manifestly, not beyond the means of Dr Wilfred Twite, an excessively bonhomous graduate in morbid pathology, who dismounted from it. He was a short man owning to hardworking sweat glands and to an amiable expression decorated with an inappropriate Mexican-style moustache and sidewhiskers, his black hair tightly ridged in waves. He had been padded to a hard-breathing fatness on the *haute cuisine* of a couple of Abbotsburn's better restaurants; his so far unpunished and equally hard-breathing appetite for other professional men's wives was seemingly unaffected. His twill suit was in suntan-sepia, his silk bow tie and matching handkerchief a flaring scarlet set off by a shirt in dark brown and white stripes.

He was a brilliant man with a scalpel or bone saw, almost intuitive in uncovering death's dark secrets, but undeniably cavalier in his wielding of them, his necropsy table often finishing like a butcher's block. He had left his case of instruments in the car – a common enough happening – and he held out his hand to Rogers who had come to greet him. 'I hope this is going to be worth it, old George,' he beamed, his grip damp and warm. 'There's not a damn decent eating-house in the place.'

Rogers liked Twite and had an enormous respect for his skill. 'I shouldn't think you'd want to eat anything after shaking hands with this one, Wilfred,' he said, leading him into the garage. 'It's a killing that someone's attempted to set up as a suicide. Crude stuff and it doesn't impress. His name's Cruickshank, by the way, and you can put him down as being in his early sixties.'

Twite moved in an unexpected light-footed manner to within three yards of the hanging body. Rogers, following behind him, heard his whispered, 'Beautiful! Oh beautiful!'

'Indeed it is,' the detective told him ironically. 'I know it's going to be difficult, but I'd be grateful for an early time of death, even for one within a day or two. And, Wilfred,' he pressed him po-faced, 'though it's probably unlikely, could you see whether there's any evidence of his having been outrageously depraved with a lady-friend within a reasonable time of his death?'

'Dear God, the bloody optimism of the man!' Twite breathed in mock derision without moving his attention from the body which was now his to do with what he willed. He stepped to its rear, giving the back of the body the same steady scrutiny he had given to the front.

Moving to within a foot or two's proximity to the front, he fumbled in a pocket for a package of his scented cigarettes, took one out and flicked a lighter at it – Rogers knew that it

31

bore an emotive engraving, *My hand on it. Pamela* – all without taking his eyes from the object of his intense interest. Then, taking the small kitchen steps used by Magnus for his close-up photography, he hefted his sixteen stones of overfed flesh on to them until face to face with his paymaster Death, there to use his pocket lens to examine at heavy-breathing length the eyes, the interior of the mouth and the rope mark biting deep into the flesh of the neck. Twisting the body around and combing his fingers through the head hair he localized an area at the back. 'Ah,' he grunted, 'he's had a hell of a whack with what I'd imagine to be your old friend the blunt instrument. If it didn't kill him – and it needn't have – it'd certainly stun him.'

'You think it might have?' Rogers asked. He wanted a definite diagnosis.

'It feels to be a comminuted fracture of the skull, so I suggest you activate a reasonable suspension of belief in your noddle until I've finished. Which won't be here because there're congested conjunctivae in the eyes with possible petechial haemorrhages which may suggest that rather than having been beaten to death he could have died of asphyxiation.'

'You mean he could have been bludgeoned to unconsciousness and then hung up to die?' Rogers refilled and lit his still-hot pipe, uncaring of calcined lips in the greater repugnance of his continued breathing in what he imagined to be odorous particles of disintegrating flesh.

'I don't mean anything of the kind.' Twite was verging on being testy. 'When I've got him on the table without your panting your anxieties into my ear, I might. Or might not.'

Climbing down from the steps and pushing them with his shoe to one side, he unbuttoned the pyjama jacket and lifted it to expose the chest and abdomen. His examination of them was brief, but viewing the back caused him to pull the elasticated trousers down below the buttocks, his cigarette jerking between his lips and spraying ash and sparks on to his shirt front.

'Look at it,' he said to Rogers, his face a big fat grin. 'Tell me now that I'm being too circumspect.'

Joining Twite, too close to noisome flesh to be comfortable and keeping his pipe going at full glow, he looked at the exposed back. Across the shoulders and buttocks were patches of pressure marks showing more pallid than the skin surrounding them. Rogers knew that at death liquid blood drained by gravitation into the capillaries in the lower parts of the body and stained it. There was an exception. The staining did not, could not, appear on those parts of the body in contact with any firm surface on which it was lying, for flattened capillaries could not admit blood into themselves. It was a post-mortem lividity called hypostasis and it showed both men that Cruickshank had been on his back for some time after his death and not suspended to choke to death from the roof joist.

Rogers said, 'I can see that he was definitely dead before being suspended. So where would he get the signs of asphyxiation? Being strangled or smothered hours before being strung up?'

Twite, dropping his cigarette end and scuffing it to extinction on the cement floor, regarding him over a short red-faced paroxysm of coughing. 'Pithily, yes, old George, though you seem dolefully short on some other causes of death by asphyxia. There's drowning, throttling by ligature and by angry thumbs; suffocation by simple deprivation of air, inhalation of certain gases; also, less commonly but nevertheless possible, self-inflicted asphyxiation from the effects of morphinism and the taking of some of the barbiturates. To mention,' he added, 'just a few.'

'Thank you, Wilfred,' Rogers said sardonically, no stranger to the majority of them.

Twite had pulled the pyjama trousers down to the ankles where he left them. 'There's more, of course,' he said, 'though not enough to give you high blood pressure. He's been hanging here long enough for a secondary hypostasis to have developed in the extremities of his arms and legs. The blood spots below him are almost certainly due to this, the veins in these circumstances being apt to become porous and leak.' He took out a white handkerchief and wiped delicately with it at his fingertips, returning it to his pocket. 'You're not going to be so happy when I tell you that he's in such a mess that I can't be certain of the time of death within two days or so. That is, not until I get him on the table, and even then having to do some lab tests.'

33

'It's important how long ago, Wilfred,' Rogers urged him. 'I'll shout you a sandwich or something for a decent guess.'

Twite lit another cigarette, then screwed his eyebrows as if faced with an imponderable something. 'Nine to ten days? At a push, a day or so either side? But that's all laboratory plod-plod for tomorrow; for today it's lunch if you've a full wallet and can tear yourself away.'

Rogers winced, having had some experience of the cost of his friend's lunches. 'It's an estimate that'd fit,' he acknowledged. 'The uncollected newspapers in the hall go back nine days to last Monday week. Which means that the last newspaper he read before his death was the Sunday one. As he obviously died during the night, he never got around to reading the Monday edition. And, you'll be happy to hear, at some time I'll need to have you specify which of your possibilities killed him.'

It was important to his sense of a supernatural justice that the dead man should have gone some way to earning his terrible death. A blameworthy death could diminish his pity for it and make any contemplation of it the less painful, though none of that would forward his investigation one iota or be capable of helpful interpretation by the pathologist.

'I hope to,' Twite said, 'but it's not always possible. They're tricky, these jobs, particularly with a badly decomposed cadaver. And more particularly with one showing secondary evidence of violence.' He shrugged fat shoulders. 'That's enough for now, old son. I'll see to him in the mortuary this afternoon. After we meet for a post-mortem conference, say at the Hog's Nose Eating House at one thirty?'

Rogers, seeing Twite to his so-envied car, needed a little more than urgently the untainted air outside the garage. That and the time to organize the routine enquiries necessary to a murder investigation and yet to be able to think what the hell was he to do next before receiving Twite's report on a yet to be done post-mortem examination. He prayed that there would come to be something to illuminate what he exaggeratedly admitted to be the darkness of his brain.

6

Casa Griot, while built to the same Spanish style of the other villas in the road, was visibly more expensively appointed. Bounded by a high wall, it possessed a facing-the-sea glassed-in terrace with, inside it, its own thickets of well-foliaged dwarf trees and shrubbery. The walls of the building were an eye-dazzling white, the profusion of wrought ironwork a newly painted black. A short gravelled drive led to a two-car garage and to an iron-studded panelled and glossily varnished wooden door at the side of the terrace.

Rogers, tapping the ash from his pipe and putting it in his jacket pocket, passed by the paved forecourt planted with palms and climbed tiled steps to use the door's black iron knocker, hot to the touch from the morning's sun.

The woman who opened the door to him was an instant physical attraction and Rogers, for a brief unguarded moment, felt his heart lurch with what was probably alarm.

Appearing to be about the same age as himself, she was tall and lean, small-breasted and narrow-flanked, her shoulder-length hair the colour of cigarette ash. Her eyes were the dark green of a deep sea, her nose femalely hawkish in a tanned face in whose structure Rogers could read what he judged to be a lurking high old feminine imperiousness. Her unlipsticked mouth was generous and inclined to show sadness, though with a just discernible cynicism. She wore elegantly a white linen trouser suit that emphasized her narrowness and looked much lived in. On her feet were well-worn espadrilles. Coltart had exaggerated about her jewellery. She wore a thin gold chain around her throat, a greenstone-studded wrist bracelet, dangling ear-rings and a tiny wrist-watch which, if sold, would probably keep him in tobacco and petrol for his car for a couple of years. There was an attitude about her that said if you weren't of a piece with her, would you please shut the door and the drive gate on your way out.

'Mrs Rhys Pritchard?' he asked smiling, hoping to God his clothing wasn't smelling of the dead Cruickshank.

'That would be a fair guess,' she answered pleasantly enough, her accent beautifully articulated with echoes of a Welsh lilt in it.

He produced his warrant card, holding it out for her to read. 'Detective Superintendent Rogers,' he said. 'I'd be grateful for a little of your time.'

'About poor Philip Cruickshank, naturally.' She stood to one side. 'Do come in.'

As he passed her, Rogers smelled the scent she wore, a musky fragrance new to his nose and which, on any attractive woman, could do serious things to his libido. For God's sake, he told himself; keep your bloody mind on the job.

'We shall go on the terrace,' she said, moving around him and leading the way to a closed door with a round glass porthole in it, a few steps along a corridor furnished with gold-framed French Impressionist prints and small tables loaded with porcelain figures of birds and animals.

Looking through the porthole and then opening the door, she pressed a hand to his arm and said, 'Go in quickly; I don't wish any problems with my finches.'

The screened terrace, more of a conservatory than otherwise, into whose humid heat he stepped, had its open windows, through which there was a panoramic view of the blue-green sea below, covered with a fine metal mesh. The trees and bushes he had seen from the road were growing from large wooden tubs sunk in moist peat and appeared to be sub-tropical. From their green shadows he could hear bird noises and catch glimpses of what he thought to be yellowish-brown and wholly white sparrows with brilliantly red beaks. The centre of the terrace was paved with enough stone slabs to accommodate a white-painted iron garden table and two plumply stuffed patio chairs. It was, he thought, a pleasantly private arbour for somebody not all that anxious for other human company.

36

'Do sit,' she said, 'and please don't make silly clucking noises at my birds. So many do and the birds naturally think them mad.'

Seated herself, she had been calmly measuring him up; much, he thought, as if deciding whether his lightweight grey suit had been decently tailored and he had shaved himself properly. He, for his part, having already taken in her externals, was wondering if she had a husband. If she had, he had not so far seen one sign of a male occupancy.

He smiled from the comfort of his chair. 'Making silly clucking noises is one of my weaknesses,' he said genially, 'though usually I confine it to my customers. To the point, however. I understand that you were told that Mr Cruickshank had met with an accident. This, of course, was properly done at the time, for we do have to be careful about what we say in connection with any person's unusual death.' Bloody hell, he inwardly groaned. Why do I get so damned pedestrian when I'm talking to attractive women.

'And you are going to tell me now? Not fob me off with evasions as your inspector did?' She sounded very self-assured, her eyes unblinkingly on his.

Rogers put on an expression of downright frankness. 'That's not what I'm here for, Mrs Pritchard,' he said. 'Mr Cruickshank was found hanging in his garage this morning by his son, Stephen; cause of death so far not confirmed. I'm told that . . .'

'You mean he hanged himself?' she interrupted him.

Ignoring that, hoping that she wouldn't be too offended, he smiled at her. 'I understand that you'd had an interest in him and that you had offered to help us.' As he was to the leeward of her scent, she seemed to Rogers to be gaining in her agreeableness. 'You were friendly with him, of course?'

'For some while until he apparently decided that I should become his mistress,' she said calmly with a glint of amusement in her eyes. 'He had, I discovered, a quite nasty mind; in fact, proving to be rather a filthy pig; ever a man to put his hands up a woman's skirt. Do you wish me to go on?'

Rogers, surprised at her unusually phrased forthcomingness, eyed her with a deal more respect as a potential source of useful information. 'You make him sound like God's blight to women,' he said lightly, intending to encourage her to garrulity. 'Perhaps being a rather filthy pig and someone able to provoke an interest in himself from women are both sides of the same coin. However, I'd be grateful for more if you have it,' he added with a growing confidence in her co-operation.

'I'm sure you would,' she agreed coolly, 'so perhaps you'll stop being so officially obstinate and tell me whether he did it himself, or he did not.'

'So far as we know, he did not,' Rogers conceded reluctantly, 'though its corollary need not be what you may think. And about this I need your discretion.'

'I imagined you would,' she said with no indication whether she meant yes or no. 'You know that he was a retired farmer?'

Rogers nodded, trying not to be distracted by the small red-beaked bird that had dared to settle on her shoulder and was pulling at strands of her hair.

'He moved into the road three years ago, having, he told me and no doubt others, sold his farm at some benighted place called Lower Penruddock. He was quite a crude man, though friendly and generous should you let him be. And quite good-looking with it. As you suggest, he wasn't without his female admirers and, before you have the gall to ask me, I was never one of them.' Her expression clearly dared him to challenge that.

To Rogers, that was almost certainly so, for he felt, admittedly fancifully, that for a man to touch her unclothed body might almost be the equivalent of committing lese-majesty. 'The last thing I'd ask,' he said soberly as if he meant it. 'Particularly with a married man. He was that, wasn't he?'

'Yes,' she answered with her inner amusement showing again, 'but he did tell me when I knew him better – and I am really disclosing a confidence – that his wife had run off with his farm manager a few years ago.' She put a finger under the bird on her shoulder, lifted it off and with a smooth motion of her arm sent it flying to a tree. 'Sorry about that,' she said, her sad mouth changing itself into a smile. 'He probably believes I'm his mother; somebody, I'm afraid, available for use as nesting material.'

Returning to the subject of Cruickshank, she said, 'I was

supposed to be talking about Philip, wasn't I? After we became friendly as neighbours he told me that he was interested in buying a sailing boat – which he never did – and I invited him to occasionally crew with me in *Lady Pink Gin II*, which is my boat. That, naturally, ended after he had made his astonishingly louche suggestion; made, I'm certain, when he was drunk. Not, under the circumstances, a very complimentary proposal.'

Apart from not wanting or being unable to visualize a tall and elegant Angharad Rhys Pritchard having an intimate association with a crude and very short Cruickshank, Rogers had been watching the deep green eyes and her expression, seeking to recognize truth in her words. 'The wife and farm manager business,' he said. 'Can you put names to them? A full name for Mrs Cruickshank?' He had long begun to ooze sweat into his underclothing, and now a sort of rising warm damp had reached the collar of his shirt. Mrs Pritchard remained, he could see, elegantly cool.

'Her name was Miriam; I think the manager's was Ashe, I believe with an "e".' She thought for a moment or two. 'Richard,' she said. 'I'm sure Philip told me that was his name. He was telling me this, I'm certain, to angle for sympathy which I'm afraid he didn't get. When I hear of a wife leaving her husband to go off with another man, my sympathies usually lie with her.'

Rogers, thinking of his own ex-wife and believing discretion to be the better part of common sense, gave her a weak smile. 'I'm sure you're right,' he murmured. 'Would he have known where they'd gone?'

'Abroad, I believe. He wasn't sure, but thought probably France or Spain. He could get quite angry about it, and in the early days, he would then be quite boring company. Anyway,' she added, 'I was never particularly interested.'

'There was a woman staying with him last year, or at least frequently visiting him,' he put to her in a kind of interrogative doublespeak. 'Possibly a relative, but I'd like to find out who she is.'

'There *was* a woman and she was visiting him for short periods from last autumn, or perhaps before. So far as I am aware there was never any secret about it, nor need there have been. After a while she lived there more or less permanently – she could have married him for all I know for certain – and called herself Mrs Cruickshank. I know this because for a week or so before it was realized she was doing it we had a half-witted postman delivering my mail to Philip's address and his to mine.'

She shook her head, mildly disapproving, and a tiny crystal in one of her dangling ear-rings reflected a dazzling prism of sunlight into Rogers's eyes. 'She's gone now,' she said. 'She has been since . . . well, that's none of my business nor needing my involvement in it. She was not quiet, you understand, but flashy and rather too obvious.'

'Not up to a retired farmer's standards?' Rogers asked lightly.

'Don't be silly,' she reproved him coolly. 'I wouldn't think she was up to anyone's standards who had room in their heads for more than going to bed with a woman like her. I met her casually twice and wondered what on earth had possessed even Philip with his womanizing to have her in the house.'

She pursed her lips, calmly speculative, staring at the detective who was now comfortable in meeting its seeming evaluation of him. 'There was something of a scene at the house – I'd say it was last January or February – when she had a visitor. I was a witness to it, seeing it only because I was walking past when it happened. I don't know where Philip was, but I certainly cannot believe that he was in the house or near it. She was standing at the front door – I could see that it was open – almost screaming in anger at this extremely large man who was standing at the gate to the drive and who was being as loathsome to her, though in a more restrained way, you understand.'

'You mean quietly menacing?' Rogers suggested.

She nodded. 'That could describe it, because in the few seconds it took me to walk past them I thought he was getting ready to hit her. I tried hard not to listen, but I couldn't help but hear that she was telling him non-stop to stuff something and to leave her alone. He wasn't getting too much in and when he did he kept his voice low so I didn't hear the gist of whatever he was saying. Enough though to know that whatever threatening

40

he was doing, it was in a lowered voice as if he didn't wish the rest of the road to hear it. I don't honestly believe that he was aware of my walking behind him.' She smiled downputtingly. 'To give the man some credit, she was behaving appallingly. Certainly she called him names I don't think would ever be accepted in civilized society.'

Rogers wondered what unheard-of frightful obscenities they would have to be to upset the society they both moved in. 'You've no idea at all about what they were fighting over?'

She creased her forehead, frowning her thinking back for long moments. 'I somehow feel – it's such a long time ago, you know – that they were at odds about money and other women. Both were mentioned, I'm fairly sure. And I remember he called her Eunice, so he did know her.'

'Ignoring the unspeakable words,' the still-amused detective asked, 'was there any suggestion that they might have been lovers? Or even husband and wife?'

Her slim fingers were playing ceaselessly with the gold chain around her throat; a possible reflection of a mood that Rogers could never attempt to interpret in a woman. 'I hadn't thought of that,' she conceded. 'There could have been some love well lost between them.'

'I'm sure you were about to tell me what he looked like,' he suggested amiably. He was finding himself being more and more fascinated by her small gestures, by the sound of her voice and the movement of her lips in using it.

'Oh dear,' she said. 'I do so hate disappointing you, but I really was hurrying past them, trying so hard not to notice them or to hear what they were saying. He had his back to me and I only saw the side of his face which just showed that he didn't have a moustache or a beard . . .' – she paused, biting at her lower lip – '. . . yes, I'm trying to remember his hair.'

'He had some of that as well?' he said in good-humoured raillery.

She laughed with him. 'Idiot,' she said. 'I didn't mean it like that. It was dark brown, almost black, and it came down over his collar.' She put a finger on the side of her neck with an expression that made Rogers decide that even if subject to a future chance delirium he would never ever wear his hair like that.

41

'Can you give him an age?' he asked. 'And describe his clothing? He's beginning to interest me.'

'I'm guessing wildly as you've probably noticed. I'd say from the back he looked thirty-five – perhaps forty. He wore what I considered at the time to be a very good camel-hair coat. You know? The army major's mufti sort of thing; fairly short and military-looking. He didn't go with it, of course. Not with that hair-style.' She shrugged narrow shoulders. 'That's about it, I'm afraid.'

'Could you make a guess at what he'd do for a living?' He could not help but notice – and he had been trying not to – that when she had on occasions put a hand to her hair to push it back from her face, the movement tightened the fabric of her suit and showed the detailed prominences of her patently bra-less breasts. He could not explain it, but he was more subject to a breast's appeal when covered than when it might possibly be thrust naked beneath his nose.

'Hm.' She looked doubtful. 'You're being rather difficult, aren't you? Let me just say that he probably makes a good living from whatever it is he does. And he had a rather authoritative air about him; something that said he'd be quite capable of looking after himself. He was a big man, big like . . . like a rugby player going to seed . . .' – Rogers went Ouch! inside himself at that – '. . . and I remember now that he must have walked up here because there was no car parked in the road.'

'Perhaps deliberately parked away from the road so his calling on her wouldn't be too obvious?'

'He was obvious to me,' she disagreed.

There were a few moments of the sounds of disturbed leaves and the squabbling chirping of small birds in the tree behind her and he waited, letting the more basement-oriented mind of his *alter ego* take in her desirability until the noise subsided. 'How was Miss Parr dressed?' he asked.

'In a cornflower-blue woollen suit. It looked expensive, so I'm sure Philip paid the bill for it.' She creased her forehead. 'There was one other thing about her. I could never place her accent. It sounded English and yet it wasn't quite. It was something like educated Cockney, if there is such a thing.'

Rogers imagined that he could accept that as Australian.

'Have you seen any other callers that you'd care to identify or describe?'

She pulled a face. 'Stephen Cruickshank, as you'd expect.'

'No others?' He sensed from her attitude that she was holding back.

She made an elegant gesture with her hand towards her side of the terrace, any view from it being obstructed by the foliage of trees and shrubs. 'I see very few from here; but there are, of course, because I do hear cars arriving and leaving. But that can be confusing because Philip has no car and frequently used the local taxi service. The others? I choose not to be inquisitive and those I have happened to see I can't put names to. How could I? His friends were not mine.'

When Rogers remained silent, well aware of its power to show that he was waiting for more, she said, 'Do forgive me. I do know of one visitor – well, two actually – in whom you might be interested, but I need to think of the consequences likely to arise from what I believe I know.'

He had already judged her to be a woman of principle and there was no hesitation in him. Amiably, he said, 'And you'll tell me after you've thought it out and decided that I'm to be trusted?'

She smiled. 'I will if I'm able, but you mustn't push me.'

'Back to Stephen Cruickshank then,' he said. 'You know him reasonably well?'

'I know him,' she replied enigmatically after a thoughtful pause.

'A nice enough chap?'

She quirked her mouth at him, neither answering nor, manifestly, intending to.

Damn, he muttered to himself. He had run up against another female inhibition or something. Aloud and changing tack, he said, 'But you have told me that his father wasn't such a nice character. Apart from the woman you've already mentioned, do you know the identity of any of the others?'

'By repute, yes.' She held his gaze steadily with a friendly return of her own. 'I'm afraid that that's as far as I'm prepared to go. I'd be treading on dangerous ground where I'd be imputing immorality as such to named persons. Too, should they have husbands or commitments of their own then, unless my conscience tells me otherwise – and it doesn't at the moment – I am content to leave them to theirs.'

'Another day, perhaps?' he said as affably as his disappointment would allow him. He eased himself upright in his chair, his back feeling as if it had been given a sponge bath. 'If and when the investigation gets a lot more serious I hope that you change your mind.'

'Say perhaps when you tell me that Philip didn't kill himself. I find it difficult to believe that he did.'

'Why?' He had come to the conclusion that she was on her way back from some past traumatic happening and, further, that the longer he was with her so the more telling was her sexual attractiveness.

'Because you are asking too many questions and I'm so sure that he isn't the type. Too egocentric for a start,' she added.

He believed – he wanted to believe – that he could trust her not to stand on the nearest high eminence and broadcast his official opinion to the citizenry of Thurnholme Bay. 'It might be,' he said cautiously, 'that the manner of his death may not be quite as it appears. It is policy that if I am not wholly sure of the cause of it, then I am obliged to treat it initially as a homicide.' He softened his voice to a request. 'You won't, I hope, let that go further than yourself.'

'Thank you,' she answered him. 'Before you ask me, as I think you must, I really do not know anything at the moment that is likely to help your enquiry.' Her gaze on him was steady, feeling to him as if it were reaching into the inner aspect of his skull.

'I'll be back,' he promised her.

She rose from her chair. 'I'll call you when I've reached a decision about naming the visitors I mentioned. Now perhaps you'll excuse me, but I do have an appointment in town very shortly.'

Rogers stood also and took her extended hand. 'I'm grateful,' he said, holding on to it a few obvious seconds too long, but unable to think of anything further to say.

Ushering him from the terrace to the outer door and pausing there, she said slightly mischievously, 'I think I should tell you,

44

Mr Rogers, that though I never practised, I did read for the Bar in my early days. I tell you so because I can appreciate the difficulties which you are meeting with me.'

Finding himself in the midday sun, he was slightly bemused and wholly uncertain whether his interview had been ended, firmly if politely, on a pretext or not. While his instincts had always been against any involvement but a professional one with those women he interviewed as potential witnesses, this particular woman had fostered in him, unwittingly he was sure, a strong sexual interest for her. Far more, perhaps, than her revealed mature persona had suggested it could.

As he was lighting his pipe in full stride, she passed him in an expensive glistening new green Range Rover, waving her hand and smiling her teeth at him before he had reached Cruickshank's villa. It did things to his never very prominent ego, making him feel two or three inches taller and bigger around the chest. 'Angharad,' he said aloud, realizing that he was savouring the name much as a pudding-faced teenager might. 'I like it.'

Down to reality, he knew that he was only a little the wiser about an apparently understandably promiscuous Philip Cruickshank deceased, his very angry ex-common-law wife of sorts and a possibly thuggish kind of rugby player going to seed who sounded as if he had been very bad news for her.

7

Returning to Abbotsburn, a minster town of mostly limestone buildings in narrow and vertiginous medieval streets and alleys, Rogers sat at his desk in one of the offices of the architecturally featureless concrete and glass County Police Headquarters. He hated his coldly metal desk and the strip lighting above it which, on a bad day, made him look – he swore – a hundred and three years old. Seven years ago he had been working in a now demolished pigeon-haunted Georgian building, using a tobacco smoke impregnated office which had history written potently in its walls and a colony of tolerated house mice – he used to leave bread crusts under his wooden desk for them – behind what wainscoting had been left by a succession of otherwise interfering chief constables in the past. Now, bar the chief constables, he missed all that when he sat in his institutionalized and computerized plastic and metal unloved no-smoking-by-order office. It was largely an absurdity, the extreme of it being the Chief Constable's latest order, banning the sticky-taping of notices to office walls, having been sticky-taped by an administrative clerk to one of Rogers's walls.

Having finished updating his notes and comments of his investigation, he found it difficult in a surround of statistical crime charts and black and white photographs of the force's *Most Wanted* on custard-coloured walls to recall whatever softer emotions had been expended on Angharad Rhys Pritchard, and he had cooled down two or three degrees from his initial fascination with whatever constituted her being. Too, he felt unusually bloated with the food and wine he felt he had been bulldozed into paying for Twite and himself at the expensive Hog's Nose Eating House.

Before leaving the garage, then bare of the dead Philip Cruickshank who was *en route* for the hospital mortuary's cold tables, Rogers had detailed the phlegmatic Coltart to visit Lower Penruddock Farm, situated in what he thought of as his bailiwick's outback. There, he was to seek out what he could of the pattern of Cruickshank's farming, social and domestic life, and the circumstances of his sale of the farm. Somewhere in his life someone had felt badly enough, and savagely enough to have murdered him, presumably in his bed, then hanging him in his garage to simulate suicide.

Although he had neither the wish nor any reasonable grounds for doing so, he had also set the hounds on to the heels of Mrs Rhys Pritchard in the shape of DC Lewis, the officer in charge of committed crime and flouted morality at Thurnholme Bay. He was to give local villains a brief holiday from his attentions and to bring into the open – that is, into Rogers's open – what he could discover of her history, of her marital or other status; of her association with Philip Cruickshank in particular though also with any other male associates; and of her activities in a boat named *Lady Pink Gin II*. Having looked into the origin of the name Angharad – from casual curiosity only, he convinced himself – and finding it to mean 'white-breasted', he had to admit that while it might adventitiously titillate his own imagination, it added little to the sum of human knowledge or help to his investigation.

So far as the man who looked like a rugby player was concerned, he passed a message to Inspector Millier, adding him to her enquiry about Eunice Parr with whom he had almost certainly been associating. Doing it, he tried hard not to feel prejudiced against him just because he had been described by Mrs Rhys Pritchard as appearing to be one of those characters he was helping to support as his ex-wife's lover.

When he had disposed of that which he considered needed doing, he lit his now forbidden pipe – he could always plead absent-mindedness – leaned back in his black imitation leather executive-style chair that squeaked in protest at his weight, and thought.

First of all, unbidden and unwanted, he knew that he wouldn't mind at all hearing again the lilting voice of Angharad Rhys Pritchard. Only, he convinced himself, to be able to see dissipated whatever it was in her persona that appeared to be affecting his judgement and, possibly, his impartiality. Damn it! He certainly wasn't the pudding-faced teenager he had postulated on the way out from her villa, and he had better remember it.

His mind moved sideways to Stephen Cruickshank, a more legitimate target for his thinking. The dormant part of his mind having been allowed to do its own reflecting, it had decided that because he feared needles being pushed into the flesh of his mouth – he called it, possibly erroneously, his acusophobia – he was therefore inclined to view Cruickshank as even more unfeeling in inflicting pain than those hypodermic syringe-happy members of the medical profession. That apart, there was something about the man he didn't trust. His perfume and his finger-length pigtail? His small thin-lipped mouth or his unconcealed malice towards Eunice Parr? He shook his head irritably. He couldn't identify with any confidence what it was, but he would definitely keep it in the forefront of his calculations.

So far as the totality of available information he had fed into his brain, his personal computer, was concerned, he remained unsatisfied with its response, having received what must have been the expected reply, 'Insufficient data to suggest a conclusion.' It was now enough to remember that he had a meeting with Twite, the dead Philip Cruickshank, the rising gorge verities of the surgical disembowelling and possibly a something else, he told himself with a wry distaste, into which he could sink his teeth.

Rogers entered the mortuary, an always chilly subterranean annexe to the town's formidably Victorian hospital, by the wide sloping approach made suitable for reversing hearses. Deliberately late and hoping that Twite would be near to finishing, he pushed open the green-painted outer door, passing through a dark corridor flanked by banks of quietly humming refrigerated body cabinets, then through an inner door marked KEEP OUT into the white brilliance of shadowless floodlighting and the intermingled odours of formaldehyde and dead flesh.

Twite, standing over the dreadfully corrupted remains of a naked Cruickshank lying on one of the two stainless steel necropsy tables, turned his head and said something that sounded like 'You're late, old son,' around the cigarette in his mouth.

'Pushed,' Rogers said, taking up a position against a working top where he hadn't unnecessarily to have the body within his view. 'Paperwork unending. Have we illuminating results yet?'

Twite, wearing his green surgical gown and red rubber apron, had already removed the scalp and the skull's hemisphere, and opened the body with a clean incision from the throat to the groin. He held a scalpel in a bloodied rubber-gloved hand, his forefinger on its spine, cutting at an abdominal organ with apparent but misleading slapdash. A black hose, dangling from the low ceiling, ran rippling water on to the offcuts and slivers of tissue, flesh and internal organs put by on the table's surface.

'If my patient's weight and height you asked for are such,' he said, his cigarette jerking and scattering ash on the body, 'then yes. He's five feet six and a quarter inches, and weighs in without his pyjamas at one hundred and twenty-three pounds.'

'Reasonably portable, then,' Rogers said. 'There'd be no great difficulty in pulling him up on to a beam.' He was stuffing tobacco into his pipe, his antidote against life's unpleasantnesses with the specific inclusion of the smell of decomposing flesh.

'Probably not.' Twite worked on in a concentrated silence, interrupted only to screw his cigarette to extinction on the floor and to ask Rogers to replace it from the packet left on the working top and then to try and light it without, he said, setting fire to his moustache.

The detective, content to wait in silence, smoked his pipe, thought about the mechanics of his golf swing and, less frequently, about what it must be like to be the late Philip Cruickshank arriving at the unimaginable Other Side in a state far from being of bodily togetherness.

Twite, having at last finished, stripped off his gloves, scrubbed his hands to a pudgy pinkness in a wash-basin and, while changing from his protective clothing in a side room, spoke to Rogers. He didn't seem to be too happy with the results of his examination.

'I'd be obliged, old son,' he said, 'if you could, in future, manage to have your customers delivered as cadavers a little earlier than a probable ten days post mortem. In view of this one's advanced decomposition there'll have to be some lengthy laboratory work before I can be definite about all that you require.' He brightened somewhat. 'The near certainties are, one, that death was caused by suffocation; two, that he was dead before being strung up; and, three, that the ligature marks on his neck were caused some hours after he had died. He frowned. 'An oddity, though. There's what I'd call a shadow ligature mark below – not beneath – the other marks I've mentioned. It may mean something or nothing and it's over to you for what it's worth. So far as the question of suffocation may be an issue, there're all the indisputable

49

symptoms of it; congestion of the conjunctivae and the brain, petechial haemorrhages and so forth.'

Rogers kept his disappointment under cover. 'The symptoms could equally apply to suffocation by ligature, I imagine?' He added quickly, 'Not that I'm querying it, of course.'

'Mostly, yes, and you'd better not.' Twite wasn't a man to be argued with over his findings.

'So could we accept that whoever faked the hanging would know this? In fact, its being the reason for not faking the death as a suicide by any other means.'

'You could have something there,' Twite conceded. 'But back to how he was actually killed. The specific how of it you'll have to find out for yourself and you might start by hypothesizing something relatively soft and pliable being held by force over the mouth and nostrils. Anyway, a something that would inhibit breathing without leaving post-mortem traces of applied force as you're certain to get in a struggle. And people being suffocated do struggle very much.'

'A pillow?' Rogers remembered the one on the floor near Cruickshank's bed. 'He'd obviously been in bed and there was one handy. Though,' he added, 'I agree with you about the struggling and it would need at least a strongish adult to do it.'

'It's your guess, old son.' Twite was being non-committal.

'I was thinking about the head injury, Wilfred. There'd be no difficulty about suffocating an unconscious man.'

Twite was lighting a fresh cigarette and Rogers waited until he had finished coughing. 'That won't go at all, I'm afraid. Done in life, I think that it'd stun him; which I believe doesn't matter in this case for I'm almost inclined to believe it was inflicted after death. I'm only inclined, dammit, because several days' decomposition do dreadful things to whatever evidence in it one wants. At a push,' he said, shrugging fat shoulders, 'I could accept that he'd been dropped accidentally on to a projecting something while being carried to the garage. You might like to look into that as a possibility. And, before you ask, he was lying on his back for some hours after he died; though how many only he would know.'

'Did you find any evidence of his having been recently entertained by a lady-friend?' Rogers asked.

'I took a swab, it's all I can do. You'll have to ask the lab people if there are any died-on-active-service tadpoles on it.' He yawned openly and gustily. 'Up late on a fatal cardiac arrest,' he explained. 'I shall have to be going.'

It was a none too subtle hint that he'd had enough and Rogers didn't, and wasn't expected to, believe him. 'I feel for you,' he said straight-faced. 'Do we have the stomach contents? They could be interesting.'

'There's a jar full for you, old son.' He looked at his wrist-watch, then beamed at the detective. 'I don't suppose you feel the need to shout me a tea at the DeReszke-Cavendish later on for services so quickly rendered.'

Rogers twisted his face into what could be taken as acute dis-appointment. 'The Chief Constable,' he said. 'He'll be expect-ing me.'

It could be, he told himself on his way out, that it might well be the truth, for one of the things events had rather driven from his mind had been the required reporting of progress, or lack of it, in a murder investigation to his often testy and unreasonable Chief Constable.

8

Detective Inspector Coltart, driving the undersprung CID so-called Q-Car – elderly, deliberately kept unwashed to deceive and sagging to one side because of his weight – was on his way to the village of Penruddock Without, isolated in the rural concealment of acres of limestone outcrops and wind-bitten trees, the scattered remains of a Dark Age forest.

Living on his own by preference, Coltart was normally nei-ther happy nor unhappy, bear-like in his personal allocation of space and generally harmless until seriously threatened, when his physical response with fists like fuzzy uncured hams could be decidedly unpleasant. For a man who had once been a choirboy with a voice alarmingly near castrato, his solidly held beliefs were a mite unconventional. One of them was that God had made an almighty bodge of things in bringing into being a badly flawed version of *Homo sapiens*, equipped unnecessarily with a disgusting means of procreating its kind, to inhabit a disaster-prone and hostile environment. Superintendent Rogers did not, he felt, set a good example by his suspected indulgence in this animal grossness.

Finding the attractively tree-surrounded village built on a steep slope, its forty-odd stone cottages attended by a walled-in manor house, a boarded-up Gothic perpendicular church, a grocery store cum sub-post office and an ancient ivy-hung pub, the Crookham Arms, he chose the pub for his first call.

Identifying himself to a surprised landlord in an almost empty bar, he bought a tomato juice stiffly laced with Worcestershire sauce. A few words about Lower Penruddock Farm brought out the name Scarton Sims. 'Call him Simmo,' the unusually garrulous landlord said. 'It might help because he's a miserable little bugger. He used to look after the pigs and chickens until he was sacked.'

Sims lived five miles along an unclassified road in a cottage isolated within an enormous yew hedge, its walls having a great need for a coat or two of white paint, and being identified by having a hollow-eyed and vacuous-looking life-sized scarecrow standing in its vegetable garden. It was accompanied by a small man who looked up from his digging at Coltart's approach.

Alighting from the car and entering the garden, Coltart said a reasonably cheerful 'Good afternoon, Mr Sims,' produced his warrant card because he was being regarded suspiciously and told him that a Mr Cruickshank – whom he had been told he would have known – had been found dead in his home at Thurnholme Bay and that there were necessary questions to be asked on behalf of Her Majesty's Coroner.

Sims was a stringy, burned up and seemingly bitter little man with greying brown hair, a beaky nose and watery pale blue eyes. Looked at not too closely, he could appear to resemble an elderly rooster. He wore a scruffy patterned cardigan over an open-necked khaki shirt and narrow-legged jeans. Coltart's initial opinion of him was that at some time he had been pickled in vinegar and that, as a consequence, he would probably last for ever.

52

Sims had listened intently to the big detective, then said, 'The old bleeder's gone, 'as he? I can't say I'm sorry, he weren't no friend of mine.' Turning away from Coltart, he pushed the spade he held into undug soil.

'But he was your employer? Pigs and poultry, I've been told.'

'Yes, he were. How'd you know that? An' what's it to you?' His attitude was resentful and he turned the spadeful of soil over in apparent dismissal of Coltart's presence.

Coltart wasn't liking this, but accepted Sims's apparent hostility as a not unusual facet of questioning procedures. He knew, too, that he should tread carefully with him, for the majority of small men, bantam cocks and pygmy shrews could too often be touchy and overly quarrelsome.

He reached within his baggy suit and produced his wallet, taking out a five-pound note and poking a heavy finger at Sims's unattending shoulder. 'This is witness expense money,' he said untruthfully in his chest-rumbling voice. 'You can put your spade down and listen to what I'm going to ask you. Right?'

Sims had turned and flinched at something in the detective's voice, then planted his spade into the earth with a heavy boot and left it there. Looking back at the cottage, he snatched the note from the huge fist in one quick movement, stuffing it crumpled into his trouser pocket. 'There ain't no need to shout,' he snarled. 'And me time 'as to be worth a quid or two.'

'Tell me what Mr Cruickshank was like to work for?' Coltart's forbidding green eyes held him like a pair of handcuffs. 'And the Coroner's man who'll want all the facts.'

'He was a bleedin' shit,' he said nastily. 'He laid me off after I'd been with 'im twelve years. He said I was too old an' needed a rest, which weren't right.'

'Was that when he sold the farm?' Over the top of the hedge behind Sims he had glimpses of undulating acres of newly grown grass with scattered clumps and groups of formidably large trees in the largely stone-walled landscape. A few hundred yards away there was a partly erected building flanked by a large and obviously ancient barn and an untidy scattering of building equipment, heavy on breeze blocks and railway

53

sleepers. There were no visible signs of human movement, but what he thought of as a hell of a lot of sky above it.

Sims's weatherbeaten features scowled. 'No. That were back four years, nearly five, long after I'd been laid off.'

'How long before?'

Sims thought. 'Two years. It were easy that.'

'Someone else did your pigs and poultry then?' He needed other names.

'The pigs they did. I 'eard he sold all me birds to the processing factory like as if they was wore out, which they wasn't, as soon as I'd gone. There was six 'undred of 'em in the deep litter barn an' he'd always said they was a small gold mine. So why'd he do it, eh? I could 'ave gone on, I ain't old yet . . .'

'The traumas of big business,' Coltart said sympathetically, stopping him in his tale of woe. 'He could have been having trouble with his finances.'

'So were I. Why didn't he sell the pigs then?' Sims demanded. 'They was worth more'n the chickens. An' Bill Anson took 'em over too. He weren't laid off; anyway, not until the farm shut down.'

'I'd better have a chat with him, hadn't I? Where's he living?'

'He ain't. He's dead an' in Penruddock graveyard. Younger'n me, too.' That seemed to give him a grain of satisfaction.

'I think I'll leave him be, then,' Coltart said with heavy meant-to-be humour. 'Are there any others about?'

'Not now there ain't, though there was four other'ns.' He gave Coltart their names, then added with seeming derision. 'They've all got jobs tha's miles away any'ow.'

'No matter, I'll find them. How well did you know Mrs Cruickshank?

'Agh!' There had been something in his watery eyes that interested the detective. 'She were a nice'n an' she 'ad enough sense to run away from 'im. She 'ad never come back. 'Ave you found 'er yet?'

Coltart answered his question with a steady stare. 'Do you mean running away with another man?' When Sims seemed lost in indecision, he said a trifle brusquely and not very truthfully, 'I already know who the man was. You're a paid witness now and I want *you* to tell me about him. Give me his name, tell me what he was doing here.' The sun was warming his back to a degree where he was beginning to sweat.

Sims had apparently thought about the five-pound note and, with it, the impressive bulk of the detective standing within reach of him. 'I reckoned there were somethin' going on with the three of 'em,' he said cautiously. 'I weren't born yesterday. She was at the farm one day an' gone the next. And so were 'im.'

'And who was he?'

'Mr Ashe, the farm manager. I knew 'e'd been soft on 'er an' I don't blame 'im one bit. It was like they was 'aving it off every time the boss went out the 'ouse and away somewhere, an' we wasn't that daft we din't notice it. The boss was a pig to 'er and it served 'im right. She was a good'un an' always polite to us, an' that's all I know.'

'Tell me more about Mr Ashe. What he did, where he slept, whether he had any family or relatives around here. Where did he come from – things like that.'

If Sims wondered why any coroner would want such dissociated trivia he showed no sign of it. He seemed to be thinking out Coltart's questions while retrieving a flat tin from his back trouser pocket and rolling himself a thin crumpled cigarette which he lit to the detective's visible displeasure. 'He were younger than 'er,' he said at last, 'an' good-looking with it. He were proper to me an' I 'ad respect for 'im. I was sorry 'e went off like that, but it couldn't be 'elped, I suppose. He were single an' 'ad lodgin's in the Crookham Arms boozer. He were a bit of a loner an' I never saw 'im with anybody else.'

'How old was he? Describe what he looked like.'

Sims scowled. 'It weren't me what was sleepin' with 'im. I weren't near enough to 'im to know anythin' about 'im.' He pulled at his lower lip with earth-stained fingers, patently thinking back in time. 'Guessin', I'd say he were near enough thirty-five an' much more younger'n Mrs C. who was gettin' on for per'aps ten or more years than 'e was. But, by golly,' he leered, 'she were a good-lookin' lady an' 'er titties were still as big as ever.'

'*Him*,' Coltart said severely disapproving. 'Not her.'

'I dunno. He was tall and skinny an' he 'ad black 'air a bit on the bushy side an' I suppose you'd say good-lookin' in a pansy sort of way which he couldn't 'elp of course. But a nice bloke for all that. I mean, 'e was polite an' not too bossy an' 'e knew 'is stuff about farmin'.'

'Was anything said by Mr Cruickshank to you chaps about him and her going off together?'

Sims curled his lip in derision. 'Not to me 'e din't, but 'e did tell Bill Anson Mrs C. 'ad gone to 'er family in London somewhere for a 'oliday an' Mr Ashe 'ad been given 'is cards because 'e'd let 'im down by gettin' a job somewhere else and nobody 'ad to mention 'is name again.'

'Just somewhere else?'

'That's what 'e told Bill.' He was irritable about it.

'Can you remember when all this happened?'

'I don't need to. It were in July six years ago like I told you. They went the day before the boss said I 'ad to go because I was too old and business was bad an' e'd 'ad a good offer for the birds. He paid me my wages for a month an' told me I could go straight away an' that I could stay on rentin' the 'ouse until 'e wanted it for someone else, an' I've been 'ere ever since.'

'Nothing other than that?' Coltart felt himself to be dodging around something significant if only he could pin Sims down. 'Even if you weren't at the farm, you were here and you'd be able to hear or see what was going on.'

Sims's cigarette had gone out and he held it between his fingers while he bit at his lower lip in irresolution. 'There was somethin',' he said finally. 'The boss 'ad let me go on trappin' 'is rabbits where they was a nuisance an' 'e couldn't keep them down by 'is shootin'. I was out early a few days after I was let go to pick up what 'ad been snared an' I saw smoke comin' from the incinerator shed near the farm'ouse. Nobody'd be workin' then an' the ashes 'ad to be damped down at night, so I thought it'd come on again an' might per'aps burn the shed down. Anyway, I found the boss in there, though 'e weren't my boss any longer, an' of course I'd shook 'im by walkin' in an' 'e was 'opping mad.'

He paused to hawk in his stringy throat and to spit out

56

phlegm, then saying broodingly, 'He were a nasty-tempered sod at the best of times, an' 'e shouted at me for a bit then told me that now I knew Mrs C. 'ad gone off and left 'im per'aps I'd keep my bleedin' mouth shut about what was bound to shame 'im or else I would be lookin' for another 'ouse to live in. What 'e was doin' there was burnin' some of 'er dresses an' shoes 'e was takin' out of suitcases. It weren't any of my business anyway an' I never told anyone like 'e asked me until now.'

'Did he say anything about Ashe?'

'No. The bleeder wouldn't think it were any of my business. Or about Mrs C. either if 'e 'ad anythin' to do with it.' He relit the remains of his cigarette, sucking in its evil-smelling smoke, the somewhat priggish Coltart only just holding back from telling him that he was charcoaling his lungs as well as polluting the air in his, the detective's, vicinity.

Instead, he asked, 'Who owns the farm now?'

'I dunno, do I?' His elderly rooster's features were expressing an inner venom and signs of impatience. 'They was making a golf course out of it, but they stopped an' now I've 'ad solicitors' letters telling us to get out of the 'ouse. An' they said I were to stop trappin' their rabbits.'

'I don't suppose the rabbits are complaining,' the animal-liking Coltart said unsympathetically. 'Do you know the names of any of Mr Cruickshank's friends? Visitors to the farm and suchlike?'

Sims snorted. 'If 'e 'ad any, we didn' know 'em. He never went to the boozer neither. Mind, I know 'e went into Abbotsburn a lot, specially on market days, but he would bein' 'as he was in the business.'

Coltart was wondering if he had covered all Rogers's instructions. He was a perfectionist and, if Coltart hadn't, life for the next few hours would certainly be less than pleasant. He nodded in the direction of the buildings he could see. 'That was the farm, of course?'

Sims didn't bother to look, impatiently pulling out the spade he had planted in the soil. 'It was,' he glowered, 'until the bleeder sold it.'

Coltart, accepting with relief the meaning of the being-used-again spade and the turned-away attention from him, said,

'Thank you, Mr Sims,' to the unresponding back of his head and left the garden for his parked car.

Perhaps, he thought as he pointed his car towards the lane leading to what had once been a farm, he should have called the surly little bastard Simmo or leaned verbally on his spleenishness towards the dead Cruickshank. After he had satisfied his curiosity about the deep litter barn, he would have further words with the landlord of the Crookham Arms about a missing lodger he was fairly certain had never been reported to the police as such.

9

Rogers, smelling off-puttingly of formalin and the dead Cruick-shank, called in at his apartment after leaving the mortuary. Though he showered, doused himself in supposedly male-compatible fragrances and re-changed all his clothing, the receptors in his nostrils still refused to accept that his externals no longer smelt of decomposed flesh.

As fate usually had it, Detective Inspector Millier was waiting for him at Headquarters. Taking her to his office on the second floor he was careful always to keep to the rear or to the imagined leeward side of her. Seating her in the visitors' chair – she was either wearing no scent or his nose was being bloody-minded about it – he sat himself in his own chair after he had pushed it as far back from his desk as he acceptably could.

Having seen two typed reports, both marked *Urgent*, on his blotting-pad, he said, 'Excuse me for a moment,' to Millier and focused his attention on them. The first was from an only vaguely remembered DC Kirkpatrick who had been given the routine detail of ferreting out reputation information about a witness of significance and had submitted a report of not very useful ordinariness, in this instance about Stephen Spokes Cruickshank. Rogers picked from it what he thought to be information pertinent to his investigation. Cruickshank was aged thirty-two years, was unmarried and a dental surgeon

58

practising with group associates K. Hoy and D. Abernethy at Lysle Street, Abbotsburn. His private residence – which he shared with his sister, Mrs V.M. Cummins, who appeared to be husbandless – was given as Apartment 7, Winslow Court, Abbotsburn. Kirkpatrick described Cruickshank as being about six feet in height, of medium build, dark brown hair, brown eyes and with a large nose. There was nothing about Cruickshank's oddness in appearance, but a reference made to his interests in sub-aqua diving and fell walking. He had no known female associates, was apparently well regarded by those close to him and his name was not shown in criminal or other records. He was known to possess and drive a silver-coloured Metro City saloon, its registration number not being given. Rogers grunted his dissatisfaction at the report's lack of anything of apparent use and, with Kirkpatrick's future in the CID having taken a hard knock, turned to the second report.

This was from Thurnholme Bay's minor clap of doom for thieves scavenging from local hotel rooms, DC Lewis, the blond crew-cut type with a broken nose; an oddity in that he believed there was a smattering of good in the very worst of the villains he dealt with. The report's subject was Angharad Rhys Pritchard whom he had already met that morning. In relatively simple policeman's prose it told Rogers that the subject was thirty-nine years of age and a widow of independent means. She was a member of the local *Club Mouiller l'Ancre* – Lewis had unwisely explained to his likely-to-be-touchy senior officer that it translated into something like letting go of the anchor – as had been her late husband, retired Lieutenant Commander Gerald St John Rhys Pritchard, DSO, DSC. He had died highly respected and well-liked eight years previously in his early sixties, Lewis's enquiries suggesting the cause of death to be the acquisition of a naval wardroom's pink gin-related hobnailed liver. The marriage had been her first and only one and there were no known children from it. There was no mention of her in any record kept at Headquarters.

Apart from owning a this-year's marque Range Rover, its description and registration number detailed by Lewis, Mrs Pritchard also owned a Swordfish 31 diesel-powered sailing cruiser called *Lady Pink Gin II*, at present moored alongside

59

the club's 2B Walkway. She was known to have sailed it with the now dead non-member, Philip Cruickshank, on four occasions two years earlier. There were other members who had crewed for her and she for them, but as the boat could be sailed single-handed in normal weather conditions these were few. Other than that, it appeared that Lewis had found little to comment on in Mrs Pritchard's social life.

Rogers looked up from the report, meeting Millier's regard on him. 'Sorry about that,' he said amiably. 'It's Lewis's report on Mrs Rhys Pritchard. You hadn't met her this morning?'

'No. I only saw her speaking to Inspector Coltart.'

'No matter. You probably will.' He noted that she was still wearing her green suit of the morning, now seeming to be much the same shade of green as had been Cruickshank's liver. 'You've something to stop my day from being wholly jaundiced, I hope?' He held up his pipe. 'You don't mind?'

She smiled at him, not answering a question that needed none. 'I've been lucky and unlucky,' she said. 'I've bits and pieces about the woman Parr – that's her family name, incidentally – and who she's been associating with, but I've not so far managed to contact her.'

'Oh!' His black eyebrows lifted. 'Not missing, I hope? Or has she found herself another lover?'

'I think it can be assumed that she's still living at the address on her car registration form. It's a detached house – very much run down, by the way – called Haygarth in St Epiphanius Road. Though I called there three times there was no answer to my ringing and knocking, back and front. The curtains were drawn, and it would have been difficult to look inside even had I wanted to. There was no accumulation of anything on the doorstep and, so far as I could see through the letter flap, which wasn't much, there was nothing.' Millier looked hesitant for a moment. 'Those could be indications, I suppose, that she had been taking in any deliveries day by day and latterly this morning.'

'And leaving the curtains closed?' he queried. 'Could be, I suppose. But then again, possibly not. There's more?'

'Yes. Her car – it's correctly registered as a red Mazda – appears to be still in the garage. I say appears to be because it's locked and I could only see the red roof of what could be any car through a small window.'

Rogers had been furtively sniffing at himself while she talked – difficult because her gaze rarely left him – to decide whether he was still giving off the smell of decomposed Cruickshank, and still not being certain. 'Stick to it,' he said. 'If there's no sign of her by this evening, try a neighbour or two. And be reasonably diplomatic about it. It'd be difficult to believe, but we may find her to be the essence of respectability.'

'I'm sure that she's not,' Millier said with spirit, 'and I've already approached a neighbour or two under a most reprehensible pretext, about which you shouldn't enquire too deeply. Although nobody's certain – how could they be? – neither she nor her car has been seen in the road for at least a week. Admittedly it doesn't make her missing in our sense, because she wouldn't have been at her own address while she was living with Mr Cruickshank.'

'No, it doesn't, but you sound as if at least you have something interesting.' He hoped that she had, for he wanted to be able to recommend her with truthfulness at the end of her stay in the department.

'I think I have in the shape of a girl who used to work with her and knew her well.' There was an air of barely held-back satisfaction about her. 'She's known to have been employed by a man called Fuller who owns the Club Midnight Blue; almost certainly having been living with him off and on at the club. He's got convictions that I'm checking on for detail . . .'

Rogers held up a stopping finger at her. 'He's Robert something-or-other Fuller and he's known to the local hoi polloi as Robbie Fuller. He does own the Midnight Blue – it's hidden away in Paper Court off Commercial Street if you didn't already know – and I'd have thought you would have heard of him. His convictions are fairly elderly and are for unlawful wounding, GBH, carnal knowledge of a juvenile and false pretences. A gaudy mixture, though I understand he's cooled down a little, but I still wouldn't trust him out of arm's reach. He's said to be particularly lavish with the charm thing, attractive, generous with his or somebody else's money and a bugger with women.' As if that were something of which he

61

disapproved, he tried to look like a man in whom no women could possibly be interested. 'Whatever it is that you women like in a man, he's said to have it in abundance.'

Rogers knew Fuller – if the man he was thinking of *was* Fuller – though only from his investigation years back when Fuller had sorted out a thug he had seen badly ill-treating a greyhound bitch. Fuller had hit the man a smashing blow that had – unintentionally, he maintained – sent him staggering into the road with a broken jaw to fall under the wheels of a passing car. Rogers, his sympathies wholly with Fuller, had reluctantly charged him with causing grievous bodily harm. He had later spoken up for Fuller at his eventual trial, this resulting in Fuller receiving a much lesser sentence than he might otherwise have done. It hadn't meant that Rogers particularly liked or approved of Fuller, but he did like dogs.

Though he hadn't had anything personally to do with Fuller after that, he knew that he had bought himself into a rehabilitated eighteenth century burial vault-cum-adjacent cellar, then a failed restaurant called The Hole in the Wall, turning it into a drinking club. Against all the odds and his nature as a dishonestly acquisitive man, he ran it as an overtly honest business that didn't overcharge more than a hundred per cent for genuinely undiluted alcohol and good food, refused to employ singers and waitresses who wished to earn a second income by after-hours prostitution – there could be a selfish motive in that though – and used two uniformed security men to keep the club free of intruding yobbos and drunks. For all that, Rogers could never accept that Fuller was anything but an essentially unscrupulous man with a short-fused inner brutality.

'I knew about the Midnight Blue,' Millier said, a shade touchily, 'but not about Fuller. Should I?'

'Not necessarily,' he tried to mollify her, 'and up to now he seems to have been keeping his nose clean, though there have been unsupported reports that he's involved in marketing drugs. What matters is that you've given me the name of a man I could be interested in. I should have known he couldn't keep out of trouble for too long.' He told her about Parr and the big man she had been lashing with her violent tongue outside

Cruickshank's villa, not naming Angharad Rhys Pritchard as his informant. 'That's something I want you to bear in mind when you find Parr,' he said.

'I'd intended seeing him anyway.' She hadn't lost her touchiness and Rogers thought *What the bloody hell!* as he had dozens of times before with unfathomable females.

'Possibly one of the chaps could go with you,' he suggested. 'I wouldn't want you to be numbered among the objects of his physical displeasure.'

Millier stiffened in her chair, abrupt rejection in her expression; not a circumstance a surprised Rogers had previously met in her. 'When you do that, sir,' she said tersely, 'I shall know that I've ceased being of any effective use in the department.'

Rogers thought *Bloody hell!* again on this encounter with the inescapable sharp edge of an offended woman's tongue. 'For God's sake,' he growled in his own irritation. 'I'm only trying to be helpful. I don't want you to be assaulted or lied about by some bloody lout.'

When she said nothing and didn't look as if about to do so, he said more mildly, 'All right, Miss Millier, have it your way, but don't hurt the poor bugger too badly if he is tempted to physical assault. You've more about Miss Parr, of course?'

Millier had recovered the calmness she normally carried around with her. 'Yes,' she agreed, 'but little enough to find her. According to her friend – or her one-time friend, for there's no love lost between them since Parr seduced her lover – Parr is an Australian and came here five or six years back from a town called Cairns to take possession of the house in St Epiphanius Road which had been left to her by her maternal grandmother who was English. I was given a rather sketchy story about Parr's parents going on a motor-van holiday inland from Cairns and just not coming back. Parr said that if they'd been eaten by crocodiles – which was suspected – then they'd have eaten the motor-van as well because they and it were never found and were eventually presumed dead, leaving her to inherit the house and some small savings in place of her mother. While Parr and my informant were still on speaking terms, Parr had told her that she had been a singer while living in Cairns and, somewhat vaguely, hinted that she'd been married to a man she'd chosen not to go back to.'

'You think she was a singer in Fuller's club?' Eunice Parr was beginning to interest Rogers.

'As well as sleeping with him, yes.'

His pipe had died on him, not yet having brought relief to his nerve endings. Putting a match to it, he was, aside from obtrusive thoughts about Millier's personal attractiveness, mentally filing his opinion on her reaction to his questions and to an assessment of her answers; for, in due course, he was to judge her professionalism and to put it on paper. 'Miss Parr doesn't make a habit of throwing herself at the ancient and arthritic, then?' he said lightly.

Her eyes were back to their steady regard of Rogers who was beginning to believe that there was something wrong with his face. 'It seems not, though she was described to me as a promiscuous over-scented slut.' Millier was surprisingly censorious for a policewoman.

'And by implication, over-sexed?' he suggested. 'It's a common enough catalyst to monumental trouble.'

'Not necessarily,' she unexpectedly disagreed. 'There are other considerations, though I'd not like to impute them to Parr.'

'Such as?' he asked, showing his cynicism.

'Affection? Love?' She was intense with her words.

He stared hard at her through the blue haze of his just exhaled tobacco smoke. 'I'll concede the first,' he said, trying hard not to sound either thwarted or misogynous. 'Happily I'm not familiar with the second. I think I'll continue to believe that Miss Parr was more fascinated with Cruickshank's money than his body.' He tapped his teeth with the stem of his pipe, thinking. 'It might be useful to consider that she may have attached herself to some other man whose financial standing attracted her affection, or whatever.' He pushed back his shirt-sleeve cuff, checking the time passed on his wrist-watch. 'Before I forget, do you have . . .'

He was interrupted by one of his desk telephones ringing. Picking up its receiver he said, 'Rogers here,' and heard the mellifluousness of Angharad Rhys Pritchard's voice which acted on him like an unexpected shot of adrenalin. Without preamble she said that she could now tell him about the two visitors to Philip Cruickshank's villa which earlier she had refused to discuss. She would be going to her boat at the *Club Mouiller 1'Ancre* – her French was, he thought, much enhanced by the touch of Welshness in it – where she would be happy to see him, given the thirty minutes it would take her to get there.

Telling her that he would be delighted to see her – it struck him then that he had seldom used that word before in connection with the interviewing of an informant – he disconnected and spoke to Millier. 'That', he said, 'was the most attractive and mysterious Angharad Rhys Pritchard, saying that she has some very interesting information for me.' He scratched his thumbnail at the emerging stubble on his chin, thinking of her. 'While we may know that my telephone operates on an unlisted number, it's not a terribly secret one. But it's also not one that I'm aware has been handed out to Mrs Pritchard.' He shrugged his shoulders, dismissing it, though only for the time being. 'I was about to ask you if you have a description of Miss Parr, or whatever it is she now calls herself.'

Millier had been watching his face while he had been speaking on the telephone, her expression enigmatic, as clearly his had not been. 'I don't imagine for a moment that she's as attractive as your Mrs Pritchard,' she said expressionlessly, 'though I'm told that she has her full share of everything that men appear to value most. She's reported to be thirty-two, her height round about five and a half feet with what I thought was politely called a sort of ample figure by one and fleshy by another. Her hair was described to me as being banana-yellow, which she wears shoulder-length, sometimes held back with a coloured ribbon in the shape of a bow. By one account she's a generous user of lipstick, eyeliner and perfume, and wears stud keeper ear-rings.'

Rogers said, 'And a woman with a nasty temper.'

'That she has. Probably a dangerous one too. I've a so far unsupported account of a noisy quarrel she had with an unnamed man in the bar of the Solomon and Sheba, and her hitting him with a heavy glass ashtray.' She smiled gently as if with some inner humour. 'They were both thrown out of the pub and though he was bleeding badly they were seen to go off together as if they'd never quarrelled.' She smiled again. 'He must have accepted it as an expression of her affection for him, don't you think?'

'God preserve me from such an affection,' Rogers murmured before asking, 'There's nothing recorded against her?'

'No, nothing, and I suppose that on paper she has to be a lady of probity and virtue. In fact, of course, it appears very much otherwise.'

Standing from his chair, Rogers said, 'I'll leave you to catch up with her wherever she is, and do try and keep Fuller at a reasonably safe distance when you see him. He's probably unaware of Cruickshank's death, so see if you can find out what his attitude to him is. It could provoke a suspicion or two that he might be somehow involved'.

Seeing her out from his office, friendly geniality in his expression, he was wondering irritably why she was making him feel so bloody uncomfortable with her whatever-it-was attitude and her looking at him on occasions as if he were something edible. Like canned snoek, he typically down-graded himself.

As he waited on the telephone for DC Lewis to answer it, he reflected that while he liked and admired Millier and admitted that she was magnificently attractive, for him she must always be disciplinarily *Verboten* and, anyway, on a much less mature sexual wavelength.

10

Rogers, emerging from the concrete and glass monstrousness of Police Headquarters on to its forecourt and about to leave for Thurnholme Bay and his interview with Mrs Rhys Pritchard, thought the afternoon's warmth just right. It was enough, anyway, to stir in him the inbuilt masculine excitement of having a sexual interest in an attractive woman. His car was parked in a white-lined space marked *Detective Superintendent*, the implication being that only God could possibly help any officer of equal or lesser rank who dared profane its inviolability. He was sliding his key into the car's door lock when the department's disreputable Q-car pulled up behind him, and Coltart climbed from it.

'I'm on my way to an appointment,' Rogers said dismissively, unlocking the door and opening it. Normally quite adequate for his own use, his hundred and ninety pounds of flesh and bone felt, as it almost always did, frail and insufficient in the presence of the huge inspector. 'It's important and your time with me is now measured in seconds.'

'I need a lot more than that, sir,' Coltart rumbled. 'I believe we've a couple of dead bodies on our shooting.'

Rogers released his hold on the handle of the door, the sun seeming to have suddenly lost its warmth. 'Just two?' he said, surprised into not taking it too seriously. Then, reading Coltart's face and deciding to do so, demanded, 'So where in the hell did you dig them up from?'

'Not dug up yet,' Coltart answered, taking his words literally, 'but I'm here wanting your say-so for doing it.'

Rogers slammed shut the car's door. 'Go ahead,' he said quietly, 'I'm listening.' Taking in what Coltart was now telling him with ponderous precision, he occasionally frowned in his manifest understanding though with a growing irritation at its probable complicating escalation of his investigation into an already incomprehensible murder.

When the big detective appeared to have finished, Rogers said, 'And you believe from that that Mrs Cruickshank and Ashe, supposed to have gone off together into a nowhere unknown to family and friends, never left the farm at all? That they were killed six years ago by Cruickshank, a man we can't now get in touch with, and buried under deep litter in the barn?' He was staring hard at Coltart's small green eyes and beefy face, trying to read what he wanted from them. 'You're sure?'

'The barn was locked and I couldn't get in,' Coltart said stolidly, 'but I'm sure.'

It was enough for Rogers. 'So am I,' he assured him. 'Get it opened and lay on a search before the evening's on us. I'll be finished by then and be with you.' He wasn't going to be surprised that, given that the bodies would be unearthed from the barn, Mrs Cruickshank and the man Ashe had been discovered *in flagrante delicto* by Cruickshank. He couldn't think of a more impelling motive for murder.

Coltart's mouth moved briefly in what could perhaps have been taken for a smile. 'I knew what you'd want, and it's already organized. Five thirty there with half-a-dozen uniformed PCs, a sergeant and a chap standing in for Paull & Norden, the agricultural estate agents.'

He paused, adding to the weight of Rogers's growing problems. 'There's more because I hadn't finished what I was telling you.' There was then a regimented rumble of words by a dogged man intent on delivering them to where he believed they belonged. Cruickshank, it appeared, had been an arable farmer mainly growing bread wheat and barley, and had, over the years, got himself into heavy debt. Forced into selling the farm buildings and land to a leisure centre consortium, he had been left able to clear the debts with a substantial sum over; certainly enough to buy himself a villa and not have to worry overmuch about the financial future. The consortium itself later ran into cash liquidity problems, cutting short the conversion of the farm into a golf course and leisure centre and putting the whole project back on the market through the agency of Paull & Norden plc, where it lay currently languishing. According to the agents, to whom Coltart had spoken, there was a snag in the marketing of the property. The snag was the farm's ancient tithe barn, a Schedule II listed building which made it one of history's untouchables and not subject to any interference or alteration to its structure by unauthorized hands on pain of some undoubtedly frightful financial penalties. Consequently, it was currently kept locked and secured against entry and Coltart could only obtain promised access to it by agreeing to have present a Paull & Norden's representative.

'I had a job to get them to agree to even that,' Coltart said heavily, which meant that he had done a measure of official leaning on somebody in the company. 'All they know is that we've good grounds for believing that two unnamed bodies are buried there, and that any obstruction to their recovery by us would, at the least, seriously embarrass them in explaining it to Her Majesty's Coroner.'

'Good,' Rogers said briskly, groping for the door handle of his car. 'Just so long as you didn't hit anybody. If there's nothing more I'll see you at five thirty.'

Coltart stood unmoving. 'There is,' he answered very positively. 'It's about Ashe's disappearance. I spoke to Dunwithy, the landlord of the pub where he'd been lodging, and asked him what was what about his leaving. It was nearly six years ago, so he wasn't remembering so well. But I think enough. He'd been surprised at the time that Ashe hadn't returned to the pub after work, or at all, for he'd not said anything to Dunwithy or taken any of his goods and chattels with him. He said that Mr Cruickshank – who he knew well enough, though he wasn't one of his customers – had visited him during the morning of the next day, telling him that Mr Ashe had been called away suddenly to somewhere he couldn't remember over family business and wouldn't be back. Cruickshank then said that he had been asked by Ashe to collect his few belongings which included books and papers from his room and to forward them on, paying Dunwithy whatever he owed for the current month's room rent and meals.'

Rogers raised his eyebrows. 'And Dunwithy believed that?'

Coltart shrugged his huge shoulders. 'I don't think he had any choice.'

'I suppose not. You told him that Cruickshank was dead?' His legs were aching with his standing unmoving on hard asphalt, though not so much that he would sit while Coltart was on his feet.

'Only then, and with no details. He hadn't heard and he wasn't all that interested anyway. Still, he did seem to think it all right then to tell me that later he'd heard that Mrs Cruickshank and Ashe had been improperly associating under Cruickshank's very nose; going off with a substantial sum of his money and never returning.' Coltart added doubtfully, 'I've only Dunwithy's word for it, but I don't think Cruickshank was much liked in the area. He apparently had a bit of a reputation for treating his wife badly; hitting her on occasions.'

'That should make me feel a little better about his being

hanged,' Rogers said dispraisingly and looking as if he really meant it. 'We don't believe that bit about the money, do we? I assume you've checked that there was no complaint?'

Coltart's look at his senior said mutely, *Of course I bloody well have*, though he confined himself to saying, 'There's no record of any complaint of theft by him, or of violence against her by his wife.'

'Did Ashe have a car?' Rogers had temporarily – very temporarily – put aside his need to dash off to a waiting Mrs Rhys Pritchard. A reasonable deferment, he convinced himself, might be good for his self-control.

'No. He went back and forth in the farm's Land Rover.'

'His description?'

'I confirmed that his name was Richard – Dunwithy called him Dick. He'd have been about thirty then, six feet tall and thin, though being a bit athletic because he used to go jogging before starting work. He had dark hair with a bit of it hung over one side of his forehead to hide a red birthmark or whatever it was. His eyes were brown and he had widely spaced prominent teeth. Dunwithy called him a quiet, well-mannered and friendly chap who said he'd come from the Stockport area – he thinks it was Stockport – and had lodged with him for just short of a year.'

Coltart paused, then said, 'He did mention one other matter I think could be important, though Dunwithy seemed not to. About six months ago, he had a telephone call from a man who said he was Ashe's brother and was looking for him, having only recently discovered that he had been lodging with Dunwithy. He told him much of what he'd told me, though keeping Mrs Cruickshank out of it. Or so he said.' Coltart was sceptical. 'Then this man – Dunwithy said he sounded a you-be-damned sort of hard man and quite unlike his missing brother – questioned him about Cruickshank in particular, though Dunwithy was careful not to say too much about him. When he'd finished, the man said, "Much obliged, friend," and rang off. Dunwithy never heard from him again.'

'It seems a long time after a brother goes missing to start worrying about him,' Rogers observed. 'It might mean something or nothing, but do a check with Southport; Dunwithy may have remembered it correctly. So what about the unfortunate Mrs Cruickshank? Her name's Miriam, by the way.'

'Ah!' Coltart looked discomfited. 'Other than Sims referring indecently to her large bosoms, I've nothing. I hadn't got around to her.'

'No matter,' Rogers said amiably enough, being already half-way into his car. He had checked his wrist-watch for the time and knew that if he could shake off the unusually garrulous Coltart now, he needn't be too outrageously late for his appointment with Mrs Rhys Pritchard who was already occupying his mind with what he imagined to be her potential for wanting to be friendly with a wifeless golf-playing detective superintendent. 'It'll probably be unnecessary after we've been to the barn, so if there's nothing else I'll see you there.'

On the way, driving into a dazzling sun and taking the twelve miles of steep corkscrewing bends between Abbotsburn and Thurnholme Bay uncharacteristically too fast, he was preoccupied with trying to tie up the as-yet-to-be-discovered murdered bodies of Miriam Cruickshank and Richard Ashe with Cruickshank's own murder. This, he had to accept, seemed light years beyond his present capacity for imaginative understanding; he knew only that he would probably finish the day with a four-aspirin-type thumping headache.

11

It was with a more than usual feeling of pleasant anticipation that Rogers reached the high approach to Thurnholme Bay, seeing far below the town's harbour with the dark green water of the marina behind it on which floated the gapped rows of tall-masted yachts and squat motor cruisers, each moored to the walkways of the *Club Mouiller l'Ancre*. His access to what he was already believing to be a circumstance-sent chance for his cultivation of an attractive woman's interest was by dropping steeply in a cautious low gear through crowded streets compressed to narrowness by geranium-decked white, pink, washed-yellow and pale blue cheek by jowl houses, hotels, villas, guest houses and shops, his foot hovering over the brake pedal until he reached the more sober flatness of sea level.

The blond crooked-nosed DC Lewis, wearing Mafia-style dark glasses, was waiting near the clubhouse flagstaff for Rogers and approached him as he climbed from the car. 'Do you have to wear your secret service disguise in a place like Thurnholme?' Rogers demanded, a little testily. 'People here don't recognize you by the colour of your eyes.'

'No, sir, they don't,' Lewis agreed, used to Rogers's disciplinary peculiarities and remaining unfazed. He pointed with his finger over the coloured umbrella shading unoccupied white tables and chairs, past the cement tubs of yucca plants, to indicate a sailing yacht. 'That's Mrs Rhys Pritchard's boat; the fourth one along.'

'Have you anything further on her?'

Lewis, looking as though he were missing out on something or other, said, 'I don't believe so. Was there?'

Rogers lifted black eyebrows. 'Not meeting her, or speaking to her during your enquiries?'

'Absolutely not, sir. I wouldn't dream of it.'

'Somebody's given her my unlisted phone number.' Rogers's gaze searched not too darkly Lewis's face, knowing even before he answered that she hadn't got it from him.

Somewhat bewildered and irritated behind the blankness of his glasses, Lewis said, 'Not from me, I can assure you.'

'Not that I thought she had, and not that it matters all that much,' Rogers said placatingly. 'It could mean that she has a friend at Headquarters. Was there anything more said about Cruickshank's visits here?'

'The bar steward remembered him, though not by name, being with Mrs Rhys Pritchard on two or three occasions. He said he was a bit of an uncouth bugger obviously on the make for her, and not the sort for a lady like her to be too close to.' Relieved of any imputation of verbal indiscretion, he showed Rogers a man-of-the-world jauntiness. 'But I know that some women, even at her age, wouldn't object to a bit of rough stuff, would they?'

Rogers shot him a hard look, concealing sudden irritability.

'If you're suggesting Mrs Rhys Pritchard could be like that, then I'm sure you're mistaken,' he said tersely. He hadn't liked Lewis's observation at all, for he knew that it could undoubtedly be true in part; and that truth was capable of casting a shadow on what he thought about her.

Turning to leave Lewis and affording priority to his instincts as an investigating police officer, he said, 'I don't want you to drop your enquiries about her, about Cruickshank, or anyone else you might identify as an associate of either of them.'

Treading the floating hollow-sounding boards of Walkway 2B, he found the yacht he wanted in the line of shoulder to shoulder boats, her raked stern presented to him with *Lady Pink Gin II* painted on it in blue letters. She was elderly, but sleek and in fine condition; enamelled in the palest of blues with a furled navy-blue mainsail, white guard rails and a complexity of nylon rigging running from the tall mast towering above him. Her cockpit in the stern was enclosed on two sides by white canvas screening set with clear plastic windows and led into the low profile cabin. A brass ship's bell hung from its bulkhead and a small blue inflatable, looking capable of accommodating with difficulty two dwarfish crew members, was lashed to its roof. The boat swayed dreamily against her fenders, giving off shimmering heat waves from her glossy surfaces and, but for the muted sound of unidentifiable orchestral music coming apparently from her bilges, had a *Marie Celeste* air of being abandoned of life.

Moving to the boat's stern, he stepped over two feet of green water and then between two yellow horseshoe-shaped lifebuoys secured to the side rails, hearing what was the now identifiable music of Delius through the open door of the cockpit. Unhooking the thonged clapper of the bell, he rapped it ringingly twice against the metal.

With Delius turned down to near inaudibility, she appeared at the four steps leading down from where he stood, smiled and said, 'Come aboard, Mr Rogers.'

In the half-light in which she stood, her sun-tanned hawkish face showed a light coffee-brown and, seeing her so, he knew that earlier recollection hadn't exaggerated her attractiveness. The slenderness, the leanness of her body, was emphasized by

73

her wearing a yellow shirt – it looked like a shirt to Rogers – and a longish black skirt overprinted with large yellow flowers. She had tied a chiffon scarf of the same pattern around her throat and put on gold ear-rings, discarding her espadrilles in favour of black flat-heeled shoes and, to the dazzled Rogers, altogether looking stunning.

Climbing down to join her, smiling his pleasure, he said, 'I like the Delius.'

She stood to one side, allowing him to pass in the discreet fragrance of her scent. 'It's on tape,' she told him. '"The Walk to the Paradise Garden".'

'I like it,' he said, 'but prefer by only a little his "In a Summer Garden".'

'Then you'd know the preface to it, too?' There was a twist of amusement to her mouth. '"All my blooms, and all sweet blooms of love; to thee I gave while Spring and Summer sang."'

'Gabriel Rossetti,' he said lightly, thinking that she had been somewhat mocking in her quoting it to him. 'But he probably lived on a higher plane of feeling than most of us.'

The cabin into which he was ushered – not too unlike an over-sized coffin, his claustrophobically inclined mind suggested to him – was obviously the saloon. Panelled in a blond wood veneer it was clearly a sitting-room cum galley cum navigating room. Two fixed blue-cloth benches flanked closely a wooden folding table, and the far end of the cabin was the partly enclosed galley. Near it was a pygmy-sized table on which was a portable typewriter with paper in it and an assortment of books, one of which was opened. The long rectangular portholes near the ceiling, built too near the gently heaving floor for a tall man to stand upright, let in the golden light of the late afternoon.

Switching off the tape of Delius, she motioned him to sit and, with his knees squeezed under the table opposite her, he had to be reasonably confident that he no longer smelled of Cruickshank's dissolution. He said, 'I do apologize for being late, but I really was held back by a necessary conference.' He nodded at the typewriter on the table. 'I disturbed your working?'

'It's of no consequence,' she assured him with what he took

to be friendliness, though her mouth still held in it the sadness he had noticed before, 'and I was expecting you. I'm writing a paper on the legal aspects of marine charter and brokerage, coupled with a symposium of the case law on marine insurance. For the Club,' she added; then, in the put-on affected voice of an *ingénue*, 'Isn't that too, too dreadfully unfascinating?'

'I'd rather read up on binary-coded decimals about which I know nothing,' he assured her. 'Or, better still, to be told about the two visitors to Cruickshank's villa.' He smiled disarmingly. 'Before that, though it's of no great importance, I've been wondering how you came to have access to my ex-directory number?'

'You aren't annoyed?' She was amused.

'Of course not. It's curiosity only.'

'Which must rest unappeased,' she said calmly. 'Like most confidences it's not for passing on, but I assure you it wasn't from anyone in your department. Nor, in particular, was it from your Mr Lewis who has been so indefatigably making enquiries about my marital status, my past and present lovers should they exist, the boat about which you already knew anyway, and, for all I know, just how close my relationship with Philip Cruickshank in particular actually was.'

The stricken Rogers, surprised metaphorically with his trousers down around his ankles, tried hard to read in her face what attitude, as an albeit non-practising barrister, she would be taking in this apparent invasion of her privacy. He forced a weak smile to his mouth. '*Mea culpa*,' he confessed. 'You know how despicably underhand we have to be when it comes to checking out our sources. A precaution, no more than that, and I hope you aren't too offended.'

'No,' she replied, not looking it anyway, 'I'm not.' Still with amusement in her face, she continued, 'Was it in Mr Lewis's brief to find out if Philip had been my lover?'

'Not after what you'd told me,' he protested, not, he felt, very convincingly and cursing Lewis in his mind for being so obviously ham-handed. 'Only your associates in general.' She was less than a yard away from him on the opposite side of the table; he a sitting duck exposed not only to the scent she wore, but also to the impact of her considerable personality.

'I could, of course, be terribly offended,' she rebuked him. 'So in order to make matters clear to you, I choose to tell you that I am a woman long done with pretence and dissimulation about what I might call my social life. If Philip had been my lover I would, under the circumstances of his death, have had no hesitation in telling you so. And that, you might guess, probably comes from having been married to a naval officer. You knew I had been, of course?'

'Yes, it was told me with the rest.' He had decided that he had no defence as such and that sensible policy for a humbled man was to take whatever more was to come from her on the chin.

'Further,' she said, now definitely amused, 'you should cease to be worried or concerned about my natural preference for male company, despicable and untrustworthy though that company often is.'

'You read me like a book,' Rogers murmured, only just audibly. Frankness from a woman was not a characteristic with which he was familiar and he decided that a little unbending, an ounce or two of openness might be called for. She might respond, she might equivocate, she might just laugh at him. It was, he supposed, all a matter of the improbability of an elusive male and female compatibility.

'I wanted to believe,' he said, staring unblinkingly at her; 'and that was partly why I had the enquiries made. A police investigation is not always a hundred per cent professional one.' He smiled hesitantly. 'I accept wholly what you told me about Cruickshank, and I'm pleased that I can do so.'

There was for Rogers an uncomfortable lengthening of a period of silence in the cabin, broken only by the inner creaking of whatever stringers and things held a boat together and the raucousness of quarrelling gulls outside.

Composed in her calmness and seeming to be scrutinizing the teeth he was exposing in his lingering smile, she said matter-of-factly, 'That is how I expected you might react,' leaving him completely unenlightened about what she meant.

Having returned to his expression some of the gravitas of his rank and about to take back some of the initiative he had lost, he said, 'To get back to . . .' when she held up a long-fingered hand to stop him.

'There's one thing more before we put aside the subject,' she said. 'Do not be too embarrassed – if you are – about the enquiries you've had made about what I do and possibly don't do. Following your visit this morning, I too made enquiries of the person supplying me with your telephone number and I, in my turn, was given a fairly detailed run-down on your own background.' She sounded warmly friendly, adding, 'Never forget *my* legal background and the connections it brings with it.'

Rogers narrowed his eyes in mock ruthlessness. 'I never imagined that I'd be driven to murder my own chief constable,' he growled.

She laughed at him, shaking her head, and he thought he had seldom heard a more fetching laugh.

'All right,' he said, 'I didn't think it was him anyway.' In a way, and unaccustomedly, he felt naked and exposed to her obtained information about him, knowing now how some of his better class of villains had felt under his own scrutiny of them. Though guiltless of anything that could be classed as criminous, he wondered whether he was to be resentful or otherwise about an unknown informant's version of his activities and peccadilloes. Because he was so physically and mentally drawn to this forthright woman, her good opinion of him was of immense importance.

Returning to the prosaics of his enquiries, he said, 'You were going to give me the names of Cruickshank's two visitors.'

'One name,' she answered him. 'As he's already been mentioned as a quite frequent visitor, I'll need your discretion.'

'As much as I'm able,' he promised, 'and you must know the limits.'

'Stephen Cruickshank; with another man I didn't know. When did I say Mrs Parr had that quarrel with that loathsome man? The beginning of the year?'

'About January or February.'

'Yes. It was three or four weeks later than that and half-way through the morning. I was about to take my car from the garage when I saw Stephen and the other man . . .' – her expression suggested that this man was definitely of a lower order of humanity – '. . . going into his father's villa from his car they

77

had parked in the drive. I knew Phillip had left on his own earlier because I'd seen him being driven away in a taxi and Mrs Parr wasn't with him.'

She paused, beginning to look to the detective's eyes like counsel laying down the case for the prosecution. 'I admit to a rather unneighbourly inquisitiveness in waiting at my garage to see what was happening.' She frowned. 'I can't explain why, but they both looked *intent*; an intent to do something that possibly wasn't acceptable to either man or beast.'

'Was that because you didn't like the look of the man with Cruickshank?' Rogers asked. He was dying several slow deaths for a life-enhancing pipe of tobacco, but did not wish to add the stain of smoking to whatever picture she had of him by asking whether she would mind.

She looked surprised, pausing in her playing with slender fingers at one of the gold ear-rings beneath her hair. 'No, I did not, though that wasn't my original reason for watching them. It was too cold to stay outside, so I went back indoors and watched from the terrace. It was at least fifteen minutes before they came out and Mrs Parr was with them. Unwillingly, I am certain, for the brute who was with Stephen was holding her arm and forcing her towards her car which was in the drive. Even from where I was I could see she was distressed and had lost much of her colour. Stephen, I must say, looked rather shamefaced. He was carrying two large suitcases and he put them in the boot while the other man pushed Mrs Parr into the rear seat and then got into the driver's seat.'

'Still obviously against her will?'

'Most certainly. He handled her quite roughly and whatever it was they were saying it wasn't friendly. Had it not been for Stephen being there, lending a sort of authority to what was happening, I could have been silly enough to have intervened. She was almost certainly being ejected from the house with the consent and approval of Philip Cruickshank who I have since considered to be a selfish . . . dammit, I haven't a word for him while you are with me, but you probably know how I felt.'

'I do,' he said, thinking that he would have liked to hear exactly what the word was. 'What happened then? Was she driven off?'

'Yes, with Stephen following in his own car.'

'You can describe the man with Cruickshank?'

She nodded, though seeming doubtful, taking her gaze from him in her effort at recollection. 'I've a pretty ghastly memory for that sort of detail, but I'll try. I'd guess him to be in his middle twenties and content with wearing an anorak and no gloves on what was a particularly cold day. His hair was dark and straight and cut short, and he wore a small dark moustache. He was stocky and athletic looking with, I thought, a quite brutish face.' She shivered. 'Not a nice man to be alone with and he must have certainly frightened poor Mrs Parr.'

'And Cruickshank was driving his Metro? The silver one?'

'Yes, he was. It probably isn't important, but it was quite noticeable that Mrs Parr was directing most of her anger, her frustration, at Stephen. I suppose because she knew him.' She smiled almost apologetically, showing very white teeth. 'I'm sorry. None of this is very much good, is it?'

'I'm grateful.' Rogers smiled back at her, not showing his disappointment. 'It could be useful.' He was silent for a few moments, then said, 'Since we spoke this morning, it's been established that Philip Cruickshank almost certainly died during the night of last Sunday/Monday week, ten days ago. It really is important that I know what callers there might have been to his villa on that Sunday and subsequently . . .' He left it hanging, an expectation of something from her clearly in his face.

That had not surprised her and she said, 'As I told you, I've a quite ghastly memory and I am doubtful that I can help you further.'

'Would you think about it?' he cajoled her. 'Forgotten memories, buried memories, can be brought back with a little effort at concentration. They're there, down in the subconscious or thereabouts.'

'You wish me to try and recollect something I might or might not have seen or heard at Philip's villa during the past ten days?' She had amusement back in her eyes. 'To put aside all else in your favour?'

He gave her a quick grin and a nod of his head as if she had already agreed. 'That's kind of you, and I'd be grateful.'

'All right, I'll try,' she said. 'I really would like to help.'

'I'm sure you'll come up with something. May I see you again when you do?'

'I'm quite sure that you will,' she said; which, again, could mean anything.

'Thank you.' He looked at his wrist-watch and stood with difficulty from his cramped seat, his bones seeming to have set solid. 'I'm sorry, but I'd forgotten. Would you let me go? I'm due at an important meeting at half-past five and I'll be late anyway.'

She stood too. 'I shall let you know if I remember anything.'

They were near each other and eye to eye. Rogers thought that whatever it was that remained unspoken between them seemed almost palpable. He had to say something more before he left, however trite or awkward, make some move towards a closer, more intimate association than that of policeman and potential witness. It wasn't an easy divide to bridge.

'Do you play golf?' he asked, self-admittedly and momentarily extremely wet.

'I used to,' she replied, looking slightly baffled. 'I still have my clubs . . . I think.'

He read nothing in that; only perhaps a polite answer to an odd and unexpected question. 'Perhaps – possibly, a game some day?' he said with a nothing ventured nothing gained intent, though immediately hearing in his mind a yelled *Bloody fool!*

'I'd like that,' she told him, as if it had been something she had wanted for a long time, then held out her hand to be shaken. 'Let's do it,' she smiled, the pressure of her hand warm and exciting. 'There is one thing, though. You could stop treating me as if you were unsure of my being a witness or a potential suspect and use my given name.'

'Such as a friendly Angharad?' There had been a shine in her deep green eyes that had pleased him.

'If we are to play golf, yes.'

He went out into the early evening's sunshine for his probable appointment with a couple of long-dead bodies, feeling much the same as if he had been suddenly told that he was no longer liable to support financially his ex-wife, and that her live-in rugby-playing lover had fallen from a sufficient height to have broken both his legs. It was a warming thought and he had even forgotten that he was dying the death of nicotine deprivation. Only temporarily forgotten, of course, for he would never be that far gone.

12

It was well after six o'clock when Rogers arrived at the Penruddock Barn, a reddish sun already dropping behind the looming bulk of Great Morte Moor. The air was cooler and the surrounding landscape and abandoned golf course looked bleakly devoid of human presence.

The barn in which his interest lay bulked large, its roof steeply pitched and stone-tiled with the eaves overhanging the ancient timber framing, bleached by time and weather, of its walls. There were opened double doors, spacious enough to allow loaded horse-drawn wagons to enter, and four narrow glazed slots in the side walls. Rogers saw fixed on one of the door posts a blue metal disc informing those who read it that the 1721-built tithe barn was an English Heritage Grade II listed building and, by implication, God help anybody laying an impious finger on it with intent to alter or damage its structure.

Outside it and unmanned were a constabulary utility van used for carrying bottle gas lighting equipment and tools, a squad-carrying coach, the CID's resolutely filthy Q-car and the Coroner's Officer's van with its rear hatch partly open and showing not too obviously two black plastic coffin shells and a neat pile of body bags.

Inside, but for two hissing floodlamps concentrated on groups of kneeling PCs in dark blue overalls scrutinizing the soil and rubble floor, the barn was twilit, its cavernous beamed roof space darkly shadowed. Coltart was there, and Sergeant Magnus with his photographic equipment; the uniformed Coroner's Officer standing by with a pallid and willowy youth owning to curly yellow hair, an almost non-moustache and, in Rogers's opinion when introduced to him by Coltart, an overly limp handshake. He was, it appeared, Timothy Stitch, sent to represent the interests of Paull & Norden Plc who were marketing what seemed to Rogers to have, in the hard times for selling anything, all the saleability of a long-dead sheep.

Moving with Coltart away from the group, Rogers turned the corners of his mouth down and said, 'I was kept against my wishes. I take it there's no finding yet?'

Coltart's small green eyes showed that there wasn't. 'The ground's hard,' he rumbled. 'Too hard, I reckon, for a spade job. And we've still got covered ground to dig into.'

Rogers took in what he could see in the hard-edged shadows beyound the brilliant white beams of floodlighting. Stacked untidily in blocks in the barn's centre were unpainted doors and window frames, lengths of raw cut timber and plastic guttering; a lop-sided pyramid of bags of cement and columns of unopened cardboard boxes, none of which gave any promise of being easy to move. The open spaces in and around these materials were occupied by the searching PCs, each with a tool like a pointed case-opener with which the consistency of the soil – under Rogers's shoes it felt like sedimentary rock – was being tested.

'The roof space,' Rogers said. 'If we get no joy at ground level, it could be.' He hadn't sounded convincing and he didn't feel it. A multiplicity of beams were just visible in the high massively shadowed darkness of the roof. There were, he saw dimly, shelved recesses at the sides. Ideal, he thought, should he be convinced that a smallish fifty-six-year-old farmer could climb to them twice, each time carrying an adult body. Still, if they weren't found in the earthen floor, some agile rock-climbing-experienced PC, properly insured against smashing himself up, would be detailed to climb the beams and find out.

Looking next at the unpainted chipboard panelling screwed on to the rough-hewn upright timbers of the barn's frame, Rogers remarked to Stitch, 'Wouldn't that boarding stuff fixed round the walls be what the Heritage people might see as damaging to the barn's listed antiquity?'

Stitch's expression was that of a man confronted suddenly with an obtuse logarithmic equation and before he could answer Rogers had left him, struck with an imagined possibility.

Standing before the panelling nearest the open doors, he saw that the board spanned neighbouring beams which were a guessed-at five feet apart and reached to eighteen inches or so above his head to an open top. The foot of the board was stained darkly to a height of a yard or so with what appeared to be dried chicken manure and stuck-on fragments of straw and wood shavings.

He rapped on it with his knuckles, hearing the expected resonance of unoccupied space. He beckoned to Coltart to join him from the other side. When he had, having lumbered over purposefully and not looking too happy, Rogers said with an unaccustomed familiarity, 'I know that you'd have got around to it eventually, Eddie, but I'd like to dive in with my own idea before it gets too dark. I see there are about thirty of these boarded-up cavities, and they're obviously easily unscrewed and removed.' He rapped on the board again. 'This one's empty, but it needn't have been, need it? Why dig a couple of graves with three feet or so of deep litter to move out of the way first when there are suitable wooden ones all round the walls?'

'Wouldn't they smell?' the yet to be convinced Coltart questioned.

'Above hundredweights of chicken manure dropped into the litter?' His nose told him that a fairly strong ghost of its smell remained; enough to convince him that its source would most likely mask the stench of a body's decay.

'You want them opened up?' Coltart was clearly of the opinion that bodies, particularly murdered ones, were best buried conventionally and wasn't too impressed with his senior's theory.

'Only the one we find that doesn't sound hollow. You do your side, I'll do this.' His feeling of being right was now strong; he was nearly enough certain that a man in Cruickshank's doom-laden situation, faced with the urgent disposal of two bodies and having the barn in mind, would opt for concealing them in an already available cavity.

With Coltart moving to the other side of the barn and Stitch rejoining him, Rogers started his knuckle-rapping search for evidence of what would be his own choice of a secret burial. He hadn't gone too far – he had found that repetitive banging on wood with his hands could be a painful activity and a tedious one – when Coltart, standing at the tenth or eleventh boarded cavity, had a triumphantly thumbed fist held aloft and was bawling, 'Sir! Sir!' He had, manifestly, found something other than empty space.

Joining him, Rogers examined the boarding that now, to his fanciful imagination, seemed to emanate a brooding of contained death which he knew to be one of the ambient properties of the mortuary's body cabinets. He rapped on it, hearing what could be the muffled sound of non-resonance. 'It might be,' he said to Coltart, 'so get somebody to find a couple of screwdrivers, will you?'

Waiting, he told Stitch – who looked to be wrapped in an unawareness of what was going on – what he proposed having done and why. 'You're welcome to stay,' he said, filling his pipe and lighting it against any chance inhalation of the foulness of human decay from what might be an exhumation, 'but I recommend that you don't.'

Clearly unenthusiastic about it, Stitch said, 'I think I'd better, if you don't mind. My company would certainly expect me to.'

When Coltart returned with screwdrivers from the utility van, Rogers stood back with Stitch at his side while the big detective set to in removing the boarding. He didn't lack a sufficient audience, for the squad of searching PCs were now standing and watching, silent but for the few lighter-flicking cigarette smokers following Rogers's example.

With the screws removed, Coltart allowed the loosened board to come towards him, enough to get his sausage-sized fingers behind it and move it sideways to expose the cavity. Rogers, though ready for what he was expecting, caught a nevertheless heart-stopping glimpse of a compacted sepia-coloured mass that collapsed outwards in a dusty disintegration of wood shavings and straw to reveal two brown skeletal figures, cocooned in clear polythene bags which fell with a crackling sound to within inches of his shoes.

A chopped-off wailing sound came from Stitch who stumbled

a few steps backwards into the shadows and noisily vomited his horror on to the barn floor. Coltart, impassive and not about to give way to expressing anything so belittling as being sickened or excited, had released the board he held and stepped out of the litter that had piled itself around his ankles. 'I'd better return the men to divisions, hadn't I?' he said, his way of conceding his senior's rightness.

Rogers nodded. 'Have the lighting arranged so that I can see what we've got here and take Mr Stitch outside before he chucks up again.' He added, looking into the shadows where the wretched agent stood, 'Don't be too hard on the poor bugger. We're paid for it; he isn't.'

With the floodlights showing the two bags in nauseating detail, he turned his full attention to what were indubitably the mortal remains of the ill-fated and grossly careless lovers, Miriam Cruickshank and Richard Ashe. The necks of the bags in which they had been shrouded had been tied with string and Rogers, working in the electronic flashing of Magnus's camera and in the shadow of the returned Coltart, brushed aside the litter on the bag containing the body wearing a blue summer dress. Holding his breath, he slit the bag from top to base, finding unexpectedly that there was little smell – and that musty – and he could stay closer than he actually wished to a sight that already cancelled out any thoughts he had of an evening meal.

The body had patently been put in the cavity in a standing position and over the years its weight had bent the legs at the knees. The dress on it had a four-inch ragged hole situated over the stomach, the approximate spread of shotgun pellets fired from a distance of four or five yards. It was heavily stained with a once liquid dark brown matter, the colour of old blood. Overall, the mummified skin was a dusty brown and deeply shrivelled. Where lifted from the tissue beneath, it was of the thinness and appearance of charred paper. An emerald-set ring lay in what looked like the corpse of a large dark brown tarantula spider with enamelled fingernails. A few sparse patches of long hair clung to the scalp. What had been a woman's face was too horrific for even the hardened-to-it detective to dwell upon, for violent death, ruinous decay and insect predation had done it no favours.

85

The male body of the presumed-to-be Richard Ashe, also exposed almost odourlessly to Rogers's scrutiny by the slitting open of the enclosing polythene membrane, was dressed in the twill trousers – he noted that the flies were unzipped – and open-neck shirt in which he had died. He was in the same state of mummification as his dead lover, though there was a difference. He had been shot in the face at close range, the blast taking away most of it, though leaving exposed a few scattered large white teeth.

'The birthmark's gone,' Rogers pointed out to Coltart, 'but the poor devil has to be Ashe.' He had known neither of them, but he felt an immense pity for the two lives cut short so brutally. Being cuckolded in one's own nest wasn't the nicest of things to happen to a man, but he wasn't sure it warranted this degree of bloody vengeance. All passions spent, he reflected sombrely, in a killing hail of lead pellets.

He straightened and stood, his calf muscles giving him hell, leaving a search of the bodies to Coltart and the Coroner's Officer, men more hardened than he would ever be to touching dead flesh. His gorge had been teetering on rising and, like the pallid Stitch, he needed the palliative of cool fresh air in the now darkened evening outside to still it. Too, he needed to do some deep thinking about the problem posed of a man murdering his own wife and her lover and then becoming, in his no doubt deserved turn, the victim of another murderer.

His headache put to one side and driving back to Abbotsburn, he knew he needed a tidying-up spell at his desk. And, now that he felt less likely to upchuck, a squeezed-in supper seemed in order. He grimaced about that, thinking that he might have the no-option choice of the canteen cook's *chef-d'oeuvre* of two eggs, chips, fried tomatoes and baked beans on top of trying to work out dispassionately in what order he might break the news to Stephen Cruickshank of his mother's death – and to his sister were she available – while also questioning him about his forcible ejection of Eunice Parr from his father's villa.

And then, he reserved for himself, not feeling so anaemic in his needs as hitherto, time to be made for Angharad . . .

13

Parking her Rover Mini at the end of St Epiphanius Road, Detective Inspector Millier, dressed in an inconspicuous dark blue jacket and skirt, walked casually, not to be noticed she hoped, into the front garden of Eunice Parr's house. Standing on her toes and looking into the garage's high window, she could see the red-enamelled roof of Parr's car in the same position in which she had seen it earlier.

Moving to the peeling varnished door of the all-too-shoddy house, she knocked loudly on it and waited; knocking again when silence was the only answer. Looking around her and being apparently unobserved, she retrieved a small vanity mirror from her clutch bag. First trying the door handle in case the lock hadn't been keyed, she slid part of the mirror at an angle through the letter flap – this on Rogers's advice – then bent and peered at what was reflected in it. On the inside mat there were five or six envelopes overlapping each other which, with the exception of a handwritten white envelope carrying an orange-coloured postage stamp with a kangaroo on it, appeared to be junk mail. Whatever else, she thought, unless Parr had gone out very early that morning, she would have at least picked up the Australian letter from the door mat.

Walking to the rear of the building and ignoring what was a manifestly empty and broken-glassed greenhouse, she checked the back door, finding it locked. Try as hard as she might, she failed to identify anything recognizable between the narrow slits between the window curtains, being only reasonably satisfied that the house was unoccupied in the sense that Parr was no longer sleeping there.

With an edgy feeling that she might have missed some

evidence that would redound to her discredit and diminish her in the eyes of Rogers, she re-entered her car and returned to the town centre for her appointment with Fuller. She had telephoned him at the Club Midnight Blue, surprised at his unexpected friendly courtesy, and falling in with his suggestion that he would be happy to see her at eight o'clock, an hour before the club opened.

Dusk was dying into darkness when she pulled into the kerb in a stridently neon-lit Commercial Street and close to the entrance to Paper Court, thought to be once a seventeenth-century mews and now a superior, if minor, shopping precinct.

Stone-flagged, iron-pillared and lit by three electrified old-fashioned gas street lamps, it went nowhere. Apart from the unseeable Midnight Blue, its intimate narrowness was host to small shops with dark green paintwork and Regency-style bow windows that sold 1920s clothes and bric-à-brac, hideously expensive antique furnishings, glittering crystal ware and flowered porcelain, artists' paints and materials, and a tiny cramped tea and coffee shop acknowledged quite authoritatively as having been eaten in and thus made hallowed by Charlotte and Emily Brontë.

A flight of descending stone steps, flanked by railings appearing to have been contrived from rows of black-painted fleur-de-lis headed spears, led down at basement level to a solid green door overhung by a matching fabric canopy. At head height was inset a curtained circular plate-glass window and the club's apparent needlessness for being noticed was shown by a modestly small number 12 in gold leaf above it.

Millier, her head now below ground level, pressed a brass bell push at the side of the door. Her mind was already determined on a list of no-nonsense questions to be put to a man she had decided was probably more of a brutish villain than Rogers had allowed him to be.

While she knew that villainy – even brutish villainy – came in different guises, the big man who had opened the door without using the inspection window, and who was manifestly Fuller, put her into an instant anxiety about her face and hair being in proper order. She thought that even his standing in the doorway's shadow showed him to be what a more impressionable woman than herself would call masculinely gorgeous in a beautifully tailored dark suit. When he smiled at her and said a pleasant 'Good evening' in a deep warm voice, she felt that Rogers could have short-changed her somewhat in his briefing.

When she produced her warrant card he barely glanced at it. 'Come in,' he said amiably. 'I wasn't thinking you were here to sell me insurance.'

Being ushered along a dimly illuminated corridor that had been lightly scented – or was it coming from him? – and passing an open double door, she saw through it into the shadowed half-lit interior of the windowless club. The ceiling was low and supported by brick vaultings which left deep niches between their columns. Small gilt tables and matching fabric-seated chairs were placed in their quasi-privacy, or exposed unregimented around a small circular dancing floor of polished parquet. A platform stood in deep shadow against an end wall with a baby grand piano on it, together with three wooden chairs and a stand-up singer's microphone. The old cellar held in it a muffled silence as if, Millier thought, somebody was waiting in there and wanting to scream.

Fuller, opening the door of an office at the end of the corridor, led her in and sat her attentively in a softskin leather chair at the side of his desk.

'I must admit that I'm agog with interest in what you want of me,' he said, brushing by her and taking his seat at the desk.

Being now in stronger light, she saw in him a rough-hewn attractiveness, his eyes large and a big cat's yellowish-brown, showing what she hoped was friendliness, his mouth full and sensual. His hair, a little too long for his type, was densely black, his freshly shaved jowls the bruised blue they would always be. His neck was thick and bullish, suggesting an overplus of masculine thrustfulness in all things. He had the air of a man used to demanding things and getting them.

'It's possibly of no great importance, Mr Fuller,' she said in a softly-softly approach, 'but I'm seeking information about a woman called Parr whose whereabouts are at present unknown. Not, I should add, that she's necessarily done anything wrong.'

As she spoke, so she had taken in as much of the office as she could without being too conspicuous about it. Small and neat and smelling of cigar smoke, it was furnished with the leather-topped desk and the two chairs in which they sat, for her in too close proximity. A small safe was set at head height in the wall behind him, together with several framed Gauguin prints of his Tahiti period. Those and a slim Chinese dragon black-lacquered cabinet were the total of the furnishings.

Fuller had noticed her quick scrutiny, at least of the safe, and he said, looking amused, 'I've never felt the need to hide it behind a picture. Any near-decent safe blower knows where to look for it, and it's only money anyway.' He showed very white teeth at her. 'I'm sorry. You were asking about Miss Parr. Eunice Parr, that is. Yes?'

'Yes,' she acknowledged. 'I understand that she works, or worked, for you.'

'She was with me as a singer for a year and a half until last February, but that was then and I certainly don't know where she is now.' He had been looking at her as if trying to read in her what she was thinking.

'She *was* a singer?' Millier echoed him, wanting more than that.

'Yes, and a good one too. She did cabaret turns; Piaf and Minelli songs which she could do well enough. I was sorry to lose her in fact.'

'Because she was that good?'

He frowned. 'She left me without a second vocalist. Isn't that a good enough reason?'

'Not really,' she said calmly. 'You knew Philip Cruickshank, I believe?' She had a brief and horrible vision of him dangling dead-faced in the garage.

Her sudden change of subject had surprised him and he frowned again, though recovering quickly his amiability. 'I see you know a little more about Eunice than I'd thought. I do know now that she went to live with him. When she left owing me money I'd loaned her, I didn't.'

'She's since repaid it?' Millier had noticed him tapping his nicely manicured fingernails on his desk, prepared to judge his reactions to her questions by it.

90

He shrugged. 'No, and it's nothing I'm likely to lose any sleep about.'

She hesitated, then said, 'But it was quite a something in your quarrel with her at Mr Cruickshank's house, wasn't it?'

'Ah!' Though he appeared not to be physically discomfited, there came from him an almost palpable emanation of unease. 'It isn't Eunice you're gunning for, is it? It's me. You're building up to tell me something concerning myself, so I'd prefer that you'd be more direct.'

Millier was annoyed with herself. Precipitancy wasn't normally her style and she wished she could smile it disarmingly away. 'I'm sorry,' she said. 'The information I have makes it an uncertainty what your relationship had been with Miss Parr. That there is evidence of a serious quarrel between you while she was living with Mr Cruickshank suggests it was more than something between employer and employee . . .'

'Go on, I could be interested.' Whatever it had been, he had recovered himself. He sounded unworried and confident. 'So far, you may be right. Partly, that is.'

'There is further information that Miss Parr confided in a friend that she was living here with you. On and off, that is.' Millier was feeling lightweightedly ridiculous, becoming unhappy with how she was coping with this unflappable man.

'Oh,' he said, a touch derisively. 'That sounds dreadfully immoral, doesn't it? I'm flattered, naturally, but it's not true. There *is* no other accommodation down here but what you've seen – it's strictly non-residential – and everything above me belongs to somebody else and has been rented out as offices.' He smiled. 'I am not a man, Miss Millier, to make improper use of my desk or my office carpet. You know the Ancient Gatehouse Hotel, of course?'

Millier nodded, anticipating a further put-down.

'Being a single man and intending to stay one – for the time being, at least – I rent a suite on its top floor and I've done so for the past seven years. I entertain my friends there, it's true, but never ever Eunice.'

He paused, apparently waiting for her to speak. When she wisely didn't, he gave her a wry smile and said, 'So be it, but the money's probably the thing. It was something she had a feeling for.'

'It might help to explain why she seems to have abandoned her home, even if temporarily.'

'She could leave it for any damned thing you might imagine,' he said shortly. 'I had her under contract here, renewable annually and generously, without, as somebody's suggesting, having anything from her on the side. She's East Coast Australian who was left a bit of a run-down house here in Abbotsburn which hadn't been lived in for years. It gave her the push to come here, which was what she had apparently wanted.' He pulled a face, indicating his disgust. 'Once she'd settled in she told me that the house was as good as falling down – roof slates dropping off, brickwork crumbling, window frames needing painting, that sort of thing – and said that unless it could be made habitable it was back to flaming Australia for her. It was then that I was stupid enough to be touched for a pretty hefty loan against her future earnings, though all down on paper in legal fashion with me holding the house deeds as a guarantee of something or other. I'd been to view the house a couple of times, never inside, without seeing anybody doing anything – she said she couldn't agree on a builder's quotation and was arguing it – and when I was becoming a little less stupid but more hot under the collar she walked out on me.' For a moment he looked savage. 'The damned bitch,' he swore, then said, 'I'm sorry. I shouldn't have let her upset me into saying that.'

'I've heard worse,' she told him. 'What happened then?'

'Nothing for months except that I was left with some house deeds I could do nothing with even had I wanted to, which I don't. She was always away when I tried to get hold of her and she isn't on the telephone anyway.' He was still in a state of irritation with his thinking of her, his words seemingly bitten off short by it. 'I'd given her up as a singer at the club, of course I had, but not altogether on the couple of thousand I'd loaned her, even though I was suspecting she'd gone back to Australia. Then, at the beginning of the year, somebody I knew said that she was living at Thurnholme Bay, having joined up with a chicken farmer called Cruickshank. I'm not a hard man, Miss Millier, but I wasn't going to forget her letting me down over the singing and then have some other bloke help her to spend my money. Can you understand my feeling that?'

'I can only listen to what you say, Mr Fuller,' she said, self-consciously priggish. She had decided already, against all the cogent reasons for not allowing personal likes and dislikes to colour her opinion on someone she was interviewing, that she rather approved of this man who appeared on first meeting to carry with him a decency and honesty of feeling, not to say a definite dishiness. But that didn't, she told herself, affect her judgement in what he was telling her.

'Yes, I respect that and I apologize for asking.' Pausing, almost imperceptibly shrugging his shoulders as though pained, he said with a hint of self-mockery, 'I did some brilliant, for me, detective work by looking in the local telephone directory, then tapping out the number to see who'd answer.' He grimaced. 'As it happened, Eunice did; not that it eventually did me any good. I recognized her voice, naturally, and closed down without speaking.' Then, surprisingly, his nose tasting the air, he said, 'You are wearing a most attractive scent, Miss Millier. I'm sorry I hadn't noticed it before.'

Millier gave him a half-smile, bereft of anything sensible she could say.

'Forgive me,' he said hastily. 'I honestly don't know why I should say that then . . . it isn't me at all. I was about to say that I went to Cruickshank's address straight away, not giving a damn whether he was there or not. As it happened, he wasn't.' He smiled, making him seem to Millier a more appealing man than the one saying that she smelled nicely. 'I must say that if the average Australian woman is anything like Eunice in a difference of opinion over money, then God help the men who live there.' He turned his mouth down. 'I'm afraid I was led into saying some harsh things by the battering she was giving me, nothing of which got me anything but a threat to put a solicitor on my tail for the return of her house deeds which she said I'd got from her by trickery. That's it,' he said. 'I haven't heard anything from her or her solicitor since, and I still have the deeds.' He indicated the wall safe behind him. 'They're in there if you want them.'

Millier shook her head. 'That would be a civil matter and not

93

for me, and the quarrel was a long time ago. You've definitely not seen her since?'

'I'd have told you, please believe me.' His fingers were tapping on the desk top's green leather again. This time, she thought, signalling an inner irritation or, possibly, an impatience with her.

Manifestly trying to read what was behind her questioning, he said, 'It's probably not important, but I had second thoughts about her a month or so later, telling myself, Goddammit, but why shouldn't I, and ringing her number again. This time a man answered – presumably Cruickshank, though he never said so – and I asked to speak to Eunice. He didn't ask what the hell did I want her for, but said quite unpleasantly that she didn't live there any more and then banged the phone down on me.' He smiled, Millier thought quite boyishly. 'After that, I put any concern I might have had about her on the back burner. You're happy with that?'

'Happiness doesn't really come into it,' she said, then immediately hoped that he didn't read reproof into it. 'My seeing you is only a means of my finding out where she might be.'

'I know,' he acknowledged amiably enough, 'but it had crossed my mind that you could be thinking I'd strangled and buried Eunice in a desperate attempt to get my money back, or in revenge for something or other. Am I right?'

Millier thought that had Fuller and Parr been lovers – and the balance of probabilities was that they had been – then in any police-held opinion he could have. She showed in her expression that she accepted his humour. 'You're reading far more into my questioning than is there. *Did* you strangle her?' she asked, far from being serious.

He laughed, showing his teeth, then said, 'I'm sorry I was teasing you. You've obviously checked on my criminal past?'

'It's part of the routine.' She had to admit to herself that she felt comfortable with him, warming to him almost, which was something she needed to repress.

'They're not half as bad as they sound,' he said. 'Almost forgotten relics of my impetuous younger days.'

'They haven't come into my considerations,' she told him,

then moved off on a different tack. 'I'm sorry, but I've forgotten what you said when I asked had you known Mr Cruickshank. Had you?' That was devious-speak, for he had not answered her question.

His eyes had shadowed at that and he said shortly, 'I knew of him, I spoke with him on the telephone, but I'd never met him.' Then he added pointedly, 'There's still something more behind all this, isn't there?'

'Not so far as you are concerned,' she replied as if surprised, watching intently for his reaction. 'Mr Cruickshank was found hanging in his garage this morning and it seems we have a responsibility for telling Miss Parr of it. Which is why I'm here.'

His eyes told her nothing. She thought he might be talented at not being disconcerted by thunderclaps and suchlike, for he cupped his chin in his hand and gazed calmly at her. 'I'm not surprised,' he said at last. 'I imagine she'd have that effect on anybody fool enough to marry her. Delayed reaction in his case, no doubt. So far as she's concerned, I'd say it's a good bet that she's deliberately gone missing and it might be a good idea for you to check on a flight or two to Australia. Yes?' It couldn't be read in his expression that he was either worried or particularly interested.

She couldn't think of anything more she could ask, though suspecting that the moment she was out of his rather formidable and unsettling presence she almost certainly would. 'Thank you,' she said rather limply. 'You've been a help.' Retrieving her clutch bag from the floor at her side she stood.

Fuller heaved himself from his chair and stood with her. Tall though she was, he was the taller and she felt that with him so physically close to her he was reacting to her as a woman. She was surprised, but not displeased.

'There's one thing more,' he said with a deep seriousness. 'I'm concerned that you could be believing that Eunice and I had been living or sleeping together. We never have been, and I'd rather not have you think that we had. I've not even been in her house, which I've been fool enough to lend money on.'

She *had* thought that and now, searching his face for the truth of it or otherwise, wondered why it mattered to her one way or the other. And, more significantly, why he had said it. 'If you say so,' she said finally. 'And I'm happy to believe you.'

Opening the door into the night for her, he said abruptly, 'Do you like horses?'

Puzzled, she replied, 'Yes, I love them.'

'And motor rallying?'

She shrugged. 'I could live without it.'

'But skiing in Switzerland, yes?'

'Why all the questions, Mr Fuller?'

He smiled. 'Tell me, please. Skiing?'

'I like it very much and I do it when I can. Now tell me why I'm being interrogated like this.'

'Perhaps, only perhaps, because I'm doing to you what you've been doing to me for the past hour.' He was too amiable to be angry with. 'I wondered . . . well, when you've finally crossed me off your list of suspects for whatever it is, I'd like very much that we'd have a meal together. At a place of your choice, if that is how you'd wish it.'

She smiled her acknowledgement of that without answering and, climbing the steps into the court, she listened for the door being closed. Hearing nothing, she knew he was watching her leave, and that, in a silly way, was pleasing her.

Driving her car back to Headquarters by a circuitous route, she found herself considering Fuller, analysing her own emotions. Not, she thought, necessarily sexual – her mind shied away from that – but an awakened need to be masculinely dominated, to have any necessity of choice taken out of her hands. She had never thought of a man that way before, certainly not Rogers, and she felt somehow demeaned by it, almost hating him for making her feel that way.

Stopping outside Parr's home as she had originally intended, she walked around it, seeing in it the chillingly lonely darkness of a house to which nobody had returned. Thinking of Parr's association with Fuller, she was indecisive, not knowing whether to believe him or not in his denial of a previous sexual intimacy with her. Even had Parr been his mistress, she knew that it mightn't make all that difference if it ever came to the wantonness of her choice. Despite the disgust she felt for

96

herself, she knew it was going to be extremely difficult for her not to do something about him.

Slamming the door of her car and driving off in a squealing of tyres was symptomatic of an inner frustrating irritation.

14

A fatigued Rogers, nursing a pounding headache – he attributed this fancifully to the activities of an unknown to science purple worm eating holes in his brain – sat at his office desk in a thickening fog of tobacco smoke, reckless in his knowledge that the Chief Constable, the Deputy Chief Constable and the cohort of Assistant Chief Constables had all gone home knowing that somebody else was keeping the force flag flying. Catching up on his reading of the investigation's incoming paperwork was a stopgap while he waited to keep his appointment as the bearer of bad news – this on top of the finding of their dead father earlier that day – with Stephen Cruickshank and his sister, Veronica Cummins. The stopgap was also a palliative in keeping his earlier viewing of death's long-term horrors from impinging too frequently on his consciousness.

A telephoned preliminary report from a late-working scientist at the Forensic Science Laboratory was confirming rather testily that an examination of the yellow oil-stained rope showed broken fibres incorporating wood fragments having been pressed forward by heavy pressure on a rope being pulled over a horizontal and unpainted wooden joist or beam. Material taken from the plantar surfaces of the deceased Philip Cruickshank's feet had been identified as cement dust containing a few blue carpet fibres, there being no finding that the feet had been in contact with either sand or stone taken from the gravel path. It had been left to Rogers to assume – as he had already done – that the dead man had been carried from his bedroom to the garage for his hanging. A pillowslip taken from Cruickshank's bed had shown traces of the saliva of a smoker of tobacco; the bed's sheets showed nothing either to support or to invalidate

97

any theory that he had been smothered by the application of the pillow or having had bedclothing forced into his mouth.

Rogers had telephoned Dr Twite, telling him of the finding of Mrs Cruickshank and Ashe, saying that they had been dead and decomposed enough to defer the examination of what remained of their bodies until the morning. That pleased the hedonistic Twite who, while cheerfully complaining that he was going without food and still working his socks off for a brain-retarded constabulary, said that he had checked and rechecked on the facts and figures of a body's decomposition, and Cruickshank's in particular, and was now prepared to say that he had died from suffocation sometime during the Saturday and Sunday night ten days prior to his examination, possibly while in his bed.

Relighting his pipe and acknowledging that the fug of smoke wasn't all that thick when he could still read the *Please, No Smoking* notice on the far wall, he knew that, however slight the suppositions he had already formed, he had to be sure. Nobody could be exempt. Not even Ashe's brother. Whether he was from Southport, or from Tierra del Fuego for all anyone knew for sure, he could know something to which he, Rogers, was not yet privy and easily be homicidally inclined. The detective pursed his lips and shook his head at that, though knowing that all things were possible in the disaster-bound civilization of which he was so reluctantly a member.

Before opening the windows of his office to let the forbidden smoke out and leaving for what was almost certainly going to be an emotionally charged interview, he anaesthetized his system with a carefully calculated below-breathalyser shot of whisky from the bottle he kept in a drawer of his desk for such emergencies.

The building now known as Winslow Court had, within Rogers's experience, been modified and prettified from its former use as a tall, narrow and yellow-bricked warehouse with a canal frontage into what were patently much less than wide-bodied apartments. Leaving his car standing on the dark forecourt, he climbed steps to open a door to a poorly illuminated vestibule, just bright enough to show him that apartment 7 was on the top floor and that there was no lift.

The three steep flights of stairs did nothing for the equanimity of his inner being, harassed as it already was by the frustrations of a long day. Nevertheless, he managed a grave and restrained social half-smile at the woman opening the door identified with a silver-coloured figure 7. 'Mrs Cummins?' he asked.

She was wholly unlike her brother in appearance. Her build was what he would call a sinewy horsiness with, undoubtedly, a horse-rider's leathery backside beneath the narrow-legged trousers she wore with a loose tan-coloured shirt. Her face was angular with hostility showing in the small pale grey eyes, her straw-coloured hair tied back in loose untidiness. The hand that held the door open could, by its size and muscularity, be a man's.

Rogers had been about to introduce himself with his proffered warrant card when she pre-empted him by saying curtly, 'Come in, Superintendent,' leading him into a sitting-room smelling of cooked fish and equipped with three bloated easy chairs, a large stuffed-full bookcase, a matt-black music centre with green lights showing and two standard lamps, only one of which was burning and failing fully to illuminate the room. A small recess was furnished with a tiny dining table laid for a meal and two chairs. Cruickshank, dressed as he had been that morning and occupying one of the two easy chairs grouped side-by-side, made a half-hearted attempt at standing. Looking sick-faced, he mumbled something which Rogers – thinking he looked sloshed – couldn't properly hear.

Mrs Cummins indicated the unpaired chair to Rogers – he hoped that she acted in a more civilized manner with her horses – and he stood by it as she herself sat with her brother. Both waited for him to speak while he wondered if he was being unduly suspicious in having been offered the chair facing the only light illuminating the room.

'I'm sorry to call so late in the evening,' he started, his gaze going from one shadowed face to the other, 'but what I have to tell you is important and may affect you badly.' He had already told Cruickshank in telephoning that he would be the bearer of bad news. 'The body of your mother, Mrs Miriam Cruickshank, has been found this evening at your father's former farmholding, and it would appear that she has been dead for several years . . .'

It was, he knew, brutal, but how else could it be? He winced, seeing their open-mouthed shock, the sudden bloodless paling of their faces; Mrs Cummins reaching sideways and seizing fiercely at her brother's hand.

'I can wait outside for a few minutes if you wish,' he offered, trying hard for a kind of solemness suitable for the occasion.

'Y-Yes,' Cruickshank said, his eyes already brimming with tears, his sister glaring at the detective and nodding her head in impatient agreement.

Sitting none too comfortably on the narrow sill of a window outside the apartment, Rogers waited, gradually filling the stairwell with tobacco smoke while the fat purple worm of his headache bored deeper into his skull. After about twenty minutes spent with a background of the subdued murmur of fraught voices, the door was suddenly opened by Mrs Cummins who stood to one side for him to re-enter.

The atmosphere in the room was now changed and, searching for something to describe it, he thought of a low dark sky with, beneath it, falling grey rain.

With her brother slumped in an apparent bewilderment of limp grief, she, being reseated and uprightly rigid, motioned Rogers to sit. She said, 'We can't understand what you have told us, Superintendent, other than that you believe our mother to be dead. We can't dispute this, but we certainly want much more from you than you've given us so far.'

Bloody hell, Rogers swore to himself, satisfied that the pair were each now fully *compos mentis*. It clearly wasn't going to be one of his better evenings. He said gravely, 'Of course. That was always intended. As a result of our investigations into the death of your father, we had reason to search the barn at his old farm. During this, we discovered concealed behind some panelling there the bodies of a woman we believe to be your mother and a man named Ashe who had been employed at the farm by your father . . .'

He stopped when he heard a low moaning coming from Cruickshank, his sister glaring her hostility at himself. When neither spoke, he said, 'An examination of the bodies arranged

100

for tomorrow will almost certainly find that both your mother and Mr Ashe were shot to death five or six years ago while your father and mother were in occupation of the farm.'

There were long moments of tension-filled silence with Rogers wondering how much, how bloody much, was he to tell them? Mrs Cummins, clearly the stronger character of the two, took over the questioning of what the manifestly disliked detective was telling them. 'Am I hearing you right?' She demanded. 'Are you saying that our mother was murdered?'

'This *is* being treated as a murder enquiry,' Rogers said cautiously.

'And you know who did it?' She was impatient with him. 'Why was she found in the barn?'

'Not only she, Mrs Cummins,' he corrected her, not happy with her seeming determination to make Ashe a non-person. 'I said your mother and Mr Ashe; both together and both killed with a shotgun.' He softened his voice. 'It must be distressing for you both, I know, but you should take into consideration that they were shot and buried in the barn during your father's occupation, and at a time when he apparently told you that your mother had left him. Nothing, I have to assume, had been heard from her since.'

The silence in the room deepened with, in tableau, three poorly lit figures, each living the cruel tragedy of violent deaths with its different impacts on their inner worlds of the mind. The acerbic Mrs Cummins's face had suffused into an angry flush, while Cruickshank, in dumb despair, buried his face in his hands.

Finally, the woman burst out, '*My father*? How dare you! You've absolutely no right nor reason to suggest that he killed my mother . . . this man Ashe you say was with her.'

'Madam,' Rogers said stiffly and at his most formal, believing that he was encountering a born-again Medusa, 'I am giving you both, as I am bound to do, the unarguable facts about the unlawful deaths of two people. My opinion on who is responsible is, for the present, mine alone and hasn't been given to you.' He changed tack to head off more of her anger. 'I imagine that you both knew Mr Ashe?'

She stared unspeaking at him, Cruickshank apparently living in a silent world of his own.

'Tell me,' he tried again. 'Had you thought where your mother might have gone? Whether she'd gone on her own?'

She had again taken his words in silence, though now appearing to be getting her anger under control, with Rogers waiting patiently for an answer. Then tersely, she said, 'We didn't think anything.'

'Mr Cruickshank?' Rogers prodded.

'No,' he mumbled spiritlessly, looking at him only momentarily and sinking deeper into his chair.

'Not with her having been gone for six years with no word from her?'

That was clearly a non-question receiving nothing from Cruickshank and only a tightening of lips from the woman, her grey eyes hating him. He stared at them both, neither of them doing much for his headache. He was having to accept that she was barely containable in terms of being told disagreeable things about her parents – and why should she not be – while he, a weak sister if ever he had met one, would always be likely to collapse in tears.

'Let me tell you a few more facts you may care to consider.' He softened his voice to caring sympathy, though it was difficult under what he thought to be their active dislike of him as a police officer. 'After your mother's allegedly leaving your father, he visited Mr Ashe's lodgings at Penruddock Without, telling his landlord that Ashe had been called away over family business and wouldn't be back. He, your father, said that he had been asked by Ashe to collect his belongings and to settle whatever he owed.'

The room was quiet again, seemingly to Rogers to be hung darkly with racked emotions; anguished emotions not only of his words' arousing. 'Nothing', he continued, 'was heard from or about Ashe until six months ago when a man claiming to be his brother was in this area investigating his disappearance.' There had been no hint of awareness of this – he had been watching for it – in the eyes of his listeners. 'We know now, of course,' he continued, 'that Mr Ashe was probably dead by then and his body concealed in the barn when your father told the landlord that he had been asked to collect his property.'

Mrs Cummins, her face blotched over the cheekbones, said, 'That is something we couldn't know and which I do not believe for one moment.' She shot what looked to be a warning glance at her brother.

'Mr Cruickshank?' Rogers prompted.

Surprisingly now appearing to have rediscovered some of his backbone, he said, 'I agree with my sister. It doesn't do to blacken a d-dead man's name with speculation.'

'As you wish.' Rogers hesitated, then thought that it would come out, had to come out eventually. 'There is something else I feel may be relevant; something probably painful which you will hear and which I can only anticipate by my telling you now. I'm sorry, but it does appear that your mother was having an affair with Mr Ashe.'

Mrs Cummins's face was hard-planed with the intensity of her feelings. 'That', she ground out, 'is a damned lie, a slander. Something which we don't believe and never would.'

Cruickshank was shaking his head as if in blind bewilderment. 'When Father told us that Mother had left him, he was c-crying. He'd have said then if she had.'

'Shut up, Stephen,' his sister spat at him. 'It's not worth discussing and it's what he wants.'

Rogers studied them both in the disparity of what he had to accept as their grief, feeling very much the butcher of what must have been long-held illusions. 'I think we should leave this who-did-what business pending the completion of my investigations,' he said, 'but I warn you that there will be an inquest and the Coroner will be asking you questions which you do have to answer. However, there are two or three other matters, one of which is the identification of one of the bodies as being Mrs Cruickshank's.' The terrible result of death's mortification of the bodies was still vividly with him and he would not wish its horror on anyone, least of all a son or a daughter. 'I advise you both most strongly against doing this, and suggest you name another person, not necessarily related, to do it for you. Other than that, there are items of clothing and an emerald ring by which you may do your part in any identification.'

Ignoring whatever her brother thought, Mrs Cummins said, 'I shall identify my mother, should it be her body, myself. Please tell me when and where it has been arranged and I will be there.' She looked directly at her brother with what had to be scorn. 'You will leave this to me, Stephen; do you understand?'

Cruickshank, staring at Rogers as if he were the arbiter of their sorrows, said nothing.

'I'll let you know tomorrow,' Rogers said to the woman. 'If I may refer to your father's death, it's been established that he died ten days ago on the Sunday before last. I'm not sure when either of you made your visits to him and it could possibly help our investigation if a visit was made immediately before or during that weekend.'

This time Cruickshank answered. 'That wouldn't be possible. Neither of us went there the week before and we were fell walking around Carrigill for the weekend.'

Carrigill Fell, sixty-odd miles north of Abbotsburn, was known to Rogers as a seasonal slaughtering ground used by grouse shooters and a haunt for back-packers and fell walkers. There was only one hotel for these – in Rogers's opinion – peculiar people, isolated in the middle of purple heathered moorland, most unoriginally called the Carrigill Fell Hotel.

'And staying at the hotel there?' he asked.

Cruickshank, blinking at the probably unexpected question, looked hesitantly at his sister who was frowning at him, then stumbled out, 'Yes, of course. A question of economy, naturally . . .' His head jerked idiotically.

'For God's sake!' the exasperated woman cut in on him. 'The superintendent isn't interested in your finances or mine. All he wants to know is whether either of us called on Father the weekend he was killed.'

She spoke directly to Rogers. 'We were weekending at Carrigill from Friday lunchtime until Monday afternoon. Neither of us had any occasion to visit Father until Stephen did so last Friday.' She hadn't lessened her hostility to him, suddenly snapping, 'Don't you understand that you are upsetting my brother with your pointless questions?' She now appeared about to shed tears, her eyes moist. 'Will you please remember that we have both suffered losing our parents today and wish to be decently left alone.'

Feeling both justifiably irritated and uncomfortably guilty of something or other, Rogers pushed himself from his chair, not having obtained everything that he had wanted. Anyway, he needed a smoke as much as they clearly needed him to be somewhere else. He said, 'I really am sorry and regret that I've distressed you. Unfortunately, questioning relatives is often necessary in any investigation of a murder and it doesn't mean that we like it.'

He stood there, his policeman's unblinking gaze trying to reinforce his mind's assessment of the reaction to grief by these two manifestly stunned, but so different people. 'Thank you,' he said at last into the unhelpful silence when it was obvious that he had already been lost to them, then turned and left, closing the door gently like an undertaker's mute.

Beating tired leg muscles into further motion, he descended the stairs, hoping that he hadn't committed a professional *faux pas* in not questioning Cruickshank about his forcible ejection of Eunice Parr from his father's villa.

Back in his car and driving away with a smoking pipe clenched between his teeth and his headache still with him, he felt a strong reluctance to give any more time that evening to worrying about the deaths of three people who weren't going anywhere – at least, not in the body – and who would no doubt be reasonably indifferent about doing some more waiting on his pleasure.

Something or somebody – though certainly not the Medusa-like woman he had so gladly left – had provoked in him the warming remembrance of Angharad and he determined that, given the merest whisper of a reason, he would let loose the shamefully lusting masculinity which had been waiting too long for its release.

15

Back to an almost unoccupied, hollow-sounding Headquarters building and ready to book off duty, Rogers found Detective Inspector Millier waiting on his return. He said, 'I see you're still about,' hoping she couldn't read in his face the vast irritation he felt behind it. Leading her to his office, he let it be known to her *en route* that ten o'clock in the evening was no time for anything but the most succinct.

Millier, having changed into an off-duty blue satin tunic shirt and a long Oxford-blue skirt, her lemon-coloured hair glossy with good health and a recent shampoo – Rogers could smell its fragrance – looked particularly attractive. It was wasted on her physically unaffected senior who was feeling that there had to be something amiss with his inbuilt reproductive instincts in not appreciating her.

On his desk – heaven-sent, he thought – was a telephone message form telling him that a Mrs Rhys Pritchard had rung to say that should Detective Superintendent Rogers need to speak to her again, she was now back at her home. He also thought – though not actually believing anything of his sardonic self-appraisal for a moment – that the gods having the overseeing of the hardworking, the deserving and the almost saintly, were being kind to him.

With Millier seated and himself in his executive chair with his four-aspirin headache and showing a false image of alert efficiency, he gave her an abbreviated account of the finding of the bodies in the barn. 'Not that I can see there's any connection with your lost Miss Parr,' he said, 'but I think you should be aware of it; for who knows? You've seen Fuller?'

She had, she said, and he had her version of the interview in a pithily constructed account of it.

During his listening, he had felt a stir of unease, not altogether at what she was saying, but with how she had said it. He remained silent after she had finished, sensing in her some kind of a commitment to Fuller. 'I hadn't heard he'd yet been elevated to honest citizenship,' he told her cautiously. 'Running a night-club such as his has certain connotations with making a dishonest pound or two, though that may be a biased view.' He smiled. 'We *are* talking about the same man, are we?'

Millier wasn't taking that so lightly. She said, bristling a little, her beautiful mouth getting her words out fast, 'Don't we have to accept that a man can change, live down whatever he's done in the past, as I believe he has? I've no reason to suppose he was lying to me.'

'Remember though,' he warned her, 'you might only have seen the face he's chosen to show you. Underneath he may be all pit bull terrier.' Believing her about to be quarrelsome, he back-pedalled a little, but only a little. 'I've always held that it's horses for courses, though I have been found fallible in holding it on an occasion or two. I'll defer to your opinion of him for the moment, knowing it wouldn't anyway affect your jumping on him if you have to.'

'Thank you,' she acknowledged, though clearly not yet won over. 'I certainly believe what he says about his relationship with Parr, which *was* the main reason for my seeing him.'

'Indeed it was.' Rogers had noticed that she no longer stared at him in her unsettling manner, and he felt puzzled relief as well as a small disappointment to his ego. 'I thought you were convinced he was exercising a night-club owner's seigneurial rights with her?'

'I'm now not so convinced.' She was looking at a point over his shoulder. 'I don't think he had any reason to deny it had he been living or sleeping with her.'

'And I don't think it's all that important. Just bear it in mind in case you're proved wrong.' He shrugged that away. 'You haven't said, but you had asked him if Cruickshank got to know Parr at the club, I suppose?'

Her embarrassment was its own answer. 'I never thought of it. I'm sorry.'

'He was the type of man to be a member,' he pointed out levelly, 'and if he had been it would link him to Fuller more closely than we realize.'

'I'll see him again,' she said tersely.

'No, leave it. Let me think about it. I may be able to suggest a different approach.' Then he said mollifyingly, 'You've probably not had the time or opportunity, but there are one or two further enquiries you can make about Parr. Belatedly, I've a darkish suspicion that she might be missing because she's become a victim, rather than just missing because she's dropped out of sight and hooked up with another man.'

Millier looked surprised. 'I hadn't that impression at all.' She bit at her lip. 'You're not saying that I should have, are you?'

'I'm older in the tooth than you,' he said amiably. 'Intuition comes with long service and a thick skin against being found wrong. There've been suggestions here and there that Parr had married the older Cruickshank at some time. It doesn't sound at all possible, but I'd like you to do a check with the Births, Deaths and Marriages office as soon as you can.'

He looked at his wrist-watch. 'I'll have to cut this short,' he said. 'I've things to do. And so have you. Very quickly then, were the upstairs window curtains open or closed?'

Millier showed sudden irritation. 'Damn,' she muttered, then louder, 'I'm sorry, I didn't feel the need to check them.'

'Were the ground-floor windows locked?'

She shook her head, still irritable. 'I'm not sure.'

'No matter. When you come on tomorrow morning I want you to arrange for a ladder long enough to reach the bedroom windows to be at the rear of the house. I shall want to have an unadvertised look inside the upper rooms for myself.'

'Where . . .'

Rogers had held his hand up to silence her. 'Don't ask me from where you can get a ladder or anything else. That's for you to exercise some sort of initiative. I want you also to find me a means of entering the garage so that I can examine the car.' He was being mildly critical. 'Had you considered that

108

Parr might be in the driver's seat stuffed to the gills with carbon monoxide?'

'No, I hadn't. You think that I should have broken in to find out?' She was disapproving.

'I think *I* should, not you. In my opinion it's time for a more direct approach. I wouldn't want us to be accused later of feebleness and indecision.'

'Apart from making a forcible entry, I consider I had done all I could to see into the garage and the house, sir,' she said, being very formal and obviously resenting the implications she was reading into the well-meaning Rogers's instructions. Pink patches had appeared over her cheekbones. 'And no, I wasn't thinking of her as a probable suicide. Are you saying I should have?'

'No,' Rogers said mildly, standing from his chair, 'but I'm sure we'll come up with some useful answers tomorrow, one way or the other. Keep in touch, will you?' In a sense he had been making the missing woman Millier's problem for the good of her soul and her future in the service. Now, he was dismissing her before the conference became quarrelsome and hard words were bounced around the office.

Millier stood, looked at him for uncomfortable seconds with compressed lips and then stalked from the office, leaving Rogers with his eyes turned ceilingwards and wondering what the hell. When, from the corridor outside, her footfalls had died to silence and he had retaken his seat, he became slowly and gloomily conscious of his bleak solitariness in a building that echoed emptiness, only giving out the remote noises of a settling down for the night.

It brought into focus his own projected settling down for the night in an apartment as vacuous of feeling, of ambience, as a tomb waiting for his occupancy. It made him want to call Angharad, gave him a need to hear her voice, as late as it was. The thinness, the inadequacy of the only question his brain could contrive from nothing much, could be an embarrassment should they not, after all, be on the same wavelength.

It seemed that somebody else had lifted the telephone receiver and pressed the right buttons when she answered his ringing. 'Angharad?' he asked unnecessarily.

109

'George?' she said, and there was what seemed a wholly companionable silence between them. For him, also, he had only to have heard her voice to know that he had to be with her, a solace for his loneliness.

Judas!, he was thinking. Six feet two inches and a hundred and ninety pounds of lawful authority, and she could make him nervous, reduce him to almost flabby irresolution. He cleared his throat. 'I'm sorry to bother you at this time of the night, but I did have a further question to ask about Eunice Parr. It's only just occurred to me,' he added lamely, 'and I may not be able to call you in the morning.'

'It couldn't be a bother.' There was a slim edge of amusement in her voice. 'You wanted the answer tonight?'

'If possible.'

'It's possible, George, as all things are possible. I did leave you a message.'

He thought that sounded non-committal. What did he say now? And she was waiting, saying nothing to help. 'Yes,' he finally said, 'and I'm grateful. This is . . . well, it's confidential stuff.'

'And you don't want to chatter about it over the phone?'

For Rogers, there was nothing in her voice to suggest that this was a bloody good idea. He swallowed; surely she must hear the banging going on in his chest. 'If it's not too late,' he said.

'I'm here, and I do keep late hours.' She paused, then said carefully, 'Tell me if we appear to be steering the same bearing, George.'

'I had hoped we were.' He wondered even then whether her words were as significant as he thought them to be. 'I may come, then?' *Please, God*, he prayed, looking up at the strip lighting tube that put ageing sallowness and melancholy creases in his features.

'Of course,' she said, amusement back in her voice. 'Isn't that why you are calling me?', disconnecting then and leaving him feeling that his sun was quite definitely in the ascendant.

On his way out from his office he had a moment of cold-footed doubt, though trying to convince himself that the apparently acquiescent Angharad must have known his call to be a

110

triviality and have recognized it as the excuse that it was for calling her so late.

It was when he was taking the steep climb over the darkened moor's edge to Thurnholme Bay that he realized his headache had fled, his old familiar the purple worm being asleep. While he hoped as always that it was the sleep of death, its ceasing to bite him was, he knew, only until next time.

16

As a road, High Ipstone View was badly lit and often a dead loss for anyone visiting it on a moonless night. When Rogers turned his car into Angharad's drive and switched off its lights, he could see only dimly the subdued starlit whiteness of her villa and the reflected dark shadows in the glazed-in terrace above him.

Walking in the darkness towards the panelled and iron-studded door at the side, he was suddenly dazzled by the brilliance of a sensor-activated security light, enabling him to grope for and to lift and drop the iron door knocker.

Aware that he would probably be under scrutiny through the tiny observation lens near the knocker, he hoped he looked the very proper figure of a man pursuing his investigational enquiries. After he heard the sounds of two locks being operated, the door was opened and Angharad stood there. In a reversal of everything he had been thinking – and much of it had to do with lechery – he knew the moment he looked into her eyes with what had been a changed perception that he didn't want any easy and cheap option with her. She was a woman who could be for ever.

So far as the dazzled detective was aware, the gold-coloured sweater she now wore over a striped black and yellow outfit could have been run up from fish netting and barbed wire, the now long dangling ear-rings no different from those he had seen that morning. Plainly pleased to see him, she said, 'Come aboard, George. It's nice to see you again so soon.'

Following her into a room off the corridor he had earlier been in, he was exposed again to the – to him – unsettling musky scent she wore. It stayed with him after she had sat him in a large seaweed-green leather wing chair which could have been the late commander's, seating herself in a smaller version of it. He was only peripherally aware of other crowding green leather chairs, of a dark-wood sideboard and a wall-length case of books; of magazines and newspapers on spindly knee-high tables, quantities of silver things gleaming from reflecting parchment-shaded lights, and walls hung closely with prints of naval ships and paintings of yachts with coloured sails that billowed like the ample bosoms of matronly women. The room was comfortable though idiosyncratic; to his heightened imagination, redolent of a naval wardroom smelling of coffee and an ocean's salt-water.

At Angharad's side was an Indian hexagonal table supporting a hot-plate holding a transparent cylinder of the steaming coffee he had smelled and two deep green French *café*-style cups matching the colour of her eyes.

'You'd like a coffee, George?' she asked him. 'It's thick, on the Casbah side of being bitter and in time it'll turn the whites of your eyes a dark brown.'

'I'd love one,' Rogers said, 'and I've no objection at all to having dark brown eyeballs.'

He watched her – attracted mainly by the fetching slimness of her body – while she dribbled the viscid beautifully smelling stuff into the cups and then handed him one. 'I feel guilty about this late visit, Angharad,' he apologized, 'though it's true I wouldn't have asked anyone else to do the same thing.'

'I rather gathered that,' she said with a dry humour. 'And for my part, I would no doubt have refused to see another in your position.'

Rogers sipped at the smooth bitterness of his coffee, deeply content and only a little short of being certain that she was too. 'There are only a couple of queries – really there are – if I may get them out of the way.' He still didn't wish Angharad to know that he had, in effect, to contrive excuses in his need to see her. 'I hadn't said anything about it to you, but Miss Parr appears to be missing from her home in Abbotsburn. When she was living up here with Cruickshank, had she her car with her all the time?'

If Angharad thought little of the significance that could be attached to the question, she didn't show it. 'The red one she was taken away in? Yes, she had. She used Philip's garage, though only occasionally. Mostly, she left it in the drive.'

'And she used it regularly?'

'Yes. Almost daily it seemed.'

'There was one other matter.' That was something that had suddenly come to his mind. 'Can you tell me anything more about the Philip Cruickshank personality and character other than his piggishness with women's skirts?'

'I thought there might be more,' she murmured, her often sad mouth showing a brief smile. After a pause given to recollection, she said, 'He was a man with an inner torment; nothing of which he shared with me. He would often brood on whatever it was he was thinking, almost to the point of rudeness where he became unaware that you were with him. He was certainly too interested, too fond of discussing the financial side of living in retirement for good taste. I hadn't any doubt but that he was well-breeched and should have therefore shut up about it.' She screwed her face into an attractive grimace. 'I honestly don't wish to talk about him; not about any personal matters he confided in me, though God knows they wouldn't be of any interest to you or any other policeman.'

'Try me,' Rogers suggested.

She shook her head. 'I'm sorry, George. Not until I'm convinced they would be pertinent to your enquiries. It's the barrister in me,' she reminded him.

'I understand,' Rogers assured her as gracefully as he could. 'I'm sure that doesn't apply to Stephen and his sister. You know her?'

'I've never actually met Mrs Cummins, though I've seen her a few times when she was presumably visiting her father. Yes, and once with Stephen when she waited in his car while he called on his father.'

'She used Stephen's car to do her visiting?'

'No. She does have her own; a Volkswagen Beetle thing. A light blue one with a white roof to it.'

'Is there anything about her that you feel you can tell me?'

'A little I've heard about her from Stephen who told me that she was the victim of a particularly disastrous marriage that left her without a home, though why it was described as such I wasn't told.' She stopped there, apparently finished, but then said, 'Ah, there is something else. She's horse-mad and does an immense amount of rescue work with those ill-treated or neglected.'

'Good for her,' he said, now believing he understood in part her hostility to him on the basis that not only was he a policeman and a no doubt doubly despised male for bringing further bad news, but probably also something on which she couldn't put a saddle. He returned to her brother. 'Stephen and his father were close? As one would expect?'

'You're digging again, aren't you,' she smilingly accused him.

'Only about Stephen. A triviality needing some confirmation.'

'I'd always thought there were differences between them; perhaps no more than a generation's apartness, a difference in standards and so on. But although they appeared not to be all that close, there was undoubtedly affection there on both sides. And I'm sure the same applied to his daughter, for he spoke of her – as he did of Stephen – always with affection.'

That, Rogers thought, seemed to be his lot, lacking, as he considered he did, a creative imagination. He said, 'You've been most helpful, though I'll probably remember a very necessary question or two as the investigation gets a little more mileage in it.'

'You don't need to have questions to see me, you know. I do lead a social life outside the limits of your investigation.' She was showing an edge of feminine amusement again. 'Though, have you never heard that you should be very careful in your dealings with naval widows?'

'And you, with divorced men? Self-evident failures with women?'

'I'm sure that neither of you could help it,' she said diplomatically.

'I suppose not.' The goatish hulk of his ex-wife's parasitical

114

rugby-playing lover had come unbidden and unwelcomed in his mind and he unconsciously frowned. 'I was away from home a hell of a lot, my job taking over too much of my time.'

'I can see that happening.' Her voice with its fascinating lilt softened, her eyes questioning him. 'You're not a terribly happy man, are you?'

'I hadn't thought about that. Perhaps moderately so; a mite solitary at times, though I'm not complaining about it.' He smiled, a man not to be seen as one seeking sympathy. 'You've probably heard from somebody's reading of my curriculum vitae that I've been twice married, though only once divorced, and that I'm the usual flawed and blemished specimen of *Homo sapiens* anyway. Did your informant deal in specifics?'

'Of course not, but generally and sympathetically; and very much to your credit.' She dismissed that quickly by saying, 'May I ask how Mr Lewis dealt with my own background?'

Rogers held her steady compelling gaze, reading in it a shared rapport that encouraged him. 'It supported completely my interest in you, my liking for you, although we'd met only the once.' In the silence that followed, he said, 'I hope that this isn't embarrassing you?'

'No,' she said simply. 'It's what I wished to hear.' Then, pushing that to one side with a quick smile, 'I assume that golf comes into it?'

'Most certainly . . . and your being a most attractive and likeable woman, of course.'

She stood from her chair, the familiarity of expression between them agreed and settled. 'You should go now before I have a quite uncharacteristic change of mind.'

Rogers rose hastily. 'Another time, then? Another place?' No sooner had he said it than he knew that it had to be the most God-awful cliché of the year, not even remotely witty; the sort of thing that could be hung around his neck for life. However, it had been uttered and he cursed inwardly his gaucheness.

Angharad had had the decency not to have flinched or laughed her head off at the naïvety of what he had said, but led him out into the corridor with its now becoming familiar porcelain figurines and Impressionist prints to the outer door. As they stood there, close together, with the door open to the coolness of night air, it was at his initiative that he took her hand and kissed her on her mouth with a quite unRogers-like chasteness and gentleness he might have used with his mother. Although this reflected little of how his baser self felt, he wouldn't have traded that moment for a £10,000 win on one of his ancient and dusty Premium Bonds; yet he remained realistic enough for even his presently besotted mind to recognize that he could later renege on that with more immediacy than an honourable intention might allow.

And later – restless in his lonely bed – he was attacked with shameful misgivings. Had he left Angharad sexually frustrated by his pusillanimous inaction? Had she expected and hoped, despite the seeming lack of any indication from which he could have known, that he would make love to her? Was she viewing him now in retrospect, in her so to speak virginal bed, as a wet and feeble ninny lacking in masculinity?

Deadly tired though he was, with what felt like ounces of gritty sand in his no doubt dark brown eyeballs, it was a long long time before he fell into troubled sleep.

17

Detective Inspector Millier, who had breakfasted unhappily on grapefruit juice, butterless toast and coffee in the flat she rented in the leafy Shady Bower area of Abbotsburn, had spent an unusually disturbed night. The cause of it was the incredulousness she experienced at finding herself drawn physically – and, she made herself suppose, also mentally – to Fuller, the type of man against whom she should be adequately fireproofed by her police training, her fastidiousness and her own standard of morality. But now, she seemed not to be that woman. In her disconnected thinking, she concluded that her being drawn sexually to Fuller had somehow been coincident with a suddenly discovered dislike for a newly revealed close-quarters Rogers; a revelation that there was little compatibility between them, that there never could be and that he had treated her with an unexpected measure of official displeasure the night before.

As she was about to leave for the office, there had been a knock on her door and a man in a pink jacket with *Clarissa Florist* embroidered on its breast pocket had said, 'Good morning, madam; Miss Helen Millier?'

When she agreed that she was, he had handed to her an expensive-looking bouquet of flowers encased in clear polythene and held together with pink ribbon and a bow, leaving her standing mute, like, she thought, a stunned idiot.

There was a card, but it bore only her name and address in typescript. It needed no more for her to identify the sender. 'Damn him!' she had said, her face flushed, returning inside to toss angrily in disorder the bouquet on to the kitchen draining-board. Leaving the flat and slamming the door after her, she had then hesitated and returned to put the flowers in order and into a wash-basin to await her return in a more equable mood.

A pipe-smoking Rogers, seated at his worktop of a desk, was not at one with the reasonably bright early morning of not too many clouds. Despite what he considered to have been a promising start with Angharad, he felt like a man waiting for inevitable rain to come drenching down.

It was, he suspected, going to be a long day with three bodies lodged firmly in the vault of his skull, problems throwing up such incomprehensibilities as the blow on the back of a man's head who had almost certainly been suffocated to death, a thoroughly searched bureau, a needed walking-stick left in the dead man's bedroom, the finding of an inappropriately placed elastic band, the surprising incompetence of the usually efficient Millier, and the seemingly civilized character that she had made of Fuller to his unbelieving ears.

Coltart was dealing with what he had inelegantly called a couple of dead ends in the sad forms of what decomposition had left of Miriam Cruickshank and Richard Ashe; dead ends, for how could it be proved now that a cuckolded Philip Cruickshank had murdered them *in flagrante delicto* and, even

117

were it possible, who – not being God or a coroner – would wish to prosecute and punish a dead man?

Somewhere in the gap between his ordering a quartet of loose-end DCs to trawl through the division's hotels, motels and guest houses in a search for evidence of a visit by the dead Ashe's apparently harder-cased brother from Stockport or anywhere else, and a call to his opposite number in the next county for a detailed and urgent check on Stephen Cruickshank's visit with his sister to the Carrigill Fell Hotel, his telephone had rung and Cruickshank himself was asking to be put through to him.

'Yes?' Rogers said not too genially, recollections of his last evening's visit still with him.

'About your call here last night, Mr Rogers.' His words sounded forced as if, the detective thought, his formidable sister stood heavy-handed behind him. 'I-I wish to thank you for what must have been an unpleasant job for you to do, and to apologize for myself and on behalf of my sister. We were both under great stress in trying to come to terms with the terrible things you told us . . . about our father being suspected of . . . well, of causing our mother's death. You do understand, I hope?'

'There was no offence taken,' Rogers said, 'and no bones broken either, though I felt I had to leave without raising one matter I had to clear with you.' He cleared his throat. 'I have to see Miss Parr about her past relationship with your father and it appears that she is now missing from her home. There's nothing too serious at the moment,' he added, 'but I thought you might have some views on it.'

'I'm sorry, but after what she did to Father I couldn't care less about where she is.' He seemed to be tightly wound up, his voice rising. 'So far as I am concerned, I hope . . . I hope that she stays missing.'

'I wondered if her being so had anything to do with your forcible ejection of her from your father's villa last February?'

'Oh.' After that there was silence in which Rogers, waiting, heard the sound of what must have been a hand placed over the mouthpiece. 'I'm sorry,' Cruickshank finally said, late in responding. 'I should have told you before, but I was thinking of Father. He wasn't a well man and that woman had lately been making his life a hell. He said to me that he no longer wanted her there, but she wouldn't go, and I promised him that I'd see to it if he went away for a day or two. He asked me not to hurt her – as if I would anyway – because she couldn't help her own nature. He gave me a cheque for five hundred pounds to cash and to give her against a written promise that she wouldn't try to return or contact him by any means whatsoever. This I did when she left and I gave the agreement to Father as he wanted.'

'Go on,' Rogers told him, putting his already filled pipe between his teeth and fumbling unsuccessfully for his matches. 'That isn't enough. Not nearly enough. She was being removed by forceful persuasion and there was a man helping you.'

There was more delay, Rogers using it to light his pipe. Cruickshank was sounding neurotic to him, though he wasn't too sure of the symptoms. But certainly an oddball to have pushing his hand around in your mouth. 'A friend,' Cruickshank said miserably at last, 'and helping me out. I won't involve him . . . there wasn't any force used. I told her that she'd been unkind to Father, a sick man; that she'd been behaving promiscuously with other men while living with him. I told her that she had refused to leave the house when asked quite reasonably to do so on a number of occasions and that she could now leave voluntarily with five hundred pounds expense money, or I suppose involuntarily with nothing at all.'

'I rather gathered it was involuntary,' Rogers interposed drily.

'Not at all. She agreed to leave.' His voice was more assured now. 'Not happily, obviously, but I suppose under some slight pressure and the promise of the money. She tried to convince me that she was Father's common-law wife or some such non-sense and that the five hundred wasn't enough. I told her that I'd see if Father would cough up a little more, though I guessed that was unlikely and he didn't. She packed up her stuff in some suitcases, gave me the house keys I'd asked for and we took her to a house here in Abbotsburn which she said was hers.'

It hadn't been quite how Angharad had described it, but Rogers held non-belief in abeyance. Cruickshank, he recalled, had denied any knowledge of Parr's leaving his father's house and of where she lived. That, he supposed, had been understand-able at the time. 'Was there any contact after that?' he asked.

'No, thank God.'

'With your father?'

'If there was, he'd have told me.' He added somewhat bitterly, 'I suppose it can be seen as a bit of rather dirty work he'd sooner have had forgotten.'

'Yes, it was. On both your parts. Does your sister know of this?'

Cruickshank groaned. 'Christ, no. I'm speaking to you in confidence, I hope?'

'I imagined you would be,' Rogers said more coldly than he had intended, knowing that were his sister within earshot then what he said could be highly suspect. 'Can you suggest where Miss Parr might now be? Or with whom?'

'Of course I can't.' He hesitated. 'Could I ask how Father's death . . . how the case is going? I know it's early days, but my sister and I . . . we're very concerned that whoever it was is still about.' He sounded nervous. 'You don't think there's any danger to us – to my sister, I mean?'

'I don't think so,' Rogers told him, wondering why he had asked and whether there was.

'If there is anything, I'm not a well man at the moment and I'm away from the surgery. If you do want me again perhaps you'll ring me at home.'

'Before you go, tell me whether your father had any connection with the Midnight Blue night-club?'

'I'd heard he'd been visiting a club here, but I never heard it called that. Is it something I should know?'

'I don't believe so.' Rogers closed down after formally thanking him, not liking him any more than he had before. Cruickshank hadn't asked him who had seen and spoken of his ejection of Parr and this probably meant that he knew it was Angharad, or had guessed it to be.

That his hitherto absent on sick leave second-in-command, Detective Chief Inspector Lingard, should unexpectedly rap on his door and enter his office gave his spirits a pleasing and necessary uplift.

Lingard, a lean and elegant man with narrow patrician features, had the daunting blue eyes that could chill the presumptions of other men, yet warm women to a lowering of their sense of caution against male predation. He wore his shaggy blond hair a little too long at the nape, his silk shirts high in the collar and a little too long in the sleeves, and his London-tailored suits and exotic waistcoats were a reproach to other men. He was a dilettante authority on the life and the Regency times of the elegant, exquisite and snuff-taking George Brummell, aping his dandyism to a point only just acceptable to his contemporaries. A bachelor, relatively wealthy from the now regretted sale of his beloved classic Bentley, he continued in his role of a highly efficient and potentially physically dangerous detective officer because he could think of nothing better to do.

With his left forearm in plaster and held in a silk sling which matched his coffee-brown barathea suit, he said, 'I'm discharged walking wounded, George, and I thought I'd like to get back into harness. I'm bored.'

Rogers eyed him with mock distaste, the peacock to his own sombre rook. 'And I thought I'd seen the last of you, David. You've disappointed me.'

'I heard you were staggering along on two cylinders without me,' Lingard said jauntily, 'so back I've come.' He swivelled the visitors' chair towards himself with the toe of one of his highly burnished Italian shoes and sat.

Rogers grinned, the prospect of drenching rain receding. 'You couldn't have chosen a better time.' He nodded at the plastered-up arm. 'You can cope?'

'I knocked on the door with it.' He wagged his arm, holding back a need to wince. 'It's nothing to make me cough up blood. Tell me what you need doing about your current cock-up.'

Rogers filled him in with a brief account of the three murders, then of the supposedly missing Eunice Parr, dealing lightly with Millier's enquiries concerning her, and of her own interview with Fuller, while Lingard deftly lodged a tiny ivory box in the flexure of his broken arm and pinched Golden Cardinal snuff from it to feed into his nostrils.

'There are papers and notes you can take to your office and read up on,' Rogers concluded expressionlessly. 'Then I'd like you to sort out Fuller.'

Lingard cocked an eyebrow. 'Egad, George! Take over from the gorgeous Helen? What's she done?'

121

'She's been standing in for you and unfortunately not doing it all that well.' This wasn't pleasing Rogers and care and diplomacy were needed. 'Now that you're back it's a matter of taking some of the responsibility for Fuller from her. With her, or without her. It's no more than that. I leave it to you to see that she's not too miffed about it.'

'It's Fuller you're not happy about?'

'Apart from whatever else I've mentioned, I believe she's gone soft on him. His supposed loan to Parr is too much out of bloody character for me to swallow. So is what he told her about not having it off with Parr when we know it'd be every other half-hour or so when he wasn't screwing money out of some dim-witted bugger with more of it than sense. And his quarrel with her. That could have been jealousy over withdrawn sex, which is always a mite more likely to provoke violence than losing money.'

He smiled benignly at Lingard. 'You know him, David. He was a client of yours some time back, so I'd like you to see him and screw something believable from him. I', he said, turning down the corners of his mouth, 'will do my own softening of Millier by keeping her busy on something else.'

'I'll beetle off then,' Lingard murmured before leaving with his bagful of instructions, 'and look for an occasion to jump on friend Fuller's face.'

With his departure, Rogers felt that he might now be able to do something useful with an unworried mind about Parr herself.

It was a further forty minutes when, with Rogers lighting up his fifth *verboten* pipe for the day, his telephone bell rang and it was Millier on the line. She was, she told him with a detectable lack of friendliness in her voice, waiting at Parr's house for him. A ladder had been obtained and delivered there, together with a large bunch of assorted keys taken out against signature from the Lost and Found Property Office. It was hoped, she said, that one of the keys might fit the garage door lock.

Rogers, having had much experience of the implacable invulnerability of bloody-minded locks to a mixed bag of keys, found, and decided to take with him, a down-to-earth extra heavy screwdriver. Then he rang through to the office of

122

Detective Sergeant Magnus – the man who, while capable of finding somebody's discarded nail clipping at the scene of a crime, could collide with an unnoticed chair – and ordered him to stand by for action with his fingerprint-searching kit and his dust-and debris-seeking equipment.

18

With Sergeant Magnus occupying the passenger seat of his car, Rogers had pulled in behind Detective Inspector Millier's highly polished Rover Mini standing outside the house called Haygarth in St Epiphanius Road. The house had, in Rogers's quickly assessed opinion, received its last coat of brick-red wash at least a decade ago, the roof slates appearing to have survived undisturbed under a blotching of green and orange lichen. The window frames were metal, needing derusting and painting. Even in the brilliance of the morning sun it was difficult to be impressed with it, grubby and neglected and patently a 1930s home fallen on bad times. It was difficult for Rogers to imagine that any of Fuller's alleged loans of money had been spent on its upkeep.

'Don't unload yet, Sergeant,' he said to Magnus, opening his door and climbing out. 'Wait until I've spoken to Inspector Millier to see whether I'll need you.'

Passing the lock-up garage on his way to the back of the house, he stopped, looking in the small side window without seeing much more than the roof of a red car through obstructing spiders' webs and thick dust on the glass. He felt no extra-sensory perception that death might be lurking in there.

He found Millier in the rear fenced-in garden, an over-grown wilderness of seeded grass, giant cabbage stalks and stinging nettles surrounding a neglected broken-glassed green-house. She had with her DC Crabtree, one of Rogers's walrus-moustached in-embryo staff, both waiting near an adequately long aluminium ladder propped against the wall of the house adjacent to a small apparently insecure window.

Saying a reasonably genial 'Good morning' to them both, he noted Millier's splendid attractiveness in spite of his immediate preoccupation with the house, and puzzled again why his interest in her as a woman was still less than lukewarm.

Doing a quick check on the security of the ground-floor windows and doors – he failed to see Millier's irritation that he should do so after she had reported them to be securely locked – he drew her away from Crabtree and said, 'I won't ask you to climb the ladder, so while I'm inside opening up the house have Crabtree fetch the screwdriver from the back seat of my car and get the garage door opened with the minimum of damage. Be with him in case there is a dead Miss Parr in the car. And, of course, show him what's what when there's a body to be coped with.'

She didn't trouble to conceal the brief annoyance she felt at his removing her from entering the house, her beautiful mouth being tight-lipped. 'I don't believe that she'll be in there,' she said. 'The door's obviously locked and I can see no key in it on the inside. There'd be the end of it showing if she'd locked it herself.'

Rogers thought that something or somebody – perhaps himself – had upset her. 'I wasn't thinking we could have a suicide,' he told her mildly, 'but key or no key, I suppose it's a possibility.' He tapped his teeth ruminatively with the stem of his pipe. 'That is presupposing somebody hasn't killed her, put her in the garage and locked the door on his way out.' Turning away, he said, 'If you're right that she's not in there, then I've been presupposing in vain; but we'd still have to know, wouldn't we? Let me have a yea or nay as soon as you can, will you?'

Alone and with a disregard for his professional gravitas, he made a cautious rung-by-rung ascent of the ladder to the apparently insecure window. Its aperture appeared smaller than he considered his bulk required for entry and gave him an indistinct pebble-glassed view of a bathroom and lavatory. The window itself was fingertip-open on the first hole of its latch and, when he had opened it and scrambled through – nearly putting his foot into a pedestal wash-basin half-full of water – his plumage had been severely ruffled and he knew that he would be unfitted for civilized company for some time.

Inside, he felt it uncomfortably hot, the day's heat having been retained in the house's shut-upness. The gas geyser-equipped bathroom he stood in was small – he could, were he so eccentrically minded, stretch out his arms and touch opposing walls – and its door partly open. Immediately, his nose, more happy when being used to inhale the splendours of a woman's sometimes dizzying perfume, now tasted, as it were, and identified, the fading stench of death's corruption of the flesh.

Discarding his intent to first open the doors below for access, he moved from the bathroom to do a visual search through the upstairs two bedrooms – only one being fully furnished and all the drawers having been pulled out and manifestly searched – the wardrobes and cupboards, and the almost inaccessible roof space. Down the narrow stairs and chasing the more rarefied stench there, he searched unsuccessfully a drab wallpapered sitting-room with a small fireplace and no central heating, an undersized dining-room, a no-refrigerator kitchen and an almost empty walk-in larder. In all the rooms the furniture and furnishings were poor and of apparent 1930/1940 vintage; uncomfortably angular, spindly tubed and distaste-fully veneered. Everything where physically possible had been searched.

He was certain that a dead body had been in the house, as certain that it was no longer there. He had, in effect, followed his nose and relied on it in searching, for the smell of death was a familiar one and had been all-pervading. Possibly, he now thought on reflection, it had been most pronounced in the furnished bedroom manifestly used by Eunice Parr.

That he had been searching for the hiding place of Parr's body had meant his ignoring for a time the material evidence of her occupation of the house. That apart, he had spent a not too unwasted several minutes in looking at and impressing on his memory an overturned framed studio photograph of, he had to assume, a much younger and startlingly blonde Eunice Parr. Undoubtedly, she had been what would be held to be plumply beautiful with, apart from a hint of selfishness in her features, a vapidness often met in young and otherwise immature women. Distinct from his professional reflections on her, and however unangelic her recent behaviour had been, he thought it a sadness that so young a woman should have died what he now had to assume to be an untimely and violent death.

With the back door unlocked and Millier and Crabtree withdrawn from their discovery of an unoccupied car and garage, Rogers let loose the ginger-haired sniffer-out of small debris in the form of Magnus to find and identify where the violence on Parr had taken place, and where her body had presumably lain for a sufficient time for the onset of its decomposition. Also, he told Magnus, he wanted more troops brought in and a rigorous search made for latent finger impressions left in the house – particularly in Parr's bedroom and the bathroom – by invited and uninvited visitors alike. If any matched Robert Fuller's fingerprints, already on file, it would be no more than he expected.

'Miss Millier,' he said, after briefing her on what he had done and his conclusions arising from it, 'there seems to be no handbag which I've always thought to be essential to a woman's peace of mind. I'd like you to trawl through the house and find it if it's here. There might be something in it that'll throw some light on the darkness surrounding us.' He smiled at her, trying to keep it friendly. 'Let me know if and when you've got it, will you?'

'How would you consider whoever it was could get in?' she asked. 'A duplicate key?'

'A knife blade to slip an outmoded window catch would do, then securing it after entry and leaving by the front door which is self-locking. Or,' he said, 'being known to Miss Parr – possibly as a friend or a lover – and simply knocking on the door. I could run off a half-dozen ways of getting in and out to our complete incomprehension, but at the moment it doesn't really matter.'

Taking for himself what had been Parr's bedroom where his nose had decided the smell of dead flesh to be strongest, he returned upstairs with his pipe burning out smoke as an intended fumigant. At the open door of the bathroom, something below the level of his consciousness provoked his interest to walking in and staring at the wash-basin into which he had so nearly put his foot. Being half-filled with slightly unclean water, it told him nothing other than that it could be odd that the plug hadn't been pulled and the water drained away.

Leaving it, he entered the bedroom where the stench persisted; possibly, he thought, retained in the stuffs of the obviously slept-in bedclothing. This was in different shades of apricot and yellow, adding a jaundiced lightness to the room and appearing to have been fairly recently purchased. Stripping it all from the bed and examining each sheet, pillowslip and blanket for signs of violence or carnality, he found nothing but a few specimens – expected to be in any bed – of genital or armpit hair. In the absence of a nightdress or pyjamas, it seemed reasonable to suppose, there being no further evidence, that she either slept naked, or had been in bed wearing night-clothing when death entered the house. Or, as likely, that the killer had been sharing her bed.

The small table at the side of the bed had on it a pink satin-shaded reading lamp, a thick paperback book titled *Slave Girl*, a nearly empty packet of cigarettes with a brass gas lighter and a glass ashtray loaded with lipstick-stained stubs. An old dressing-table holding cosmetics had nothing of interest on or in it, though taking an exploratory sniff at one of the scent bottles convinced him that its contents were designed to goad into action any normal male's sexual aggressiveness. The large free-standing wardrobe, greasy with age, was empty of anything but women's clothing, and this mostly in strongly printed primary colours.

He had earlier peered back-achingly into the eighteen inches of empty space beneath the bed, but this time was prepared to be content with establishing where the body might have been, rather than where it now actually was. His pushing the bed to one side exposed a dusty rectangle of bare floorboarding. Crouching, he examined in it a saucer-sized blotch of a deep brown staining, recognizable as dried blood. On it were five minute pallid-white maggots; three being motionless and obviously dead, the two others twitching feebly and appearing to be dying.

127

Straightening his legs and moving to the window, he opened it to the fresher morning air, noting the flies, living and dead, occupying the inner aspect of it. After several minutes of pushing his thinking around fly-associated matters while scratching matches at his still-hot pipe to disinfect his lungs of the cloying smell of the dead Eunice Parr and her perfume, he called down the stairs for Millier and Magnus to join him.

'I think', he said to both, 'that our unfortunate Miss Parr was killed almost unbloodily in this house, possibly not while in bed and almost certainly some few nights ago. This could mean, though not with certainly, that her killer was known to her and invited in. Once dead, she was hidden – I'm sure as a temporary measure – under her own bed here, still bleeding a little and probably from her head. Any comments?' he enquired.

Magnus said, 'Excuse me,' licked the tip of one of his fingers, reached down and dabbed it on the brown stain. Showing the resulting moist pinkness on his finger, he said, 'It's blood all right.'

'Miss Millier?' Rogers asked.

'No. I follow you.' She was giving him nothing at all.

'I'm on some fairly dodgy ground in trying to put a time sequence to all this,' he continued, 'though I've a previous occasion or two to support me. These maggots we see come from eggs laid on dead flesh by a fly; possibly a bluebottle fly. There are two dead ones in the window to suggest that it's most likely, though it doesn't really matter what kind. The maggots are the larvae of the fly and hatch from the eggs in eight to twelve hours, starting to feed on the putrefying flesh immediately.' He lit and applied a match to a pipe that was exasperatingly intent on dying on him. 'A maggot will feed for about eight to ten days before it charges off to find somewhere to pupate and turn into a fly proper. These have almost certainly been feeding on our unfortunate Miss Parr for something less than ten days. They aren't known for sure to stop for a rest between meals, and if that's so, being removed from their food source means they'd not survive.' He grimaced. 'I don't know how long that'd be, of course, or for how long, having been disturbed from the flesh they were eating, they would stay alive on a diet of dried blood. If at all, but not, I'm reasonably certain, for too many hours.'

Rogers was in the chair, and Millier and Magnus watched and waited while he did his thinking in trying again to relight his recalcitrant pipe. 'With the three of them dead,' he said, 'and the others on the short list to join them, I've a feeling that Miss Parr's body, having been under the bed long enough for corruption to be well on the way, was removed and taken away as late as last night. Are we in some sort of agreement about that?'

'Encapsulated fact,' Magnus said, definitely a man with a future and anticipating Rogers's coming instructions. 'I'll have scrapings of the blood and the dead and dying taken to the laboratory before there's any starving to death.'

Millier said, 'Couldn't Dr Twite give us the times with more accuracy?'

'He certainly could.' Rogers smiled again the confidence he should hold her in, guessing that she might need it later when showing a female *frisson* or two when Lingard came into her reckoning. 'However, he's very unlikely to want to be called out to examine a couple of barely alive maggots, some dried blood and a nasty smell. It's her dead body he'll want, so when you've found out about the handbag and anything else of hers you think might be relevant, it'd please me immensely if you took off from here and bent your thinking to where her body might conceivably be.'

When he had finished all that he could do there – his parting words to Magnus were that a water-filled wash-basin he would find in the bathroom might pay for some examination and that he'd like him to give it some attention – he left what he felt to be a house still haunted by the ghost of the as yet unknown to him sexually permissive night-club singer.

Driving back to his office with the prospect of a fourth body to bugger up his already complicated thinking, he let rein to his what-the-bloody-hell's-happening-now?mood, always with the danger that he would take it out later on inanimate objects by hurling empty drinking glasses into his mock fireplace or slamming the doors of his much disliked apartment.

19

One of the requirements of Rogers's office as Detective Super-intendent was the imperative that when reachable he keep the Assistant Chief Constable (Crime), Joffre Burt, informed of the serious crime position in his bailiwick and what he was doing about it.

Sitting in conference with Burt, who had hospitably offered him coffee, Rogers had filled him in with a few optimistic-sounding facts about the three dead bodies and the possi-bility of a fourth under investigation – already he felt awash with corpses – then reported on Detective Inspector Millier's expected satisfactory progress in her trial posting.

After expressing his 'I knew she had it in her' at Rogers's optimistic assessment of her progress – her posting had been on Burt's initiative – he had said, 'Is there anything I can do to help you with your investigation, Mr Rogers?'

This was an offer definitely not to be taken seriously, and Rogers hadn't done so. 'I don't believe so, sir,' he had declined gravely, knowing that by doing so he was committing himself to a successful conclusion.

His pipe being naturally prohibited and the coffee being milkily tepid, he sat impatiently with the sun uncomfortably on his back, remembering a previous occasion when the ACC had slung himself around his neck like a querulously unhelpful albatross. 'I'm grateful, of course,' he said, 'but I believe I've things pretty well tied up.'

Burt, a wholly clean-living smoothie with his ambition set firmly on being the Chief Constable of any force that would have him, and by definition a dangerous man to have as an immediate superior, persisted, though looking pointedly at a well-laden tray of files. 'I mean,' he said, 'if you *really* want me, though I do have a Crown Court case pending I've to oversee for the Chief Constable . . .'

'No, there are no problems I can't cope with,' Rogers insisted, wisely concealing the irritation he felt at having to undergo this fatuous ritual. To admit to them anyway would be to admit to an unjustified ineffectiveness.

He had pushed his chair back and stood, anxious for release, but having to listen to a five-minute well-worn homily on how thoroughly evil and godless Burt found the county in which he served and how, present company excepted of course, the service needed a fresh and original look – his, naturally – at its problems. Finally, he said, 'I shall be looking forward to hearing of an early arrest, Mr Rogers, as the result of all our efforts.'

Back at his desk with the flat yellow bars of the sun coming through the window louvres and bouncing unwanted heat off the office walls, a relieved Rogers set about the unavoidable paperwork of his investigation and the tying up of what he considered to be some carelessly neglected loose ends.

While reading and noting all that he decided was relevant to his needs, he heard from Magnus on the other end of his telephone that he had found and processed a number of latent fingerprints, some of which were almost certainly male. So far as the wash-basin came into the picture, Magnus had found in the water – which he had preserved – two yellow hairs. These, he said, somewhat disparagingly, would be expected to be in a bathroom used by a blonde-haired woman. Rogers, for reasons intuitive rather than logical, and accepting the possible triviality of it, found it difficult to accept that a woman could go to bed without draining a wash-basin she had manifestly been using. But it was a niggle in him, though little more. Millier had, it appeared, failed to find Parr's handbag – assuming that she had one – and that seemed to add problems to his thinking.

Returning to his papers, he chose to read a fax flimsy sent with a pleasing promptitude by a Detective Inspector Straker detailed by his superintendent to do the Carrigill Fell Hotel enquiry. It was endorsed for Rogers's personal attention and said that a Stephen Cruickshank from Winslow Court,

131

Abbotsburn, had stayed at the hotel from midday on the Friday referred to until 4.30 p.m. on the following Monday, signing the register as being accompanied by his wife, Mrs Stephen Cruickshank, and occupying Room 4.

They had stayed similarly at the hotel on three earlier occasions, always accepting a double bed. Mr Cruickshank's sister, Mrs V. Cummins, referred to by Mr Rogers, had not registered as a guest for the same period, or on any previous occasion. Mr and Mrs Cruickshank had been walking the moor as guests of the Carrigill Fell Walkers' Association on the Saturday and Sunday, and it seemed certain that neither would have had the occasion to return to Abbotsburn. The owner of the hotel had said that, as was customary, the keys to their car – a light blue, white-fabric-roofed Volkswagen saloon, number not recorded – had remained with the reception clerk for the whole of their stay.

Straker had finished – apparently with a troubled mind – by asking whether Superintendent Rogers wished to advise him concerning the apparent confusion of relationships arising from the Cruickshanks' stay at the hotel.

Lingard, entering the office while Rogers had been reading the fax sheet, had been waved into a chair to wait. When Rogers had finished, he passed the sheet to his second-in-command. 'Read it, David, and see if you agree with me about that which Straker seems to have stumbled on to and cares not to name.'

While Lingard, resting the sheet awkwardly on his lap, did a one-handed sniffing of a supportive charge of Golden Cardinal into his nose before reading it, Rogers picked out and read a preliminary report from Dr Twite on his examination of the two bodies found in the barn. He had recorded that though both were partly mummified, he was giving the age of the woman to have been between forty-five and fifty years; the age of the man between thirty and thirty-five years.

With what Rogers recognized as friendly mockery behind the words, he said he had deduced from his examination that both had died from the effects of gross gunshot wounds, inflicted from a distance of only a few feet and several years earlier, though probably less than a decade. There was, he had finished in the short report, no evidence to confirm that the two might have been engaged in adulterous or any other kind of sexual intercourse at the time of their deaths.

Finished, Rogers turned his attention back to Lingard, being returned the Carrigill fax sheet. 'Do we share overly dirty minds, David?' he asked.

'Egad, George, it's interestingly steamy. You had a suspicion or two before?'

'No. Though I do remember when I asked where they were over that weekend, Cruickshank blurted out something about staying at the hotel being a matter of economy.' Like a male Delphic Oracle he was apparently looking for the truth in the ash-filled bowl of his pipe. 'With a single room and a double bed it undoubtedly would be. With hindsight, I now realize that his sister shut him up much too savagely for it to be only that. I must have been in one of my more naïve periods and I didn't then latch on to its significance.'

'You're going to push it?' Lingard asked. 'Straker seems to have his nose full of the smell of incest most deplorable.'

Rogers was casual about it. 'I've already decided to keep Straker on his back burner, whatever that is. I'm only interested in that weekend so far as their father's death is concerned. Their domestic circumstances – at any rate, hers for sure – suggest that they're both sexually deprived or hung up or whatever. As they're fully adult, presumably *compos mentis* also and finding a private comfort for each other within their own consanguinity, who am I to . . .' He shrugged his negation of it. 'I've dealt with far worse conjoinings on the lawful side of the sheets to propose doing anything about it unless I'm forced to.'

He smiled. 'Personally, David, I'd sooner sleep with a female hedgehog with her spines erect than with Mrs Cummins.' He brooded for a moment, then said, 'So far as her brother's concerned, could you find time to dig into more of his recent comings and goings than we have in the papers I gave you? I don't know what it is, but I've the feeling he's holding back on us.'

133

With Lingard gone to arrange for his intended interview with Fuller, Rogers put aside temporarily the unread remaining papers, filled and lit his laid-aside pipe and to hell with any very senior officer beating down his door. Leaning back in his squeaking chair with the supposed nest of invisible mice somewhere in its interior, he set about thinking his way through the small bucketful of information he had gathered together merely by sitting in it.

He was not doing too badly until Angharad intruded herself warmly into his thinking, that possibly stirred by what he had been discussing with Lingard. It led him, neglectful of his duty, into dialling her number and getting into aural touch; which, he considered, was a damned sight better than the nothing at all of her he now had.

When he asked her with all the recklessness of a man throwing the next month's rent at a roulette wheel to join him that evening for a meal at the Minister Hotel, she had immediately agreed. There had been a proviso. Afterwards, she said – it seemed to him with a ghost of a hint of strong-handedness in her voice – she would be delighted to be invited to his apartment for a coffee and a last-for-the-evening drink.

A surprised Rogers thought he saw in that either a woman's natural wish to see in what state of hoggishness he lived, or, almost breathtakingly, a woman's determination to put a carnal seal on their association. Instead of closing down in an exhilaration of masculine expectation, it had left him unsure, and therefore unhappy, of her intent. In his uncertainty he could easily make the mother and father of a sexual misjudgement as had, apparently, the late Philip Cruickshank whom she had consequently dubbed a filthy pig.

Returning to the scrutiny of his paperwork with what he thought to be an ongoing warring of his emotions, he reached and recognized without too much interest the regularly faxed *Daily Crime Bulletin* issued by a neighbouring force and usually stupefyingly uninteresting in its reading.

About to reject it unread, his eyes caught the words 'body of a woman'. His attention now focused pin-sharp, he read what had been printed on the green paper sheet:

BODY FOUND. *Found in a rail wagon of road ballast travelling from Ulverigg Quarry siding to Thurstoneleigh and recovered at 0520 this morning when signalled to stop at Wrynose Bottom Halt, the body of a woman as described below, believed to be the victim of a violent, possibly fatal, assault.*

Appears to be about 30 years, 5' 7", light blonde shoulder-length hair, full figure, fingernails and toenails lacquered pink; digital watch on left wrist, chased silver bracelet on right; wearing gilt keeper earrings and ruby-set finger ring; dressed in orange-coloured satin pyjamas (badly soiled). The woman appears to have been dead for some days and the trunk and face are disfigured, possibly partly by the fall on to the road ballast.

Suggestions as to identity are urgently sought. Any information to D/Superintendent Simon Samways at Rooksby Castle Divisional Headquarters: telephone 0023 191676.

For those few moments, all thoughts of Angharad being regrettably fled, Rogers felt that the world was suddenly an eminently satisfying place in which to live, and he himself surely a sweet smell in the ineffable nostrils of his god, before it all lapsed into the matter-of- factness it had always been.

In a way, the information contained in it was a window opening on to a positive something for him, if not for poor dead Eunice Parr. The railway line to Thurstoneleigh passed no more than a mile north of Abbotsburn, climbing a gradient in doing so. He knew of two little-used road bridges crossing it at points where a loaded quarry train of many wagons would be travelling very slowly indeed. Nothing would be easier than to lift the body of Parr over a parapet of either of the bridges and to drop it into one of the wagons passing below.

Without hurrying, he relit his pipe before lifting his telephone receiver to catch Lingard before he left his office, then getting through to Rooksby Castle for words with Detective Superintendent Samways. Though he knew him only as a name in the *Police Almanack*, he now felt for him a warm and grateful friendship.

135

20

Lingard had lunched rather extravagantly on a haddock soufflé and cold lobster in the Minster Hotel's private dining-room. Because his car had been damaged beyond repair, he had walked to Paper Court, waiting at the basement door of the Club Midnight Blue, and listening for a response to his ringing against the unsubdued noise of traffic moving above him in the street outside.

Rogers's calling him back to his office to tell him of the finding of what was unarguably the body of Eunice Parr had pumped adrenalin into the prospect of his meeting a man he still held in an unremitting dislike.

Years before Fuller had acquired the cellars he had later converted into a night-club, Lingard had, armed with a warrant for his arrest on a charge of unlawfully wounding a woman with whom he was then living, found him drinking in the bar of the Solomon and Sheba inn, his known watering hole. The then more youthful and stupid Fuller, not having met the elegance and Beau Brummellism of Lingard in any other policeman he had known or had suffered to question him, had reacted unwisely to the detective's quietly discreet invitation to surrender himself outside without fuss.

Adopting a hostile attitude against what he must have known to be the inevitable, he had said loudly and publicly that he wasn't to be arrested by any bloody upstart of a poof like Lingard. It had earned him some brief laughs from his drinking friends present, but brought down on his expensively coiffured head some bitter and unnecessary suffering while resisting arrest; though not without Lingard losing much of his dignity and a lot of blood in the process.

Lingard had telephoned Fuller on this occasion, asking for an interview to follow on that given to Detective Inspector Millier. Fuller had remembered him and put bloody-minded difficulties in his way. 'It's all right with me, chum,' Lingard had said tersely and ruthlessly. 'Just so long as you don't object to my having a uniformed PC with me to hammer on your door and my showing you up for what you are by making some pretty pointed enquiries among your immediate neighbours.'

So two o'clock it had been and he now waited with an easy nonchalance, though sweating gently in the confined heat of the basement steps, for Fuller to answer his ringing.

When the door had been opened by him it was clear to Lingard that behind the mostly unreadable face the old antagonisms had not been forgotten and that his own dislike was being returned full blown. Sizing him up, the detective saw that he had put on weight without being fat and that he wore well an expensively tailored summer suit. Being wholly masculine-oriented himself, Lingard couldn't see what might, in Fuller's appearance or persona, push Millier into going soft on him.

'Nice to see you again,' Lingard said not very truthfully, but reasonably affably. 'I hope not to keep you too long.'

'Anything'd be too long,' Fuller grunted, leading Lingard along the windowless, twilit and noticeably scented corridor into his glaringly illuminated office. There was a simulated leather easy chair and a gilt wooden dining chair to one side of the desk and Fuller pushed with his foot at the wooden one. 'Sit in that one,' he said, then taking his own softskin leather chair behind the desk and waiting.

If there was anyone else in the dead noiselessness of the basement, he or she was, Lingard thought, a soft-footed, light-breathing mouse-like creature. He said, 'As I mentioned on the phone I've been detailed to do a follow-up on your chat with Inspector Millier. The picture you painted for her lacked here and there a touch of reality.' He smiled briefly without warmth.

Fuller shifted in his chair. 'I said, make it short, Lingard. I don't like the smell of you and I'm only seeing you now to get you out of my hair.'

'Your association with Miss Parr,' an imperturbable Lingard said. 'I'm given to understand that it was rather more carnal than is usual between employer and employee. That, in fact, you were cohabiting at your place and hers as a sort of routine. Something you apparently denied to Inspector Millier. There have been,' he murmured almost absently, 'some useful finger impressions – male, of course, and yet to be classified – found at her home. And', he reminded him, 'we do have yours on file.'

'So?' Fuller looked uncaring. 'Why should that be any of your business? And it was months ago anyway. I was rather impressed with Helen – that's her name, isn't it? – so why should I have to explain to her an off-the-cuff affair that meant bugger-all to me, to you or to anyone else?' His face suddenly showed suspicious puzzlement. 'What were you doing in her house anyway?'

'Inspector Millier told you that Miss Parr was missing, didn't she?' Lingard noticed that Fuller wore characteristically a northern university college tie to which he knew he wasn't entitled.

Fuller relaxed. 'So she did. I forgot.'

'What were the circumstances leading to Miss Parr leaving you for Philip Cruickshank?'

'She bloody well didn't. I tossed her out.'

'She didn't leave you short of a singer then? And also owing you money?'

'Work it out for yourself,' Fuller growled. 'She owed me money when she went.'

'Will you show me the house deeds you offered to produce for Inspector Millier's inspection? Those you say you have as security against a loan.'

'You think I'm that stupid?' The liquid yellowish eyes that had played their part in charming money from the bank accounts of susceptible women were now coldly despising the detective.

'I think you'd be stupid not to.' Lingard fixed him with his own daunting stare. 'I'll tell you what I think. Cruickshank used to visit here while Miss Parr sang for you, got to know her and whisked her away from under your nose.'

Watching Fuller, he noticed his face tightening and then his forcing out an angry 'You're asking for trouble, aren't you?'

Fuller pushed his big fist into a cedarwood box and withdrew two long and slender cigars, tossing one across the desk where it lay contemptuously unaccepted under Lingard's glacial stare.

The detective, had he been off duty and therefore less constrained, would have probably stuffed the cigar into one of Fuller's ears. Instead, he flipped it with his forefinger, sending it flying across the desk to hit into Fuller's lap. 'In the absence of a specific denial,' he pointed out, deliberately offensively, 'I shall have to accept the truth of what I'm asking. Such as, I see you as a short-tempered thug with an overblown self-regard and a reputation for enforcing its acceptance with violence, having had your nose put out of joint in realizing that you'd lost a singer who was an asset to your club. That, together with losing the sexual favours of a woman who obviously had enough sense to prefer a man probably more free with his affections and money than you would ever be. That wouldn't exactly flatter your ego, would it?'

Fuller, three-quarters turned away from Lingard and having tossed the refused cigar into a waste-paper bin, snapped a lighter at his own cigar with painstaking attention while showing no signs of having heard what had been said to him.

Undeterred and knowing that Fuller was storing in his mind – and probably on a concealed tape recorder – everything he had said, Lingard continued with his version of what he could assume had occurred. 'I've no doubt at all that there was a fair bit of unfriendly to-ing and fro-ing between you both once you'd discovered that she was living with Cruickshank at Thurlestone Bay. That wouldn't have been too difficult, would it? She was apparently flinging that which she had in abundance at the local studs, as no doubt she had when she was here with you.'

For all the effect it had on Fuller showing anything in his face, Lingard might have been watching for movement to show on a photograph of him. He battled on. 'It seems to me that something happened back at the tail-end of last winter that pushed you into telephoning her and later calling on her at Cruickshank's home – almost certainly not the first or last time – where you both appeared to have reverted to type and had a good old slanging match, laced on your side

139

with unwise threats that were heard by a neighbour. You remember?'

Any remembering that Fuller was doing was done in silence while ostentatiously studying one of his Gauguin prints of bare-breasted women, and he didn't bother to respond.

'You told Inspector Millier', Lingard continued, noticing that there was some sort of a reaction from him when her name was mentioned, 'that this was about the money she was supposed to owe you. That's something I'd question with the same disbelief I have of there being an occasional spark of decency and generosity in you and your like. I'd hazard a fair old guess that you were sour with jealousy and ready in one of your belly-kicking moods to sort out both Miss Parr and Cruickshank; the man who had it in him to take her away from your profitable use of her talents, if you can grasp what I mean . . .'

Only just on the edge of audibility there was a low rumbling coming from Fuller's broad chest; a primeval rumble threatening the possible charge of a primeval male.

Lingard, pinching snuff into his – he felt – famished nose and waiting, despite his visibly useless left arm, for some extravagant form of protest, had nothing other than the warning growl and the increasingly familiar profile of his uncooperative interviewee. 'You're just the man to lash out at somebody ill-mannered enough to take a woman like Miss Parr away from you, aren't you? What sort of courage does it take to do over a sixty-year-old man with a worn-out hip, eh?' Lingard taunted him. 'Wasn't that enough? Was he roughed up until he died and then had a cover-up job done on him by stringing the poor devil up to make it look like suicide?'

There was a ticking silence between them in which Lingard knew that he wasn't by miles on the right track. When Fuller turned his attention back to the detective, seemingly having come out of his put-on *longueur*, he said, 'You're bloody mad. I don't know what you're talking about. That's your lot, is it?'

Lingard believed that he was reading a kind of relief behind the man's about-to-be-angry expression, but wouldn't bet money on it. 'Perhaps as much as I care to tell you at the moment,' he assured him. 'Do we have disagreement?'

He had, he knew, exaggerated the few facts with which he had been armed, but sometimes there was a vulnerability to be hit and, anyway, the little suffering Fuller could have received from it might be good for his soul; if, of course, he had one.

Fuller pushed himself up from his chair, managing a half-smile, though not one he was sharing with the detective. 'I expect you've got other things to do without needing to bother me?' he said, surprisingly equably.

Lingard, remaining seated, said, 'I haven't as it happens, old son. I suppose I'm idiot enough to expect you to tell me something about your real association with Miss Parr. Such as, could she have been putting the screws on you concerning something or other dodgy about the club's affairs? Concerning your not quite so private or fragrant social life? Perhaps even a suspicion of dabbling in something a little stronger than cannabis?'

Fuller appeared now unable to conceal the signs of mental unease, though Lingard knew that this need not be anything connected with Parr's death. 'This is for your pocket-book,' he said, 'and there'll be nothing more. Miss Parr was my employee and I sacked her for letting me down by being absent on too many occasions. I had loaned her money which she was reneging on and I tried to get it back. If I threatened her – which I don't admit anyway – it was with legal action to be taken through a solicitor. Now,' he growled, very much less reasonably, 'you can bugger off because I've finished listening to the bloody crap you're dreaming up.'

'There's just one more thing which might be of interest,' Lingard said almost pleasantly, not moving from the uncomfortable hardness of his chair, but looking up at him. 'Miss Parr is no longer missing. In fact, I'm afraid that she's dead. Murdered, I believe.'

There had, he could swear, been something like sudden alarm in Fuller's eyes, though his immediate response had been open-mouthed surprise followed by a tight-faced outburst of anger. 'You bastard!' he ground out. 'You bloody tricky bastard!' He sat abruptly back in his chair, quite definitely disturbed. 'You're trying to fit me up for it!'

'The inevitable defence of a villain unmasked,' Lingard murmured as if to himself, but by no means inaudibly. 'I'm afraid

141

your reaction to the news didn't impress me overmuch. Is this the extent of it?' he asked when Fuller remained in a glowering lip-chewing silence, clearly having serious thoughts. 'I mean, when somebody is told that his one-time club singer who was doubling up as his doxie has been found dead and he shows no obvious signs of curiosity or even sorrow, it does become rather suggestive of something or other, doesn't it?'

Fuller was lighting another cigar and the hand that held the lighter had a perceptible tremor in it, though that could be from some furious thinking behind a hardly repressed anger.

Lingard, who was now thinking that Fuller's mother must have told him never to lose his temper in any interrogation by the police or let the bastards get him down, was now considering as a fact that Fuller wasn't reacting as would a man with bloody hands; that he – Lingard – hadn't that indefinable inner recognition he was dealing with that sort of guilt. He couldn't be certain about it and it wasn't nearly enough for him to let go, though he had decided that his leaving him alone with whatever guilt he suffered might provoke him into some useful revealing step.

He stood, believing his buttocks to be bloodless from sitting on the hard wood of the chair Fuller had provided for his discomfort. 'I'm going now, old son,' he said, as though they were the best of friends. 'Why not toddle off to see your solicitor if you've anything calamitous on your mind?'

A surprised Fuller, his beefy face flushed, gaped at him. 'Aren't you going to tell me what happened? For Christ's sake . . .'

Lingard held up his unplastered arm and stopped him. 'Not now,' he told him, shaking his head in mock sorrow. 'You've had the opportunity and that's something which, if not grasped when it's put in front of your face, you can lose for ever.' He turned, then checked himself and looked back at Fuller, smiling now without humour. 'I'll be seeing you again, of course. In fact, I may have you brought in for further questioning. We must all have something to worry about, mustn't we?'

On his unaccompanied way out, recharging one-handed and awkwardly his sinuses with his aromatic snuff, he thought that while Millier hadn't done all that bad a job on a bloody-minded brute like Fuller, she must be out of her mind if she had gone soft on the bastard that the detective knew him to be.

Fuller clearly had a nastiness pressing on whatever conscience he owned to, and Lingard thought that whatever it was might see daylight when he had in his possession the circumstances of Parr's death.

21

In his car, *en route* for Rooksby Castle which lay south some thirty-five miles from his office, Rogers chewed thoughtfully on the stem of his pipe as his mind dodged and danced around the factors affecting the colourful life and the squalid death of Eunice Parr. He sought for significant connections between her and the man who had used, or might have used, the easy availability of her apparently generous body. While knowing a little something about Fuller and the dead Cruickshank, he believed he was still short of information on Stephen Cruickshank whom he was now beginning to believe had been less than open about his relations with Parr. Further, despite the scorn that Millier had poured on Parr as a promiscuous over-scented slut, he thought, admittedly a little sloppily, that she might well be a very much put-on woman, and possibly one of life's undeserving victims.

It didn't help much that unbidden mental vignettes of a smiling, a talking and once an undressed Angharad interrupted some of his more professional thinking about the investigation in hand.

Rooksby Castle, reached through a largely unpicturesque landscape of barley and wheat stubble where there weren't extensive plantations of dark green conifers, was a once-medieval town now being strangled by traffic stuffing itself into its narrow streets. Its centre was made visible by the ruins of a grey castle set on a massively steep hill, this overshadowing the Divisional Police Headquarters – as contemporarily bleak as

Roger's own, though manifestly having had more money flung at it – to which he had been directed.

Detective Superintendent Samways had, in Rogers's rather exaggerated opinion, to be either a close relative of his chief constable or to be in possession of a sufficiently dark secret likely to affect adversely his chief's chance of becoming one of Her Majesty's Inspectors of Constabulary, for the superintendent's office, its furniture and furnishings, were surely more suited to a man holding a ministerial post with the government. On the debit side, there were no lingering smells of tobacco smoke or handy ashtrays likely to give Rogers licence to smoke his pariah's pipe.

Samways himself, seated on the other side of his leather-topped desk, was a pleasant and friendly smoothie of a man with a thin black moustache and precisely waved hair. He wore a sharply cut light grey suit with the air of somebody waiting to wine and dine an attractive woman with money and bursting to tell her knowledgeably that the wine he had chosen tasted magnificently of creosote and blackberries with a subtle hint of wood ash. He ordered a tray of coffee to be sent to his office and listened to Rogers's claim on the body of Eunice Parr with undisguised relief.

'She's definitely yours, my dear chap,' he said when Rogers had finished. 'She's a number one job without any doubt and lately I've had a bellyful of them. Let me tell you how she was found. British Rail had a couple of their chaps working on an urgent breakdown of something or other on a signals gantry way back up the line. One of them – Witherspoon by name – was watching a train of road ballast passing below them when he saw this woman's body sprawled out on top of the ballast in one of the wagons. Of course, he didn't know whether she was then dead or just injured and he commendably got on his portable blower and shouted to head office or similar to have the train stopped. Which it was *tout de suite.*' His accent sounded impeccable and well practised. Rogers thought enviously that he probably owned a house in France on top of it all.

The coffee had arrived and Samways, pausing, poured it steaming into uncanteen-looking cups, passing one over his desk to Rogers who began filling his veins with its hot fragrance.

'BR had nous enough to stop the wagons when they reached Wrynose Bottom,' Samways continued after he had tasted his own coffee and wiped his moustache dry with his forefinger. 'Wrynose Bottom is a godforsaken village and, as it happens, is unhappily on my patch. I was there early this morning getting set up for a woman assumed to have been murdered on our territory.'

He smiled broadly. 'I'd be lying through my teeth if I said that your claiming the body as one of yours distresses me immensely, though her being found here is for our Coroner to look into. On his instructions I've laid on a post-mortem examination.' He pushed his shirt cuff back from a wrist-watch. 'That's at two fifteen and Obergruppenfuhrer Dr McGlusky is in the chair. I should warn you that you may question her pathological findings only at some risk to your life and limb.'

Rogers raised his eyebrows. 'You said *her*. She's a woman? A Scot?'

'Yes, she's a woman and, no, she's not Scottish.' Samways put the tips of his fingers to his lips and made a kissing sound. 'Against my best interests I have to admit she's very lovely and elegant, devastatingly sexually aloof or frigid – I don't know which – and unfortunately owns to a husband, though he's somewhere in the bush in Nigeria fighting malarial mosquitoes and has been for some time.' He suddenly looked alarmed. 'All this just between the two of us, naturally.'

'Naturally. Why Obergruppenfuhrer?'

'I shouldn't have said it and I exaggerated a little, but she can be terribly bossy.'

Rogers was recalling information he had been given about a woman pathologist he had once known and who was now thought to have returned from America to this part of the country. 'Her name's not Bridget, is it?' he asked, hoping to God that it wasn't.

Samways frowned. 'Yes, it is. You know her?'

'She was in our county some years back before going off to the States and getting married. I'd heard she was back in your county, though not here in Rooksby Castle.' He wasn't about to add that he and the then Dr Bridget Hunter had been on and off lovers who hadn't hit quite the right note for a meeting of minds or temperament, that they had each torn emotional strips from the other and sensibly realized that a fury of sexual comings together hadn't too much to commend it. He had been badly bruised and wasn't all that happy at the prospect of meeting her again.

'I see,' Samways said as if he wasn't quite sure that he did. For a moment he looked hunted. 'I'm not unwittingly treading on your toes, am I?'

'No, you aren't,' Rogers said dismissively. 'What's your opinion of the cause of Miss Parr's death?'

'Um. She's had what appears to have been a bad bang on the side of the head and, sticking my neck out, she looks to me as if she's been suffocated.' He was distinctly apprehensive. 'Don't quote me, for God's sake. The McGlusky can be stupendously furious at anyone pre-empting her own opinions.'

'I have met up with it,' Rogers said wryly.

'You must have, I suppose.' Samways was patently trying to work out the politics of the association. 'I'd better leave a message for her, hadn't I? Telling her you're here and giving her your name?'

'Why not?'

'No, I suppose there's no reason why I shouldn't,' a now uncertain Samways said, then changed the subject. 'What's at the back of your woman's killing?'

Rogers shrugged. 'To be honest, I'm struggling. She's been distributing her favours willy-nilly between a couple of dubious characters and a handful of young studs around Abbotsburn. She went missing from her home there about a week ago and was not heard of until you turned her up dead.' That, he thought, was enough for a detective superintendent who wasn't now required to lose any sleep in finding out who did it. He said depreciatingly, 'It is connected with some local blood-letting, but not close enough to give me much help.'

'She wasn't a bad looker,' Samways prompted him, obviously having time to show a professional interest in another CID man's problems.

146

'It makes a difference? Can I see her now for an identification, and before Dr McGlusky starts chopping her up?'

'Of course.' Samways pushed his chair back and stood. 'She's in a cabinet still as found if I got home to that thick-headed bugger of a mortuary attendant the McGlusky has had wished on her. It'd better be now before lunch – you're my guest, of course – in case he anticipates us and undresses her.'

The graceless square brick building that was the town's mortuary and pathology workshop stood a short trundle in a wheeled body trolley from the hospital, its rawness partly screened from any patient destined for it by a row of churchyard conifers.

Passing along a corridor and through clear PVC flap-swing doors marked *Authorized Personnel Only*, Rogers and Samways entered a further short but wider corridor, quiet with that atmosphere which Rogers attributed as coming from the brooding dead. It was broken only by a low humming coming from a row of deep green body cabinets stacked at one side.

Four of the cabinets had white tickets slotted in their fronts and Samways led Rogers to the one showing that it contained the body of an unknown white woman, about whom reference was to be made to Dr B. McGlusky and/or Det. Supt. R. Samways, the day's date and a red-letter note, *Clothing to be retained*.

Pulling open the drawer to its full extent and adjusting its folding legs, Samways said, 'Your lost Miss Parr – I hope,' and stood aside.

Looking down at the body in its clear polythene bag, Rogers noticed first that the badly soiled and torn orange pyjama jacket had been unbuttoned and opened to expose the trunk; that the trousers had been pulled down to show the stomach and thighs.

Drawing fiercely at his smoking pipe against the smell of a body's decay which the bag was not containing, he saw a greenish staining of an inner decomposition on the swollen abdomen, a scribbling of green surface veins running from it. Its progress would agree roughly with his own attributed time of her death.

Changing his scrutiny to the face – the eyes were partly

147

open, looking up at him with the indifference of the dead – he searched for the signs of suffocation mentioned by Samways and found them. He saw too a bruising mark over the right eyebrow which could have been caused by a sharp-edged blow. There was a lacerated wound on the right side of her head which had discoloured the hair. It had manifestly been inflicted by an instrument while she lived and could bleed. She had lost the puppy-fat immaturity he had seen in her photograph, her face being thinner and more knowing; a possible greediness and discontent having left their stamp on it, readable even in death's terrible impassivity.

Samways had noticed his shift from the trunk to the face and said, a little anxiously, 'You can identify her?'

Rogers nodded. 'I've only seen a photograph of her as not much more than a girl, but it's her all right.' Flippantly, to clear up his suddenly sombre mood, he added, 'She was an Australian whose parents, their motor-van and its contents were said to have been eaten by a crocodile. I suppose that drove her to come to England where I don't think we have any.'

Behind the broken, discoloured and fouled with ballast dust externals of her, he could see that her body had been a magnificence of female flesh, and its destruction and loss, its coming demolishment under Bridget's scalpel, saddened him. She could have been so much more than her ending implied.

'Her jewellery's gone,' he said to Samways. 'Even her ear-ring keeper studs. You knew?'

'That's routine here,' he explained. 'It was whipped off and taken into the almoner's safe while I was still sorting myself out. You'll be given it after the post-mortem.' He added unhelpfully with a grin, 'That is, if you can find the almoner or whatever it is they call her now.'

'I think I've seen enough.' Rogers, conscious of being surrounded as it were by the unburied dead, still felt depressed.

'Lunch,' Samways said, baring his wrist-watch and scowling at it. 'We haven't much time.'

'If you don't mind, friend,' Rogers told him, following him out, 'that's something I'd be better leaving until long after we've finished with our exhibit number one. In the meantime

I think a double scotch in the nearest bar might do much for my well-being.'

He needed time to brood on what he had seen, to think about any connection he could contrive between Parr's death and the three men he had earlier thought most close to her in their different ways. And then there was Bridget. That had been a bit of a shaker. How in the hell was their meeting again going to go? Married she might be, but they still had the memories of a couple of years of mutual carnality to push behind them before a civilized amity could be attained.

His whispered 'Oh, bloody hell,' hadn't, he hoped, been heard by Samways.

22

A mortuary, strongly redolent of death and decay, had always seemed to Rogers to be a theatre of the macabre. Even as one of whatever audience authority required to be in attendance there, his was a role to which he had never become wholly accustomed; nor ever would while it displayed to him so many gruesome intimations of his own mortality.

The mortuary to which he came with Detective Superintendent Samways was cold, mainly white-tiled and brightly lit. It was furnished with white melamime working tops and a sink, glass-fronted cabinets of glittering and frightening instruments, wall shelves of labelled jars containing the collected bits and pieces of human tissue so beloved of pathologists, and a single necropsy table of glistening stainless steel.

On the table, startlingly pallid under the shadowless light from above, lay the naked body of a newly washed Eunice Parr, water dribbling along her sides from a hanging hose. An attendant, lumpish and non-communicative in a brown jacket, stood near it.

From a door marked *Strictly Private* on the far side of the room, Rogers could hear movement, guessing that it was Bridget Hunter – he couldn't think of her as Dr McGlusky

– putting on her working clothing. When it opened and she came out he was momentarily stricken by her very familiarness and, until now, the emotions he had long suppressed.

Dressed in her green surgical gown and cap with a white plastic protective apron, she was a tall and strikingly handsome woman with tawny hair and deep orange eyes; an elegant dominant woman of exceptional pathological skills. It was difficult for Rogers to now accept that she was the same woman who had once said to him after their lovemaking that should she ever get him on her mortuary table she would remove the most interesting part of his genitalia and bottle it in formalin, labelling it as *un specimen formidable*. He had never had many illusions about her. Her own body had been beyond ordinary comparison as, he had often painfully suspected, a few of the younger internes of the hospital already knew.

Smiling white-toothed and carrying her rubber gloves, she took his hand. 'Lovely to see you again, George,' she said, with Rogers replying, 'It's been years, Bridget, and we've missed you.'

It was all very sociable ordinary, during which he thought that while her looks had weathered the years very well, there was a hardness in her features which may well have earned for her, however unfairly, the soubriquet Obergruppenfuhrer.

After the inconsequential small talk, she put on her rubber gloves in small clouds of talc while listening to a somewhat ingratiating Samways's account of Parr's finding and recovery and why Rogers's county had a later claim on her body. While Samways talked, Rogers held out his pipe – she was more than familiar with his use of it – and raised his eyebrows questioningly. She frowned and said, 'Sorry. Not here,' squashing his request peremptorily.

With Samways finished and after dismissing the morose attendant, she selected a scalpel and bone shears from a cabinet and approached the table. Doing her detailed examination of the body's exterior under the brilliant light, she tested with her fingers, pinching, poking and stroking at the stigmata showing on the pallid flesh. Turning her attention to the head she felt the sides of the skull as a doctor might do on a suffering patient, returning to the right side and pressing heavily at it. 'I think a

150

fracture,' she said. 'I shall know what sort and whether it was inflicted before or after death when I've stripped the scalp.'

'The mark I've seen over the eyebrow,' Rogers pointed out to her. 'Is that significant?'

She felt it with her thumb and shrugged. 'It might be. That too when I've seen what's underneath.'

Peering closely at the eyes, she turned back the eyelids. 'Congestion of the conjunctivae,' she said, 'with punctate haemorrhages. They suggest an asphyxial death.'

Rogers tried to look surprised. 'You've an idea how caused?'

'I will have if you'll allow me time to find out.' She picked up her scalpel and pushed the head backwards as Rogers turned his, avoiding what was always for him the bloody and emetic slicing open of the body.

Samways, apparently suffering with Rogers, though with no unarguable reason for being an observer, muttered his apologies and something about an overlooked appointment and was gone. And, in being gone, it was the worst thing à propos Bridget he could have done to Rogers, he having earlier feared being left alone with her.

After Samways's departure and the sounds of the bone shears ceasing, he reluctantly returned his attention to what Bridget was doing. Already delving into the opened chest, she was emptying it piece by piece, a process at which he looked only peripherally. But he did note her rubber-gloved hands, fouled now to the wrists, an uninvited reminder of her using them ungloved in making love to him.

Bridget, examining what she would call body material lying on the table, said, 'Engorged and oedematous. Further support for an asphyxial death, and I'm certain that is what my finding will be.'

'Would you be able to suggest how?' He wanted more.

'Not yet. Perhaps not until tomorrow.'

'Would you then be able to confirm that she had drowned?'

'Almost certainly. If she was. Was she?' She was cutting into more of the material she had extracted, not looking at him, nor he at what she was doing.

'This is guesswork, Bridget, but imagine this woman being knocked insensible, or nearly so, at night and in her home.

151

In that condition she's dragged into the bathroom where a wash-basin is filled and her head pushed face-downwards into it and held there.' The thought of it still gave him a horrifying feeling of suffocation. 'While that's being done there could be the possibility that her forehead could have come into hard contact with the handle of one of the taps.'

'Are you guessing? Or have you something behind what you're telling me?'

'We've examined a filled wash-basin in her bathroom and found two of what appear to be her head hairs in the water. That's fact.'

There wasn't much showing in the good-looking face, but Rogers had the feeling that she didn't see such a hell of a lot in what he had been saying. She said, not very encouragingly, 'It could be.'

After that, she went ahead with her decanting of Parr's body with Rogers avoiding any too long a scrutiny of it, pleased that he had turned down a lunch. Instead, he watched her, trying to recall the strong attachment he had for her when she occupied a two-room suite on the top floor of Abbotsburn hospital, and what there was now left of it.

She had represented – and probably still did – sexual lust in its most attractive formalin-smelling and predatory form. And though that lust and her physical attractiveness were now having a like effect on him, even in the forbidding presence of death, he fought it, refusing to regard her as other than a woman against whom he could measure what he felt for Angharad. And in that thinking, he saw himself for what he felt he was; a middle-aged, reasonably conventional, not terribly brilliant man, appropriately weathered by life and experience and wishing to spend it with the attractive, but not too attractive, widow of a long gone naval commander. He didn't consider himself a man with an inflated ego in believing that the odds were on Bridget – separated by a continent, if not by something more, from her husband – hunting him down and enfeebling his will with all the single-mindedness of a flesh- eating praying mantis.

Mere bloody man, he muttered in his mind as Bridget dropped her scalpel on the steel table and went to the instrument cabinet. Choosing an electric bone saw, she said, almost affably, 'It's looking very much your way, George. I'll do the head now.'

That was the final straw operation for which he had little stomach and he turned away without apology for, dammit, he thought, he desperately needed a smoke against the assaults on his sensitivities by this butchering of a dead woman.

Outside the door, he absent-mindedly smoked his pipe without tasting it in the company of whoever were the remaining three occupants of the green cabinets, realizing with something of a personal belittlement that he was becoming too affected as a police officer by the horrors of bloody death. To fight it, he tried to put out of his mind any thought that the tortured and broken body which he had just left was that of Eunice Parr.

When he returned, he received a curious sidelong glance from Bridget who was about to strip off her gloves. She said, without commenting on his absence, 'She's had a single before-death blow to the left temporal portion of her skull just above the ear which resulted in a simple fracture.'

'It didn't kill her then?'

She stared frowningly at him. 'I've already said that she died from asphyxiation.' Her frown went. 'I was about to say that there was a partial engorgement of the brain, again suggesting that she suffocated to death, almost certainly by immersion of at least her head in water.'

'I'm grateful,' he said. 'You'll let me have a copy of your report?'

'Yes, though what I've told you is subject to some laboratory testing.' She had untied her apron and dropped it on the table with her gloves.

'I'd like your estimate of how long she's been dead,' Rogers said, in imagination getting ready to run, feeling now the absence of Samways.

'Five days? Six? It depends. Being under a bed in a presumably warm room doesn't help.' Removing her cap and exposing her glossy hair, she moved to the sink unit and began scrubbing her hands. With an apparent softening in her manner, she turned her head to him and said, 'I did the wrong thing in leaving, George.'

'I can't imagine you ever doing that, Bridget.' With his

departure in sight – he hoped – he was refilling his pipe with life-enhancing tobacco.

'Don't be an idiot.' She said it inoffensively. 'I did. That was when you told me that there was no such occasion as *après*-stalemate.'

He wondered what she was getting at, not remembering why he had said it. 'And there is?'

'There is if one wants there to be.' Her orange eyes were holding his in a steady, almost mesmeric, stare.

He wanted to say, 'For God's sake! You've probably got Samways, even though he's scared witless of you!' Instead, having his pusillanimity with women well to the fore, he mumbled, 'Well, I suppose there is. It's all been a surprise and I haven't come to terms with it yet.' He tried a smile which wasn't returned; had, in fact, seldom been, for she was basically a fairly serious person. And that could make her dangerous.

He simulated sudden exasperation, looking at his wrist-watch. 'Damn,' he said brusquely, 'I've to get back to the office or I'll miss the assistant chief who apparently needs to see me before he goes home.'

If Bridget saw through his evasion, she didn't show it. 'Keep in touch, George,' she told him, showing an unusual touch of sadness. 'I am on the phone.'

Outside, away from the oppressiveness of the mortuary and lighting his pipe, he felt a pang of guilt about her. He thought he might have misjudged her, had been ungracious and could have responded to her wish for a renewal of at least their earlier friendship without the distinct lack of generosity he had shown.

Hell! he protested to himself. He didn't have all that number of women making signals at him that he could be so bloody choosy. A brief, simple and uncomplicated excursion into adultery rarely hurt anyone but a husband or two who would have, no doubt, deserved it; and it was said to be certainly beneficial for one's physical well-being.

23

Millier, certain that the dreadful smell encountered in Parr's house was clinging to her skin and hair like a film of oil, had returned to her flat in mid-afternoon for a shower. She was also suffering from a heaviness of the spirit, only partly recognizable as a feeling of personal inadequacy and a need to see Fuller again. Whatever his reputation or present intent, he appeared to be the only man with an interest in her that wasn't tepidly ambivalent.

Arranging her flowers in a jar – they had been on her mind all day – hadn't helped and, afterwards in the shower, she had brought forward in her imagination a life not bound and disciplined by Police Regulations and the force's restrictive customs and modes of behaviour.

Later, when she had written up her notes about the missing Parr woman, the remembered image of Fuller – it centred on his mouth and the echoes of his voice – returned to haunt her. With having no immediate enquiries to make – they were lower rank stuff and feeble, she considered – and with nothing too settled in her mind, she tapped out the telephone number of Club Midnight Blue. When it was answered, she recognized the voice that had been so unsettling to her.

She said, without preamble, 'I believe I have you to thank for the flowers. They are lovely, but that doesn't excuse your sending them.'

'Please don't be offended.' His voice held amused contrition. 'They were nothing to do with what we spoke about, but meant to show my admiration.'

'As it happens, I am not, though I could have been.' She kept her own voice impersonal. 'It isn't done between a police officer and anyone she happens to interview.'

There was a short silence before he said, 'I can't promise I won't do it again when I've not been interviewed. May I say something about your coming here?'

'It depends on what it is.' She thought she was being unnecessarily bitchy – though only so much – and softened her voice. 'I'm not speaking officially to you now.'

'I wanted to say I was disappointed – hurt too, I suppose – that you sent Mr Lingard to interrogate me about what I'd said to you.'

She felt the blood draining from her face in a sudden anger that teetered on the edge of fury. 'When was this?' she choked out before getting herself under control. 'I don't know anything about it.'

'After lunch.' He sounded concerned. 'Wasn't I meant to tell you?'

'It's not your fault.' She was silent in worrying thought for a few moments. 'I'd like to see you again. Not officially, but it would be about your interview with Mr Lingard. Would you mind?'

'Of course not. I'd be delighted. But it's not possible at the club. What if I managed the Bay Tree Tea Rooms at three thirty?'

'I'll be there,' she promised, disconnecting and saying, 'The bastard!' though not directing it at Fuller.

The Bay Tree Tea Rooms were the much modified and built-on remains of a medieval wool merchant's home, its presence in the High Street being marked outside for any thirsty tea drinkers by two tubbed bay trees. The three upper rooms, heavy on head-banging ceiling beams with an uneven floor of highly polished planks, had been knocked into one and equipped with eighteenth-or nineteenth-century – nobody was certain which – reproduction furniture to go with the small undoubtedly seventeenth-century windows fitted with greenish bull's-eye glass. These had the effect of encouraging a private sort of twilight between the green and white Regency striped wallpaper inside and the cosy intimacy of the deep gold shaded table lamps. During late afternoons an elderly pianist and his equally elderly lady violinist played hugely appreciated low-key Ivor Novello and Noel Coward music while the patrons drank Earl Grey and Lapsang Souchong teas, or an especially aromatic coffee which could be smelled out in the street, and ate home-baked cake and spicy buns. For men taking tea with other men's wives and for parties of talkative women, it was perfect. It was expensive, pleasantly quaint and meant to be so.

Millier, who had taken exceptional pains with her appearance, walked from the street through an undistinguished open door to climb twisted stairs which creaked with the arthritis of ancient timber. At the top, she saw, with a sudden thumping of her heart, Fuller rising from a corner table and approaching to meet her. Even then she did a policewoman's taking in of what he was wearing: the palest of blue jacket with off-white trousers, a darker blue shirt with an Oxford-blue tie and a much exposed breast pocket silk handkerchief. Oblivious of others in the spacious room, or what music was being played, she knew there was in her a thrill of excitement she had long forgotten.

'I'm glad you came,' he said, showing an air of confident capability and leading her to his table which had visibly been reserved. It was small and, seated, they were within touching distance; close enough for her to see that he was freshly shaved and that his shirt was in its first wearing.

'As I told you,' she said, 'I am not here in my official capacity, though that doesn't mean that you should forget I am a police officer.'

'Point taken,' he conceded, his eyes only leaving hers as a waitress approached.

She chose tea on its own and he followed suit, exchanging nothing much against the background of undemanding music and the subdued conversations of other people – mostly women – until it was brought to them in cottage-rose-patterned china. Doing nothing, Millier had pushed Fuller into incongruously pouring out the tea. He did it with a slight smile as if understanding why she had done it and seemingly content with it for the moment.

'You told me on the phone,' she started, quite formally despite how she felt, 'that I'd sent Mr Lingard to interrogate you following my interview with you. That I never did. Nor was I in the position to do so. It was a matter, though, over which he should have consulted me, and he hadn't.' She bit, as if in doubt, at her lower lip. 'I'm not asking you what was said, but I am anxious that you don't think I was a party to it.'

'I was surprised,' Fuller said. 'I thought I was doomed and damned for evermore.'

'About what?'

He looked bleak. 'First, that I was suspected of beating up Eunice and then the old man Cruickshank; then, so far as he was concerned, that I'd killed him in the process from jealousy and strung him up somewhere. Not exactly murder, but near enough.'

'In his garage,' she said, watching his eyes and getting nothing from them. 'I did tell you.'

'Wherever,' he shrugged. 'The man's mad. What would I want to do a thing like that for? He's never meant anything to me and when he took Eunice over he was welcome to her.'

'But not the money?'

He looked blank for a moment. 'Oh, that. I'll tell you about it later. No, Lingard suddenly told me she'd been found dead. Murdered probably, he said, and then tried to fit me into the frame for it. I'm not that . . .'

'Found?' she interrupted him, her blue eyes darkening. 'He told you she had been found?' She felt her face burning.

'Much the same thing. He told me she was no longer missing.' He frowned. 'I'm sorry. I assumed you'd know.'

She shook her head. 'I've been away from the office and out of touch.' It sounded lame to her, but she showed nothing of how deeply offended she was. Not only with Lingard imposing himself unethically on her enquiries; but also with Parr's body having been found and nobody choosing to have her contacted and told of it. 'I've a feeling,' she said, 'that Mr Lingard had more to question you about than I had. Is that so?'

'Yes. You think I lied to you?'

'If you did, I'd want to know.' She realized suddenly that he

158

had laid his hand on her forearm, something she couldn't have objected to even had she wanted to.

'On a personal basis?' He was holding her with his intense dark amber stare. 'Not as a detective inspector?'

'Not as,' she agreed, 'but I'm still thinking like one. I rather think you took me for a fool.'

If masculine man could ever look hurt, he managed to do so, taking his hand from her arm and standing. 'I'm sorry,' he said softly, fishing in his jacket pocket and putting a ten-pound note next to the bill on the table. 'I rather thought we had an understanding. Forgive me if I'm mistaken.'

She was looking up at him surprise, knowing that this was not what she wanted or had anticipated. 'You don't have to go,' she said. 'I'm trying to believe you, not to sit in judgement on you.'

He remained conspicuously and embarrassingly standing for several bars of the hitherto unregarded music, looming huge and misunderstood before finally taking his seat again, crumpling the banknote in his fist and stuffing it back into his pocket. 'I apologize,' he said, 'but I thought I'd lost out to your sense of duty. I really am talking to Helen, am I? And not to Detective Inspector Millier?'

'You'll have been speaking to a committed ex-inspector by tomorrow,' she said bitterly. 'I shall be resigning and don't think that it's anything to do with you. I've been considering it for some time.'

He reached and put his hand over hers, she allowing it to stay there. A strange hand with immaculate nails and feeling right. 'I'm sorry if it's a personal unhappiness for you, but somehow I feel that it won't be. I don't, I really don't, wish to have you dislike or mistrust me.' He cleared his throat. 'You say you need to know if I lied to you. Well, I did. I lied to you as a policewoman interviewing a suspected villain. I wouldn't have lied to Helen Millier.'

He looked grave, his hold on her passive hand tightening while she felt a pulse throbbing in her throat. 'The truth now and nothing but,' he promised. 'I was a bit of a big-headed tearaway when I first came here, and Lingard does have some justification for disliking me – but not to the extent of pushing

Eunice's murder on to me. I can't think that he was serious about it, but it did make me angry. Which, I imagine, it was meant to.'

'Not perhaps the best way of answering or not answering,' she suggested, not yet having made up her mind about him.

Without dissembling, he had been letting his gaze take in those aspects of her visible above the table; the pale gold of her hair, the sensuousness of her mouth when she spoke and, almost with rapacity in his eyes, the bounteousness of the breasts hidden behind her jacket. Were he a dog, he might have been panting with his tongue out.

'No,' he admitted ruefully, 'perhaps not, though that's not on my conscience as much as you are. It puts me in a pretty poor light that I've to admit that I lied to you on two counts about my association with Eunice.' He released her hand with a downturning of his mouth. 'I told you that I'd never slept with her and that is, I suppose, strictly true because I've never been in bed with her. But I do admit that early in our association, when I first employed her, there was what you might call a fully dressed affair in the club's storeroom.'

The two could have been in the middle of a treeless plain for all they were conscious of the others in the room.

'I'm sorry, Helen,' he said. 'I didn't admit it because I found I needed to look something other than a leg-over man to you. That was it. No emotion, nothing between us but a shared lust, for that's all it was. It burned us up for a month or two, then it went.' He grimaced. 'If you think the less of me, if I've earned your contempt, then that's only what I deserve.' He waited, appearing anxious, his eyes looking as if they had parried a lifetime of difficult questions.

'It doesn't surprise me,' she said, though in a way it had. 'There's more, you say?' She felt a strong rapport between them, though why there should be was hard for her to imagine. Was it that she didn't give a damn what he had done with other women? That she would rather not know?

'I lied to you about funding repairs to her house. That amounted to a couple of hundred I advanced her when she first came to me, and which she was to repay out of her earnings. Not that she did, of course. Dammit!' he burst out.

160

'I do have to trust you on this one.' He put his hand into an inner pocket of his jacket, glanced at the small chevron with the nauseatingly unctuous *Thank You For Not Smoking* on it, then took it out again.

'Eunice was blackmailing me,' he said, 'over Inland Revenue and VAT returns which alone could appear near enough criminal to you, I suppose. But on my conscience it isn't, for before Eunice arrived on the scene I'd employed a secretary who subsequently left for parts unknown, having milked me of more money than I could afford. He had, of course, cooked the books, ensuring that there was no way in which I could complain to your people about his thefts without involving myself – because I'd signed things unknowingly – in some unpleasant stickiness with the Inland Revenue. Whichever, it left me up to my neck in trouble with the prospect of even worse should a suspicious IR decide to drop in and look at my books.'

With Millier listening deadpan, his fingers toyed restlessly with a teaspoon. 'When Eunice had been with me for only a few months and we'd finished being on any terms you could call improper, she began looking after the office when I had to be somewhere else. In view of what had happened between us, I trusted her.' His face took on the expression of a man admitting to serious brain damage. 'In fact, I as good as *told* her, for God's sake. Anyway, she'd been sneaking through the books and papers in my desk and apparently found enough and knew enough to catch on to what had happened. Who would ever suspect she'd go to the trouble, or have the brass neck to use it when she had?' He paused as though she were about to say something.

'I'm listening,' she told him, 'but I don't feel I should comment on it yet.' Neither, she noted, had touched the poured-out tea.

'I understand,' he said, though he didn't look as if he did. 'Eunice sprang this on me cold-bloodedly by saying she'd been busy with my photocopier and some interesting papers and account books she'd found in my desk. She told me that the photocopies were sealed and had been dumped on somebody else she refused to name. In case, she said, I'd . . . well, that would be a pretty fanciful happening so far as I was concerned.'

161

He looked around him at the other customers as though searching for his Eunice, a hint of contained savagery in his expression. 'Two hundred pounds a week loan was what she wanted, on top of the money she earned as a singer. A *loan*,' he growled. 'She thought that clever and I suppose it was. She even made me hold her house deeds for what that was worth, for she told me not to count on keeping them either. I paid the money in cash to her each week and entered the amounts in my accounts as such. I thought that if I fell, she'd have to fall with me. Having her still working for me under those circumstances was unbearable and I was thankful when she walked out on me and latched herself on Cruickshank.' He took a white handkerchief from his pocket and dabbed at his forehead with it. 'While she told me I could stuff my money for the time being, she made it clear that she was holding on to the photocopies in case. That "in case" again,' he said bitterly. 'I knew what that meant. And now, if she wasn't bluffing, I'm to believe that there's somebody out there who's unknowingly, I hope, still holding trouble for me.'

'All this is the reason for your calling on her at Thurnholme Bay and threatening her, isn't it?' Millier was inclined to believe him, apart from wanting to give him the benefit for the time being of any doubt over the grey areas in his explanation.

'Yes,' he admitted, 'but who'd believe what I've told you and not also believe that I'd killed her to shut her up? When you came to interview me and told me that Eunice was missing, I knew then she must be dead and that I was going to be suspect number one. That's true, isn't it?'

'Not quite, but near enough. And not enough for me to think I should have been more pushing than I was.'

'Well, Lingard made up for that. He definitely suspected me and made no bones about it. I had to hold on to that story about having loaned Eunice the money for her house in case the payments came to light.' He took a deep breath. 'I'm really trusting you now, Helen. I wasn't fool enough to believe lock stock and barrel that she'd planted the photocopies on somebody else, so when I knew she was definitely living with Cruickshank I made it my business to break into her house one night. I climbed in through a window which I'd found unlatched and searched the place.' For a brief second he showed a little of the ugliness he held in his persona. 'I couldn't find them, probably because the b ... because she really had dumped them on somebody else.'

'Were I Chief Inspector Lingard,' Millier said calmly, 'and I'd heard what you've been telling me, I'd believe that I had found the motive behind Parr's death.'

'That I've already accepted. But what about Detective Inspector Millier?'

'I told you that she wasn't here today. I can only say you don't act the guilty type, but that only puts you on hold while I wait and see what happens.'

'I'm happy with that.' He leaned forward, his whole personality being directed at her. 'Apart from that, have we something in common?'

She gave him a long cool stare, short of discouragement and mindful that she shouldn't be affected too much by the eroticism his very nearness provoked in her. 'Whether anything comes of it will depend on your attitude and on my continuing interest in you.' She took a pen from her clutch bag and wrote figures on a paper napkin, giving it to him and saying, 'That's my telephone number. If you've anything to say to me when you may be in the clear, use it.'

She stood from her chair. That this man would try to dominate her, give her small choice in what he wished to do, seemed not to offend too much against her sensibilities. His attitude, the forcefulness of his innate hardness, would be what she would choose in a lover. She said, 'I want you to stay here until I've gone. For obvious reasons we shan't meet again in this town until my retirement takes effect.'

He pushed himself upright. 'I want you, Helen, and I'd break anyone in two to have you. Is that all right with you?'

She smiled at him briefly, not quite liking the flamboyance of his remark, and leaving, said, 'It will only be all right when Mr Lingard is satisfied that it is, and when I agree with him.'

Returning to her Rover Mini in the nearby car-park, she knew that she would have few reservations about accepting such a bullishly attractive man as a lover, though she would hesitate about any further commitment. He would be containable, while she remained, as she intended, her own woman. But none of that made her terribly happy. There was too much present bitterness in her about how she had been treated by both Rogers and Lingard.

24

Rogers's rough night was catching up on him. Returning to his office towards the end of the afternoon, he felt he should eat in order to keep himself standing upright and in some sort of fettle. Seated alone in the Senior Officers' Mess, he picked unenthusiastically at a canteen prepared meal, drank to its dregs the pot of mouth-scalding coffee sent with it, abandoned the meal and pulled out his pipe to fill it. The unconsciousness of sleep came suddenly as he sat there, his head hanging and the half-filled pipe still in his hand.

Aeons could have passed him unheeded in his timeless sleep. He was woken unrefreshed by a faraway knocking that echoed boomingly through his brain. Snapping open his eyes, he saw an amused Lingard sitting opposite him, gently rapping his plastered arm on the edge of the table.

'They told me you were dead, Theophrastus,' his second-in-command quoted from somewhere in the classics.

Rogers blinked, snatched at a returning awareness and said, 'Not dead, David; just feeling like it. Don't tell me you've problems?' The purple worm was back with him, appearing to be rhythmically and painfully copulating with a nerve in the side of his head.

'Only a right and proper desire to know something about the recovered Miss Parr. She has been identified?'

Rogers stifled a yawn at its birth, retrieving his pipe from the floor and completing its filling. Putting a match to it and sucking in smoke, he gave Lingard, punctuated several times by his relighting a suddenly recalcitrant pipe, the details of the recovery of Eunice Parr's body, the findings of its examination by Bridget – she had once been Lingard's lover for a brief and unsatisfactory few weeks, though he had always assumed a pretence to Rogers that she hadn't – and his opinion of the circumstances of her murder. 'She's the fourth on our current list of sudden departures, David,' he finished, 'and how the devil each ties in with the others – if they actually do – seems beyond me in my present condition.'

'I don't think Fuller's going to help us,' Lingard said with an unwanted cheerfulness.

'I didn't believe he would. He wasn't talking?'

'Not only.' Lingard gave him a summary of his interview. 'To be honest,' he admitted, 'while I gave the fella a fair bit of stick – enough, I thought, to give him licence to take a poke at me – I don't feel that he's Miss Parr's killer. But I do that he's dodging having to come out with something sensitive and therefore probably nasty.'

'I'm with you there. Pushing her head into a wash-basin of water was a cold-blooded drowning, and though he's a brutal bastard, he's a hot-blooded brutal bastard and more likely to give somebody he didn't like a bashing.' Rogers grimaced his revulsion. 'Can you imagine the horror of it? Of what went through the poor woman's mind?'

A bit hair-trigger over the throbbing in his head, he asked, 'What did Miss Millier think of it?'

'Ah!' Lingard sniffed at a recent ingestion of snuff. 'La belle Helen wasn't there to think of anything. I looked for her, naturally. She'd booked out to Miss Parr's place first thing this morning, though when I went there and later to her flat, she was in neither. I couldn't leave Fuller and his sins to dangle unattended, so I saw him without her. Is she complaining?' He looked unconcerned.

'I don't know, but she will. I haven't been here to see her since early this afternoon.' Rogers showed his teeth in forced geniality. 'Don't worry yourself into a toothache about it. I rather think she'll take it out on me and my back's broad enough.' He shrugged fatalistically. 'Let's go back to Parr. Whoever killed her, killed her during the night, she being found in her pyjamas. Whoever it was either had a key, was let in by her or knew enough about slipping window catches to break in.' He felt morose and had difficulty in hiding it.

'Your guess, George. I'm still trying to find my way into it. Didn't you mention that the ancient Cruickshank died of asphyxiation? And now Miss Parr?'

'It hadn't escaped me. But the causes are different in kind.' He fretted irritably about asphyxiation for a while with Lingard waiting patiently while he did it. 'For all that, David, you could have a point and I'll think about it.' He changed tack. 'What about a motive for the lady's killing? I can imagine three, though none that I'd care to wager real money on.'

'To shut her up because she knew too much about something? An old-fashioned attack of jealousy? Vengeance is mine saith a somebody who is not to be confused with the saintly? I have to leave out unrequited passion, I imagine? She wasn't apparently given to turning it down.'

'Loosely,' Rogers said as if it wasn't of much importance, 'I've been trying to attach one or more of those to Cruickshank the younger. I like to think that any man braving sexual intercourse with Mrs Cummins, sister or no sister, must be capable of bigger and more self-serving enormities than that, and deserving of a closer inspection.' He added, 'Neither he nor she will grieve overmuch for our unlucky Miss Parr. They detested her for what she was supposed to have done to their father, though that could never have been too much for the murderous old goat.'

'That's one of your motives, is it?'

Rogers was sardonic. 'Only that he's also a bloody dentist and probably enjoys sticking needles into people.'

Lingard was easing himself from his chair, aware that Rogers wasn't in the happiest of moods. 'You've nothing more?'

'You're going?'

'Only for a quick fix before I drop. My arm's giving me a bit of trouble.'

'Be careful that Miss Millier doesn't do something damaging to the other one,' Rogers warned him.

After Lingard had gone, Rogers returned to his office, sitting at his desk and feeling dissatisfied with what he had done, unhappy with whatever conclusions he had drawn from it. Even thinking of Angharad and his meeting with her later that evening failed to send his adrenalin pumping, convincing himself that only doing some major damage to a bottle of single malt could slow that little bugger of a worm down from whatever it was doing.

For want of anything else and faced with what amounted to a brick wall of incomprehension, he thought he would revert to what he used to call his Switch Thinking. It was illogical, but in suitable cases it worked; more successfully when his brain was a lot younger, his thinking more vivid – particularly when it concerned long-legged women – and much less inhibited. What he had to do was to switch the known facts, forcing himself to look at the problem from a tangentially different viewpoint and to see where it led his thinking.

His first switch was that in the beginning was Philip Cruickshank, the man who, for reasons possibly connected with the long-ago murder of his wife and her lover, was now to be thought of as having taken his own life; there had been a crude and apparently managed simulation of a suicide committed by a different means. While that didn't make sense, it did lead him to consider asphyxiation in its different forms and why, as there was clearly with Parr, there was no evidence of how death had been effected.

Suddenly there was light – a dimmish sort of light – with the rubber band fitting into the use he had now provided for it. Why an asphyxial suicide – were it such – should be disguised as a hanging suicide which, in turn, was designed to be revealed as a cover for murder, was something to make a normally sane man go outside and howl at the moon. So far, what he had wasn't worth a casual spit when it came to proving anything. He had to light a firework of sorts under the backside of whoever it was he thought to be the guilty party, hoping that he had identified the right one.

Lifting his telephone receiver, he tapped out Sergeant Magnus's home number, finding him about to take his wife out for a meal. He told the unfortunate sergeant that he was sorry to interfere with the eating habits of man and wife, but he was to meet him at the late Cruickshank's villa in thirty minutes together with his camera and exhibit-carrying bags. He heard Mrs Magnus sounding off her meant-to-be-heard displeasure before he could replace his receiver.

With thunder rumbling and grey rain sheeting down far out over a restless leaden sea, Rogers braked his car to a halt outside Cruickshank's villa on the heights of High Ipstone View. Sitting in the sticky heat of the car's interior, blinking at the occasional flash of lightning, he beat his purple worm into a sort of submission with two codeine-based nerve-stunning tablets – swallowed dry they went down like sand-sprinkled walnuts – from a forgotten packet he found in the car's road-map compartment.

When the ginger-haired Magnus pulled his car in behind him, he was wearing in his expression all the fortitude of a man permanently at crime's beck and call, his senior officers justifying themselves by believing Magnus must surely want it like that. Waiting while Rogers locked his car, he failed to look surprised when he was told that they were there to look for a kind of bag into which a man might put his head were he to wish to leave this world by an undragged-out and painless dispatch.

Unlocking the door with the key left with him by Stephen Cruickshank and leading the way to the kitchen, Rogers said to Magnus, 'Without wanting you to agree with me, you've a bit of an idiot for a detective superintendent. I'm of the opinion I should have given more thinking to *how* Cruickshank was asphyxiated. It wasn't by the readily available pillow or bedclothing, for either would have shown the residues of vomit, froth or bloodstained mucous we'd expect from a suffocation. So it has to be a bag with a ligature to exclude the air, wouldn't you say?'

'We're looking for a ligature as well?' Magnus asked non-committally.

'I've already found it. It was in his bedroom. A thick rubber band; sufficiently constrictive, I'd imagine.'

Sensitive to the atmosphere of places, he felt there was something of the essence of the dead Cruickshank still left in the villa; as if, he fancied, it reflected what must have been his unhappy and despairing spirit.

In the kitchen, the light being switched on against the

growing twilight of the approaching storm, Rogers located a white PVC waste bin with a swing lid. 'Open it, Sergeant,' he said, unsuccessfully trying to relight the dead ashes of his last smoke, 'it'll be on the top if my theory's any good.'

Magnus pulled the bin out into the light, then levered off the lid with the blade of his pocket-knife. Peering into the bin, he said, 'I think we've got what we're looking for.'

Looking himself, Rogers saw a crumpled-up green plastic shopping bag, the top item on a noisome accumulation of emptied tins, screwed-up kitchen roll, tea bags, plastic containers and uneaten food scraped from plates. 'Only half-way there yet,' he told Magnus. 'Photograph it as found, then dig it out and we'll have a look at it.'

While Magnus flashed his electronic light at the bin's interior, Rogers refilled his pipe and lit it, his fingers crossed in imagination.

'This'll take prints as well as the bin,' Magnus said, lifting the bag out between finger and thumb. He unfolded it carefully, revealing its origin as *Cripps and Co., Tailors and Outfitters, 14 Kirby Street, Thurnholme Bay*, then opening it and examining its interior before displaying it to Rogers.

'It'll be dried coffee stains and snail slime if I've ever seen them,' Rogers commented, trying not to express the jubilation he felt.

'Not a bad guess, sir.' Magnus was grinning, happy to play it Rogers's way. 'Perhaps it'd be better if we let the laboratory staff have a quick and unbloody-minded look at it?'

'Quick it has to be,' Rogers said, feeling that life was suddenly having a few satisfactions going for it. 'After you've dusted its outside for prints, take it there in a hurry. I'll phone the Director from my office, impress him with its urgency, tell him we've a murderer on the loose, and it'll have doors opened for you.'

'You don't believe it's suicide then?' Magnus looked baffled.

'I certainly do, but I'm also thinking of whoever it was killed Miss Parr, for I'm certain the two deaths are related.'

Outside, having seen Magnus off in a tyre-skidding hurry, he breathed in deeply of the cooler sea air now being pushed inland by the towering black clouds which threatened the late afternoon's hazy brightness.

He thought he might now be reasonably equable and content just so long as the purple worm, apparently comatosed, didn't recover too quickly from its chemical stunning. He was a man with the opportunity of inflicting his own thunderclap of doom on a villain or villainess, using Philip Cruickshank's self-destruction as a starting point. He had an ill-formed idea of who it had to be, though not the motive. The plastic bag with its signs of bloodstaining and mucus indicated a fatal suffocation, only pointing uncertainly an identifying finger.

The only serious niggle occupying his mind was not to have the investigation get in the way of his never-to-be-missed meeting with Angharad later that evening. 'Dear Lord,' he said under his breath, not too servilely, 'I'm asking you not to do that to your otherwise reasonably obedient sorter-out of society's hellishness who needs a bit of time for himself on the odd occasion.'

And, being very much inclined to outspokenness, he meant it.

25

While Roger's preoccupied thinking on the problem of Philip Cruickshank's almost certain suicide posed something of a driving hazard on his way back to Abbotsburn, he survived without the accident he had probably earned. During it, he had tidied up his thinking enough to accept provisionally that what he was now investigating was a deliberately botched attempt to make a contrived suicide by hanging appear to be a homicidal death by suffocation and not a suicide by the same means as it actually was.

When that had been fixed in his mind – and that not too surely – he turned to the matter of Cruickshank's bureau which had been searched, it appearing that the arranged deception might be associated with the searching for and possible theft of documents. Apart from dismissing – for the time being – his first thought that the theft had been of a will, he put it to the back of his mind with a preference for believing that Stephen Cruickshank may have been the man rifling through his father's papers and consequently could be a front runner in his hypothetically short list of possible suspects.

Back in his office, heavy rain now battering at his windows and rattling the venetian blinds, he made up his mind to set in train a situation likely to lead to a loss of nerve in the guilty and lead perhaps – the 'perhaps' was extravagantly theoretical – to some compromising action. In trying to locate Lingard and Millier he found himself up against Sod's Law wherein it was laid down that the greater the need for anybody's presence the correspondingly diminished was their availability, resulting in his detaching Coltart from his worries about the bodies found in the barn and Ashe's wraith-like brother and telling him to stand by.

His tapping out of Cruickshank's telephone number was answered by his sister. Given his name, she sounded unwelcoming of the call and cautious. 'What is it you want?' she demanded.

'If I call on you shortly, would you both be in?'

'Why do you want to see us? Haven't you upset us enough already?'

'I'd prefer not to discuss it over a public line, but it's about Miss Parr.' He was heavily official and insistent. 'It is extremely important, so may I say in fifteen minutes?'

After a short silence – he could hear her uneven breathing – her 'If you must' was a dragged out, only just audible assent as she disconnected from him.

Replacing his receiver, Rogers knew that he had hit something affecting her self-possession, and that gave him the confidence of an assumption of rightness.

When trenchcoated against the rain he left his office with the massive Coltart, the evening's light had darkened to a glistening pewter greyness beneath lowering clouds and the flashes of lightning with their accompanying thunder were not too far from being overhead. Parking his car on the forecourt of Winslow Court and noting the lighted windows in the

171

top-floor apartment occupied by Cruickshank and his sister, he forced himself to climb the three steep flights of stairs without stopping to ease his lungs or admitting to Coltart close behind him that it was doing painful things to his calf muscles.

Knocking at the door of number 7 he waited, keeping the possibly menacing bulk of Coltart in his dripping blue raincoat to one side as a kind of neutral observer. He had to knock again before a still-trousered Mrs Cummins opened the door, it needing no penetrating insight to realize that she was badly shaken, though none of it appeared to lessen the suggestion of aggression towards him shown in her pallid face.

'I'd like to speak to your brother, please,' he said, stiffly formal. He nodded at what he could see of the room behind her. 'May I?'

'What do you want to say to him?' Her attitude said that there was to be no invitation to enter.

'Miss Parr has been found and I wish to speak to him about her.' He made it non-committal, for he need do no more than break the news of her death to him should he feel it inexpedient to go further. He was, as he reminded himself, wholly without evidence to connect Cruickshank with either of the deaths.

'He isn't here. He went out.' He thought she was lying, that it showed in her face and in her voice. 'Why can't you leave us alone,' she suddenly spat at him.

'You know where he went, of course?' he said, his face impassive. He was keeping an ear cocked for any sounds of movement from behind her.

'No, I don't.' She seemed to have bottled her momentary show of anger. 'He won't be back until later.'

'Where does he go this time of the evening?' He put significance in his words. 'It *is* very important that I see him.' It was hot and humid under his trenchcoat and his shoulders felt warmly damp.

'I said I didn't know.'

'I'm sure you do,' he said firmly. 'I have to know, otherwise I shall be forced to wait.'

The alarm in her eyes was obvious and she bit at her unlipsticked mouth for a few moments of irresolution. Then

172

she said, 'I'm not sure, but sometimes he goes to his club; the Liberal and Democrat.'

He stared at her for long seconds, seeking some confirmation of the lie he was sure she was telling him. 'Thank you, Mrs Cummins,' he said. 'I may see you again.' He could almost feel sorry for her suffering the strain he was putting on her, for she was beginning to look hagridden.

The door was closed almost before he had turned away from her. He stood silent for a while listening, hearing nothing but imagining that she herself could be standing listening behind the door, and then beckoning Coltart to leave with him.

Outside and re-entering his car, he drove to the end of the road where they were out of the field of view of anyone in Winslow Court, then braked to a halt. Handing his personal radio to Coltart at his side – it seemed no bigger than a cigarette packet held in his huge fist – he said, 'Go back and keep watch on whatever happens now that we've gone. I think Cruickshank's there so if he dodges out while I'm at the Liberal and Democrat, grab him and wheel him in on suspicion of having committed an arrestable offence or somesuch. Whatever else, use the radio and leave a message for me at Headquarters.'

Coltart, tight on words, nodded and climbed from the car, slamming its door hard enough to send shock waves through it and to detach from the inside of the windscreen a stuck-on road tax disc. Rogers winced, then moved off for the club and an already lost cause so far as Cruickshank's being there was concerned.

Reaching it through the town's now waterlogged streets, he had words with the club's secretary who checked the rooms and the lavatory area, assuring an unsurprised Rogers that Cruickshank, a respected member of the club, was not on the premises, nor had he been that day.

Returning to Headquarters not much frustrated, for this was how he had imagined its development, he was handed two message forms by the Enquiry Office duty inspector. One was from Coltart advising him in telegraphese that at 1938 hours – thirteen minutes after Rogers had left him in the drenching rain – Mrs Cummins had come out from Winslow Court, almost running to the rear of the building and looking as if she were crying, then emerging a minute later driving a blue Volkswagen Beetle with a white roof and a then unreadable registration number. Exiting from the forecourt she had turned left, possibly towards the mile-distant road junction with the A593 and B5343. There had been no sign of Cruickshank and lights were still burning from the top-floor windows.

The second message, received seven minutes after Coltart's radio-transmitted report, contained a telephoned request from a Mrs Veronica Cummins, address refused, that a message be passed to Detective Superintendent Rogers. It was that her brother, name not given, had left their apartment shortly before he, Rogers, had called there. He had been very distressed about the unceasing police harassment and had said that he was driving to Great Morte Moor to get away from it all. Frightened of what he might do, she was now going there herself to find him and might need help, though Rogers should come on his own. The telephone operator recording the message had added a footnote to the effect that the caller had been extremely agitated, sometimes not clearly audible, and was probably using a mobile telephone because there had been a constant background to the call of a car's engine.

There was a possibility, Rogers judged, that she was still lying; that Cruickshank was still in the apartment, that she was attempting to draw him away in the foolish chase of a man who wouldn't be there on the moor at all.

On the other hand, the B5343 road referred to by Coltart was the second-class road crossing the moor and, with her driving her car towards it, it gave support to the truth of at least a part of what she was saying.

Pusillanimously, in the full knowledge that it might be thought he was back-pedalling on a regretted commitment, he left a brief message apologizing for his absence on duty to be passed to Angharad by the duty inspector. Then, collecting a DS and a DC, both of whom had been avoiding going out in the rain by remembering some absolutely necessary report writing needing to be done, he piled them into the back seat of his car and took off for his appointment with whatever destiny had up its sleeve for Cruickshank and his sister.

The worm was still comatosed and, until it came to, he supposed that he was now as satisfied with the course he was taking as he ever would be. That this was an illusion subject to a sudden death ending he was well aware, but it sufficed for the moment.

26

From his sodden appearance, Coltart had not found a sheltered vantage point for his watch on the Cruickshank apartment. He shook his head when the in-a-hurry Rogers asked him if he had anything additional to report. 'Nothing,' he rumbled *basso profundo*, not a man to complain of a touch of wetness.

Rogers, leaving the DS and DC to take over from Coltart with explicit instructions about covering the front and back of the building and what to do about Cruickshank should he emerge, took off on the road to the moor with the huge detective inspector in the passenger seat.

The storm was now over the town, the clouds dark and swollen-bellied, seemingly low and blotting out the last lingering grey twilight that could, Rogers thought, reflect something of the fleeing man's private hell. Rain came down in slender silver spears, drumming on the roof of the car and splashing small explosions of water in the pools already flooding the roads. With the forking of lightning, each stroke bathing the landscape in its immediate periphery with momentary stark lividness, came the cracking thunder. It was an Armageddon of the heavens, Rogers fancifully imagining himself being not too surprised were he to see the Four Horsemen of the Apocalypse riding the storm.

With the road rising to the moor, he strained his eyes to see through a streaming windscreen and the sweeping wipers what his headlights were showing him of the glistening road. After twenty minutes of driving into the lashing rain and howling wind, neither encountering any traffic nor catching up with the pair of tail-lights he was searching for, he told Coltart to radio back to Headquarters and find out if there were any further messages from Mrs Cummins.

When he had done it, the answer, hissing and crackling with thunderstorm static, came over the air to the effect that Mrs Cummins, having sighted what she believed to be her brother's car and giving chase, had skidded and collided with one of the few trees managing to grow on the desolate wind-swept moor, losing her brother who, she thought, may have turned off near the crossing at Blackstone Spout.

This, Rogers knew, would now be at least three miles of wet darkness from him and marked where a track crossed the road, arriving from one heather-covered wilderness to enter into another. He was becoming even more convinced that things were not as they were said to be, that he was without the comforting predictabilities of logic. Coltart, having confined most of his activities to the entombed Mrs Cruickshank and her lover Ashe, and now not being an occasion for an idle discussion on the weather, wisely stayed silent, tending only to the radio.

When the two stationary hazy red lights emerged from the streaming blackness, Rogers decelerated and let the car roll to a halt some thirty feet behind them. In his headlights through the streaming rain he identified, though none too positively, the car as a Volkswagen Beetle in a blue and white livery. Almost immediately, lightning burned through the blackness above them, revealing in stark detail that the nose of the car was held against a short scrubby-looking tree at a slight angle to the road, though showing nothing of the interior of the car. He couldn't see why anybody not drunk should hit a tree as Mrs Cummins – were it she – certainly had on the virtually open stretch of road.

Uncertain of the situation confronting him, Rogers edged his car forward until he was a few feet behind it, then cutting the engine. He could now see that the Volkswagen's driving seat was occupied, though the head restraint and rain on the rear window put paid to any identification.

'Keep the headlight on,' he said to Coltart. 'If it isn't Mrs Cummins I might have a problem. Or even if it is,' he added as an afterthought.

176

When he climbed from his car into the drenching rain, the wind snatched the door from his hand, smashing it back on its hinges and doing nothing to improve a getting-wet Rogers's underlying irritation. Moving to the Volkswagen, he glanced at the front wheel housing which appeared to be only in slight contact with the trunk of the tree. Then, looking through the passenger-side window, he recognized the slumped figure inside as that of Mrs Cummins.

Turning her head to him as he opened the door, she said, 'Have you seen him?' Climbing in, finding it no easy fit for his body's length, he said 'No, I haven't. Do you mind my coming in? It's a little damp outside.' Then, having settled himself in the car which smelled of whisky, he asked, 'You're not injured?'

'No, I'm not,' she answered. 'Have you looked for him?'

'No further than this.' He suspected that she was going to be difficult. 'I got your message. When was the last time you saw him?'

'I told you. When he turned off on to the track and I bumped into the tree.' She was brusque with him, her eyes blinking away from his gaze.

'Why did he come up here, Mrs Cummins?' He had no intention of letting her lead him in what was to be said.

'I told you. He was being harassed. He couldn't stand it any longer.' Whatever trouble she and her brother were in, it hadn't softened her hostility towards him, and his was still the apparent status of horse manure. She made him feel sorry for her no doubt discarded husband.

'You know that's nonsense,' he said easily. He wound down his window a few inches, preferring rain on his face to the smell of her whisky. Apart from which, he was in golfing terms about to pitch a blind shot to a green he couldn't see. 'I needed to tell you both that I now know that your father committed suicide and that your brother, or your brother and yourself, arranged for it to be taken as a murder.'

He waited there in the deeply shadowed interior of the car, hearing the steady drumming of rain on its roof with, below that, the uncertain breathing of the woman whose shoulder was all but touching his.

177

Taking her silence as a tacit admission of something or other, he said gently, 'That's so, isn't it, Mrs Cummins?'

She turned on him then, viciousness in her voice. 'I know exactly what you're trying to do – you're making me responsible for what my brother's done, when I've only tried to shield him. You should be looking for him now, not cross-examining me.'

'You mean I should go on harassing him? Perhaps if I returned to your apartment I might do that there?'

'*No!*' she snapped, agitated at his suggestion. 'Why should he when I've followed him up here?' She reached down, retrieving a small flat bottle from a compartment at her side, unscrewing its cap jerkily and drinking from it. Recapping it and putting it back, she turned to the silently watching Rogers. 'Fuck you,' she said without any particular expression. 'You're making me tell you why he was forced into doing it.'

'If you say so,' he agreed, concealing his surprise. With her whisky drinking giving him some licence, he retrieved his already filled pipe from his trenchcoat pocket. 'Do you mind?' he said, showing it to her. 'I'll blow the smoke through the window.' Without waiting for an answer, he scratched a match at it, using its small flame to study her face. It still represented a sharp-planed dominance, her pale grey eyes suggesting a lack of warmth towards her fellow *Homo sapiens* and, in them, he thought he read that he still represented something for her to despise.

He gave her what he thought might be taken as an understanding smile. 'You were shielding your brother from exactly what?' he asked. Not too optimistically, he was mentally willing her to garrulity.

'When Stephen visited Father after we'd returned from Carrigill, he found him dead in his bed. He ... he told me he had killed himself with a bag, but that it had been quite a peaceful death. There was a note to us both about his intention to do it, that he was going to join Mother ...' – Rogers squirmed at the hypocrisy of that – '... and that one day we would understand. Stephen told me he'd burned this as it seemed to be a matter only for us. We thought about it and discussed it after you told us about Mother's death and understood why he should feel that way as he got older.

'Oh, damn!' She was chewing on her lower lip while Rogers was holding back on interrupting her. 'Stephen left Father there while he came back home to tell me what had happened. Father's papers needed to be considered and I went back with Stephen to see him and to look for those we knew he would wish us to deal with.'

'Such as, say, his will and a life insurance policy with an exclusion against suicide?' It was a guess, but the only thing that made sense.

She looked surprised. 'Yes,' she said. 'You knew?'

'You found them missing from the bureau?' This was all coming too easy to be believable.

'Yes.'

'You knew you were the only legatees?'

'Yes.' That came reluctantly after hesitation. 'Father had told us some time ago.'

'What was the amount of the life assurance premium due on his death?'

She shook her head, something of her earlier antagonism returning. 'That's none of your business.'

'Substantial enough for you both to worry about the suicide clause invalidatating the policy, though?'

She appeared to be resigned now. 'Not for me. We'd be getting the villa and Father's capital holdings anyway. It was different for Stephen and he told me to go home while he arranged that Father's death wouldn't appear to be anything he had done himself . . . that he'd be shamed.' Her eyes were suddenly brimming with tears as if realization had belatedly come to her, and she squeezed them shut. 'Oh, Father,' she whispered miserably, and to Rogers she was suddenly somebody humanly pathetic.

'Did Stephen tell you what he's done to the body?'

She shook her head violently, opening her eyes to glare at him. 'No, damn you, no! I don't want to know!'

'I wasn't about to tell you,' Rogers assured her, some of his sympathy fled, but still deciding he couldn't, not about the blow inflicted on her father's head after death to simulate an attack. 'I'm happy with your denial. Was there any suspicion then . . .' He stopped as a flash of lightning illuminated the inside of the car with a flaring white intensity, followed a few paralysing seconds later by a violent double crack of thunder like the wrath of God.

'I think we were rather lucky there,' he said, relighting his pipe and regarding again in the flame of the match her pallid and now incongruously tear-stained face. 'I was going to ask you if there was any suspicion shared between you about who might have taken the will and the insurance policy in particular?'

'I don't believe so.' She was trembling slightly; Rogers thought surely because of the lightning strike and not because of his questioning.

'Miss Parr wasn't mentioned? The woman you must have known was your father's common-law wife, who was thrown out of her home by your brother and who might have had some claim on the estate?'

She was gnawing at her thumb, almost childlike, and not answering him, but staring through the windscreen out into the darkness. When she did speak, she said, 'She was wrong for Father. You must know what a cheap money-grabbing bitch she was. Nobody else would know where they were kept; there's nobody else who would have taken them anyway.'

'Your brother knew that, of course?' It was a time to take a leap in the dark, and he did. 'And so it was understandable that he should go to her house to recover them?' So close to her and her breathing out of whisky fumes, he thought that he could also detect the more acceptable odour of horse.

She hesitated. 'Why should I know? He didn't tell me everything. All I knew was that they were important to him. He was about to lose his partnership in the dental practice and needed the money to set up a practice of his own.'

'I'm sorry, Mrs Cummins, but with you both living together . . .' – he tried not to make that sound censorious – '. . . I find your not knowing difficult to believe.' He was also finding it difficult to believe that she was deliberately giving her precious brother a motive for killing Eunice Parr.

Waiting for her expected remonstrance, Rogers pulled at a now well-behaved pipe, blowing the smoke out of the window to see it whipped away in the wind. His legs were aching in the

180

cramping seat he occupied and, despite the occasional breath of fresh air entering the window, he sweated.

'No,' she said finally, patently wary. 'I didn't know and I don't wish to speak about it.'

'But I do,' he pressed her in a change to implacability. 'When I told you that Miss Parr had been found, I would, had I been given a hearing, have told you that she was found dead. In fact, undoubtedly murdered.'

'Murdered!' She gaped at him – to her, he supposed, a largeish dark bulk smelling of tobacco smoke and bearing down on her with dangerously menacing questions – then cried out, 'No!, putting her hands over her ears with her head bowed over the steering wheel. 'Oh, Jesus! Stop it! Stop it, I tell you!' she wailed, then appeared to switch off from him. There was little of her horsiness left with her now, only the beset helpless femininity which could make Rogers feel harsh and brutal.

He waited, putting hitherto unthought of theories together while leaving her to suffer her personal Gethsemane without interruption.

It wasn't too long before she raised her head and turned to him, looking calmer than she had ever done before. 'Why do you call it murder?' she asked him. 'He told me that she had died accidentally, and I believe him. Why shouldn't I? He went to her house late one night – I didn't know where he was going until afterwards – and accused her of stealing the papers from Father's bureau while she had been living with him. Neither of them were much good to her, you would think.' She was slurring some of her words and Rogers watched her closely. 'God knows how, but she had been going to use them against Father, and while she didn't deny she had them she refused to give them up despite Stephen offering her money. He said he only meant to frighten her into handing them over . . .' – she swallowed – '. . . so he took her to the bathroom and told her he would put her head under water – he was only pretending, of course – unless she told him where they were. Then . . .'

She swallowed again, finding difficulty in getting her words out. 'I couldn't understand why, but when Stephen said that to her she went a queer colour and collapsed. He thought she'd

181

had a heart attack and tried to revive her because he does know how to do it professionally, but he couldn't and he had to leave her. He was quite certain she had died.'

She reached and fetched out her bottle, unscrewing the cap with shaking fingers and drinking from it, then winding down the window and flinging it out. With her not yet being in his custody, Rogers was not about to make an issue of it, though he could anticipate being criticized for it.

'What did he do about disposing of Miss Parr's body?' He still felt that this incestuous sister of Cruickshank's was bent on throwing him to the wolves and, in spite of her no doubt genuine anguish, doing so deliberately. So far, she was managing not to say anything likely to involve herself as an accessory.

'He said he'd hidden her under her bed and didn't really know what to do. He cried so much when he was telling me, but you wouldn't understand that, would you? Then, after you had come to see us last night and questioned him about Father's death, he felt that he was in danger of being arrested. He went out at midnight, saying that he was going to bury her body on the moor where it would never be found, which he said he had done.'

'And the documents?' With the storm clouds having moved on and a half-moon appearing sporadically from behind the wrack, her features became more visible to him, her pallidness more noticeable.

'He found them in her bedroom and we have them back in the apartment.' She hesitated, then said, 'You haven't told me why you should believe she was murdered.'

'No, I haven't, have I? I think that's something I shall have to take up with your brother.' He stared his will at her. 'Now it's time that you told me where he's gone; that is if he's anywhere but back in his apartment.'

'You haven't been there?' Her voice had risen.

'You know I haven't,' he said grimly. 'But now I think it's called for.'

Climbing from the car on stiff legs that felt as though they had set rigid under his wet trousers, he opened the door of his own car. 'Cruickshank's in his apartment and God knows what

182

he's up to,' he growled at Coltart. 'Get a call made to Mr Lingard on the Headquarters telephone – tell them he'll be at home – give him my compliments and ask him to go to Winslow Court, apartment 7, immediately and arrest Cruickshank on a charge of murdering Miss Parr. I leave it to him how he's to get into the apartment.'

Rejoining Mrs Cummins and settling himself in his seat, he saw that she was holding herself tight, staring hypnotically at the rain-splashed windscreen. 'Are you all right?' he asked, uncertain whether she was passing out on him.

She turned her head without answering, looking at him with haunted fearful eyes and not answering.

After waiting patiently for what was a non-response, he said, 'Your brother's still in the apartment, I gather, and you've brought me up here on a wild-goose chase. Why? And, please, no more lies.'

'I've been trying so hard not to think of him.' Her eyes were flooding with tears and she looked anything but the hard-faced woman of his earlier meetings. She reached, surprising him, and grasped his hand. 'He was my brother and even though he was weak I loved him. I couldn't stay there, could I, and see it happen? He wanted . . .' She trailed off into an anguished silence as Coltart appeared at Rogers's window.

'They've contacted Mr L.,' he said, 'and he'll be ordering a patrol car to take him to where you said.'

'Good.' Rogers felt happier now. 'Hang on to the radio; we might get something back soon.'

Hoping that Coltart hadn't noticed his hand was being held, he released it from her grip as inoffensively as he was able. He had noted that she had spoken of Cruickshank in the past tense, and he suddenly had the answer. Or some of it. 'What are you trying to tell me?' he demanded.

'Stephen,' she whispered, her voice broken. 'You're going there . . . I think he must be dead. Dear God, I do hope so . . .'

When she went no further, leaving him unsure of what further incomprehensibilities he was to hear, he spoke gently. 'I'm sorry, but you'll have to tell me in detail if I'm to understand you. Why do you think he's dead?'

Not looking at him, the slurring in her sad voice more

183

noticeable, she said, 'When . . . when you told me that the woman had been found, Stephen realized that you would know. Then he told me that he hadn't buried her at all, that as she was now found and identified it was all over for him and that we should go together.'

She paused, the flesh on her face appearing to have tightened her expression into a rictus of remembered anguish. 'I knew he had already prepared two hypodermic syringes with some drug of his . . . it was supposed to put us to sleep with no waking up. Before, I hadn't really accepted that to be anything but words, but when he said we should do it now I knew that I couldn't. There was no reason why I should, other than that I loved him.'

She wiped at her eyes with the back of her hand, silent for long moments with Rogers needing to hurry things along for a man who was apparently dead or dying. When she spoke it was broken with soft weeping. 'He gave me one of the syringes and I stood there holding it.' She was briefly fierce. 'Don't you *understand*? He wanted me to do it to him while he did it to me. He was watching me . . . so dreadfully sad, and I couldn't. Then he shouted at me . . . *Do it, do it!* . . . and dreadful things that I'd never thought he would ever say to me. Dear God,' she moaned, 'he was watching me, his poor face twisted and doing it to himself . . . so quickly that I couldn't do anything. I don't know. I should have done, but I couldn't bear to stay and see it . . . I had to run and leave him to die as he wanted to and I shall never be forgiven . . .'

'You were sure he would die?' he asked softly. He could see it now. She'd been buying time for him to die. There was a sort of love and loyalty in that and it softened his opinion of her.

She nodded shakily. 'He said between quarter and half an hour at the most. I didn't really know what I was doing, but I had to stop you from going there . . . I had to let him die in peace as he wanted to. But then I never went with him and I shall never forget it.' The enormity of what she had been a passive party to seemed then to hit her hard and she broke into further spasms of shuddering uncontrollable weeping.

Rogers, helpless as always in the face of a woman's weeping, climbed from the car as inconspicuously as he could, though getting a last thrust from her when she said savagely through her tears, 'Damn you! Damn you! I hope you're satisfied with what you've done to us!'

'I suppose you could say that,' he muttered, more to himself than to her. In fact, he was far from satisfied with what was supposed to have happened between brother and sister. But it would do for the moment. It would bloody well have to.

Detailing Coltart to take Mrs Cummins to Headquarters pending the outcome of what she had told him, he sat for a quiet and undisturbed ten minutes or so in his car, getting into his second wind before starting again. At least he had something more than just another body to lighten his present personal frustrations, for the moon was now fully out and though the landscape was still waterlogged. the night air was fresh, a reviver of a tired brain and almost pleasant to be in. On top of which, his head-worm had apparently knocked off for the night and he was feeling positively optimistic that he might be seeing Angharad. For the moment.

27

Returning to Abbotsburn and splashing his way through its dark and still flooded streets for Winslow Court, Rogers felt deflated in what he considered the amorphousness of that so far achieved. Little about the result of his investigation appeared to be clear-cut enough for the Queen's justice to be achieved.

When he had climbed again and not too briskly the stairs to Cruickshank's apartment, the door – splintered at its lock and showing all the signs of the use of a policeman's boot – was opened for him by a uniformed PC. The elegantly unflappable Lingard, sitting in one of the easy chairs, was doing his difficult one-armed writing in his official pocket-book. He stood, saying with an easy nonchalance, 'We were too late, George,' not needing to indicate the nearby body of Cruickshank to illustrate what he meant. 'Our medico's visited and certified that chummy's been operating in a different dimension for

185

at least an hour, though what he stuffed himself with to do it needs a chemist to identify.'

'That was expected, David.' Rogers moved nearer to the body and took in what it could tell him.

The apparently despairing Cruickshank, wearing trousers and a shirt with a sleeve pushed up on one arm, was inelegantly on his knees staring sightlessly into the seat cushion of the second easy chair. His face and the nape of the neck sporting his mini-pigtail were lilac-covered and, from his expression, it was clear that he had died unpleasantly. A hypodermic syringe lay near his head on an arm of the chair, a small puddle of what appeared to be vomit stained the fabric of the seat. A similar syringe containing a yellowish fluid lay on the carpet near an open door leading to a bedroom. A framed studio photograph of Veronica Cummins, its glass smashed and scattered, lay near Cruickshank's body. Rogers, looking for them, saw tiny splinters of glass glinting on the heel of one of his shoes. Other than one of the dining chairs having been toppled, there was no other disorder, though what there was suggested that Cruickshank had met the finality of his death in a rage.

'Sergeant Magnus?' he queried to Lingard.

'Found out of house and home, but now on his way. Everything's catered for, as you'd know.'

'It's why I sent for you,' Rogers hastened to say, though not adding that that was what seconds-in-command were for. 'I'm bushed, and as you've obviously got yourself well involved I'd be grateful if you'd take over what you can of it. Mrs Cummins will be awaiting your attention in one of the policewomen's offices and should make your day.'

He told him in fairish detail as much as he remembered of what she had admitted and had denied. 'She's a bit of an enigma, David,' he finished. 'To give her her due, I believe she was really suffering. But watch it, she's no fool and I'm satisfied that she was more than capable of pushing her brother around and being his guiding light. There is one thing I'm not too happy about. I find it hard to believe that Cruickshank was able to haul his father up to the garage rafters without assistance.'

'His sister?'

186

'Why not? She's a sturdy handful.'

'No, why not.' Lingard hesitated, then said, 'I was going to leave this until *mañana* when you were back to being your bright and sunny self. It's fairly bad news, I'm afraid. The gorgeous Helen bearded me on my way out from seeing you and tore me off a fearsome strip for interviewing friend Fuller without her being present, or seeking her co-operation for doing so.' He pulled a face. 'She is, she told me, putting in her resignation to the Chief with the reasons for it directed, I gathered, mainly against me but with you included. A bit of over-reaction, I thought.'

Rogers frowned. 'Let's worry about it tomorrow, if we have to worry at all. If she *is* too hooked on a villain Fuller, then her putting in her ticket may not be such a bad thing.' He turned to leave, jerking his head at the dead man. 'You're happy I'm leaving him with you, David?'

'He's already with me, George. Toddle off home. I'll feel much better when you're in your hammock and not about to collapse on me.'

Leaving him to it, Rogers returned briefly to his office to deal with the recording of his own notes. In between, and several times, he tapped out Angharad's telephone number, receiving no reply to any of them. She had obviously left the house and he felt that he could as fruitlessly have beaten his head against a metal door. She was, he feared. out with somebody else – possibly a very hairy and well-off retired rear admiral with a forty-five-foot yacht of his own – and that was damping to the spirit. With any feminine mind having its own laws, she could have considered him a bad bet as a future reasonably constant lover, as had his ex-wife for somewhat similar reasons. He hadn't expected it of Angharad, and his earlier optimism was well fled.

Feeling below par in terms of emotional well-being – no rejected man with wet trouser ends and socks could be otherwise – and being in the mood to throw his telephone handset through one of his apartment's windows when he got there, he drove from the Headquarters' hard-standing bound for what Lingard had called his hammock.

On turning into the street in which his apartment was

situated, he saw with astonishment and irritation that some thoughtless bugger had left a large car in his resident's designated parking space, its owner, a formless shape, apparently occupying the driving seat.

Drawing alongside it, ready to identify him and vent his vast outrage over this flouting of his personal prerogative, he recognized it as a recent marque Range Rover and wondrously, euphorically, in its driver's seat a shadowy female figure that could only be the bewitchingly appealing Angharad.

'You are late,' she said through her open side window and there was a casualness in her voice in which he could read nothing. 'I'll have to borrow your door key if you intend going on like this.'

Pulling into a neighbouring resident's unoccupied parking space, he went to her, holding the car's door open as she stepped from it and handed him a heavy coolbag to carry. 'I assumed you'd be hungry,' she said, smiling gently at him.

Though the night was dark and damp, for Rogers the sun shone and birds sang. He wanted to say imprudent words that a forty-three-year-old man should be careful about saying to an attractive widow who could set his heart pumping suffocatingly merely by looking at him with her sea-green eyes. Instead, he took her hand speechlessly, preceding her through the the door leading to his apartment.

As he climbed the stairs, the only worry he now had in the largely lawless acreage of his bailiwick was whether he had made his one and only bed in his one and only bedroom before leaving it that morning.